Meridian Chronicles:

Fairy Nymphs & The Demon Court (#3)

By
MD Fryson

AMF PUBLISHING
ISBN 978-0-578-51831-2
UNITED STATES
Copyright © 2019 M.D. Fryson & AMF Publishing

All rights reserved. No part of this publication may be reproduced, stored in a retrieval system, or transmitted in any form or by any means, electronic, mechanical, recording or otherwise, without the prior written permission of the author. This is a work of fiction. Any references to historical events, people, or real locales are used fictitiously. Other names, characters, places or incidents are the imagination and product of the author. Any similarity to real persons, living or dead, is coincidental and not intended by the author.

Book Cover Design by Todd Engel
Manufactured in the United States of America

Also by MD Fryson

Meridian Chronicles Series

Hall of Souls & The Book of the Fairies (#1)
Black Widow Curse & The Coven (#2)

Acknowledgements

I would like to thank Todd for the time spent finding a cover. It's always fun getting to work with you.

I would also like to thank the beta readers
Kari Lynn Isidori
Athena Engel
Savannah Bakker
Katie Thompson

To my editor
Finding a good editor is like finding a needle in a haystack. Thanks for helping me get better!

Thank you, Sam Wright

For my boys

You rowdy and boisterous boys are the biggest wonder to me,
Sometimes I sit and watch you in amazement that I have you three.
No matter where you go or what this life puts you through,
I am always here by your side to endure it with you.
Thanks for the laughs, the comedy and the fun you bring,
Even though somedays you make me feel I am hanging by a string.
Keep your wit, your sense of humor and your laughter,
I promise it can get you through any disaster.
Chase your dreams, always have hope and keep your curious mind,
Anything is possible. Just look and your dreams are there for you to find.

I love you now and always. Love, Mom

Dedication

There is a lot of work that goes into writing a book, with the behind the scenes.

I wouldn't have the time to even write without the help of my husband, Austin. With very busy lives and limited time at every turn, you always picked up the slack for this hobby I have. Couldn't do it or anything else without you. Not to mention you put up with my bold and blunt talk at home and you love me through the waves. I always knew you wanted to be a surfer!

I don't know what I would do without our sarcastic verbal sparring sessions at home that brings a smile to my face and makes me giggle. I love you very much.

Be good to one another, we are not promised tomorrow and if tomorrow arrives, you never know what tomorrow may bring.

Meridian Chronicles:
Fairy Nymphs & The Demon Court
By
MD Fryson

Chapter 1

The crimson flamed portal opened and hurled immense heat packed with indisputable winds. For a fallen, even he could barely resist its powerful waves of confoundment. Talon held the portal open and with his free arm, motioned with silence for Luna and the rest of the spirit guides to jump through. His red-skinned profile heated, and his left eye squinted tight as he bore the heat.

The roar of the wind continued as the main speaker as the group toggled through to the grand portal. Each took a deep breath and looked back over their shoulders after their first steps in. As they dragged their feet with dread, the audible crunching of the hardened dirt opened the floodgate of memories that filled their minds from the first time they visited the dark realm.

Moral was low and left only hope for each one to make it back from the dark realm. As they trudged through, the scenery remained as it had before, when spirit guides had their first encounter with the dark one and the demons. The same howling winds and a crimson atmosphere. Every bat of an eye to shield from the grit was like sandpaper to their eyes as they pushed through the heavy sulfurous air. With only a distant light to guide their way in through, it was nearly impossible to continue.

Fear for what they all anticipated spread from one to the other. Without the quiet confidence of Caius and his calming words, collectively the group ambiance was grim. The guides' thoughts ran away from each of their minds, they each relived the first time a demon's riddle was presented to them when they arrived with Meridian in the dark realm. Without her and the aid of her gifts, the tension grew thicker with each stride.

The group continued to push through the high winds and dust that showered them, giving each spirit guide a dusky hue. The dim light they pushed toward soon became a bright spot to focus upon.

"Why aren't the demons swarming us?" Pramlee asked. "The last time we were here, they were relentless in their psychological warfare."

"I can't say, that was the first thing I was expecting," Talon's amber eyes were suspicious.

The group tightened their circle, reaching their arms across to one another for protection. As they continued to move through the dark realm, the winds died down. Their vision was restored and the landscape appeared to be the same place from before, on their first trip where Relic was the first to take punishment for his sarcasm.

Pramlee stood close to Luna, taking her by the hand. Luna returned the gesture giving a nod accompanied by a comforting, firm squeeze leading Pramlee in their steps.

The dark and sinister voice spoke, echoing through the realm from all directions. Shivers traveled down the spines of the unwelcomed visitors with every word from the dark one.

"I see that you have returned without Caius who has taken his journey." The dark one brought out his guttural laugh. "What of Meridian, your special one? I would love to see that ethereal being. What has ever happened to your dear Meridian?" The dark one laughed once more in provocation. "To what do I owe the pleasure of your company? What are you willing to provide for my gracious sentiments?" his voice held notes of pleasure.

Discomfort increased amongst the group. Answering the dark one came naturally to Talon, though with hesitation. "We value your graciousness and it did not go unnoticed that we entered without challenge. I come to you again in need of your assistance."

Relic's discomfort ironically did not mirror his trusted friends. He stood, a half-cocked grin on his face, in the same place the dark one's fury had descended upon him not long ago. His memory of his last visit didn't seem to be a point of tension for him now. Scratching his head, he whispered to Luna, "Did he say gracious?" He leaned further into Luna who was nervous, however, she rolled her eyes and sighed without a verbal response. Relic continued. "So, sentiments? Really? I didn't think demons had all that." Luna gave a quick jab with her elbow into Relic's side. Stumbling as he grabbed his side, he straightened up his demeanor as the dark one answered Talon.

"Well, the last time you and I spoke, Relic seemed to want to offer entertainment, as he appears to want to again. You fled with him during the prior visit. You disappointed me stealing what was mine." The dark one's voice shifted as he recounted their prior visit when Meridian and Caius accompanied them into the dark realm. It was light in tone, like an attorney leading the opposition on the stand, waiting for an opening or an excuse to pounce, as though the lord of the dark realm needed an excuse.

Talon's confidence was fading. Admonishment flashed in his eyes as he cut them down at Relic. His shoulders stooped leading his head to follow suit. "I couldn't just leave Relic here. We answered your riddle, and we escaped. We deserved to leave if we could, and we did." Talon tilted his head slightly looking up into the red sky continuing to speak out to what he could not see with his own eyes.

"Yes, you did. You seemed to have forgotten the other riddle that has gone unanswered. It seems to me that a witch from your world called upon one of my demons from the high court. The humans have yet to answer that riddle."

Talon watched to Relic and Kieren who stood silently during the exchange. Relic lowered his head without eye contact and whispered as they would not hear if his voice by the dark one. "I was there for that calling. Raina, the witch. She called upon a demon for answers who could break Meridian's curse. It made not a bit of sense."

Relic shook his head and nodded to Kieren. Talon was silent with his thoughts as his eyes were carefully surveying the ground at the hardened dirt beneath his feet. His yellow eyes darted back up into the red and gritty atmosphere. "There was not an answer to that riddle!" Talon shouted.

The dark one laughed. "So, you think you are smarter than you appear to be?"

Talon continued, "Why would I trust a demon that was called on by a dark witch to answer a riddle?" Talon's rhetorical question struck a chord. Pacing back and forth, he continued to look upward for a response.

"A glimmer of the truth within a riddle remains, it is the answer to the riddle that sets the truth in motion. The fact of the matter remains you may not have the ability to make those distinctions, fallen!" The dark one grew louder and quick with his speech. He recounted the riddle.

> *"The being whose work is dark can only be stopped with the twin soul.*
> *The being you seek is hard to hold.*
> *Spirit guides who engage with a mortal are not pure of heart in that act,*
> *but in the face of true love all remain intact.*
> *Meridian does not trust herself in her choice.*
> *She will not listen to her inner voice.*
> *So many can enter her mind;*
> *Her greatest challenge in the true find."*

"So fallen, have I brought you back to the memory? What was the answer to the first riddle? Who would be responsible for finding her own twin soul? What is it Meridian lacks? You see, it does not matter who you call upon for help. In the end, it is only she that has her fate in her own hands," the dark one said.

Talon's anger rising, he shouted back to the dark one, "Who was the demon Raina summoned?"

The dark one laughed. "Why does it matter?" he continued to laugh and shake the entire dark realm. The deep baritone laughter struck their ears and coursed within their bodies, setting in motion a flurry of emotions.

"Who was it!" Talon shouted.

The dark one's voice shifted. His speech quickened, lighter, and aroused from deep rage with a venomous hiss. "The demon that was called upon was Pyro!" he hissed back.

The guides and Talon fell to the ground as it shook. The dark one's anger was unstoppable; he was on a journey of torment. "I am finished with your questions. What gifts have you brought this time, fallen? Your soul is banished, and a banished soul does not bring a benefit for me here."

Talon and the guides were writhing in pain on the heated crusty ground, barely able to speak. The dark one continued. "I do see that you have brought a fairy. I believe this is the first time I have had the chance to see a fairy." Luna froze with fear hearing the dark one speak of her, calling her out individually. She crawled holding herself in pain, making herself small as she reached for Relic, who remained motionless with fear. As she drew closer to Relic, her posture loosened and she slowly stood upright, drawing as close as she could to Relic while helping him to his feet.

"Oh no, I have been here before, with Lahash." Luna unlocked her tight jaw.

"Ah, yes, Lahash an up and coming favorite of the court. Yes, but your nymphs managed the distraction, didn't they?" The dark one asked. "I can summon Lahash for another try. I don't see your nymphs here. You are not as powerful as they. Is your fairy my gift, Talon?"

"We have not brought gifts, we have nothing to offer you." Talon was quick to his feet and moved to stand in front of Luna.

"Very well, I have other alternatives to appease me and bring pleasure. But first, what is it you desire?" the dark one asked.

"We have come for Chance, Charity, Janus, and Cora. We were told they were in Etheria. We also need to find out what has happened to Meridian and why the guides cannot communicate with her anymore." Talon begged his questions.

"Those are some grand requests and unfortunately, without gifts, I cannot help. Although I have been gracious, I will accept Luna to stay with us. We could use her gifts here in the dark realm. She would be a treat." Relic froze with fear, afraid to speak. "Or how about you, Relic, we started a game that we could not finish?" The dark one continued his psychological warfare.

"I will stay," Talon announced.

"Unacceptable. Your soul is already dark. I want something special. Something that will come in useful as I can see where things will be. I accept Luna here. Do we have an accord, fallen?" the dark one asked his question.

"Why do you want Luna?"

"Quiet! My reasons are not your concern. I accept your gift, Talon," the dark one said as Luna floated into the air, suspended and incoherent. Wisps of her hair brushed her blank face, her eyes turned black as she remained in suspension. The dark one laughed as her companions trembled watching their friend stifled before disappearing.

"Great! What are we going to do!" shouted Kieren. The laughs of the dark one grew into a crescendo. The ground shook beneath their feet once more. Stumbling to maintain composure, they all succumbed to the sequence of the dark one's pleasure of riddles. Talon who had kept his feet underneath him looked around to find only he and Relic stood with their wits. The dark one made no apologies for his fairy hijacking and only offered their question with a question.

"Answer the dark one's riddle and very soon you will find,
the solace you seek is hindered by a mark entwined.
Which direction will margana go?
Symbols and letters scramble to and fro.
The deceiver arrived in the time of new,
the birth sign is a part of a word, finding the word is your clue."

The dark one continued his warning. "You have one human week to return with your answer. Do it not and your friend will be mine forever." he laughed and slowly his laugh dwindled in sound as though he was moving away.

"Did he refer to himself in the third person?" Relic popped off. "You say I am the peacock?" Relic threw his hands up and looked to Talon.

Talon didn't feed into Relic's banter, they all quickly ported out before the dark one took any more of them to keep.

There had not been a peep from Warrick since the meeting he called. The lack of indication and silence had all minds wondering. Farrah and Arianna had gone missing right along with Slaten, Charity, Janus, and Cora. Back in the fairy realm, Ridge had been waiting for any clue about Warrick and those missing. Most importantly, he was awaiting Talon's return with Luna and the other guides with answers from the dark realm.

"What happened?" Ridge did not give Talon hardly any time to ask before the portal closed behind him. Talon did not speak, he turned his head away at Relic who appeared agitated and upset.

"What happened? I will tell you what happened, a repeat of the last time we went to the dark realm, only this time it wasn't me he wanted or Talon, he took Luna!" Relic hollered out. "Oh, and lucky guess another moronic riddle that we have one Earth week to figure out."

"Or?"

"He keeps her." Talon's voice was low and cross. Ridge said nothing in response. In disgust, he turned away and opened the door. Relic stood in front of Ridge. "Where are you going?"

"Where do you think? Selena needs to know this." Ridge attempted to walk but he came to a halt when the cat-like eyes that only Selena could have, stopped him in his tracks. She moved forward past the pair squabbling and sat down at the table that Ridge had been impatiently seated at, awaiting their return.

Selena quietly took a seat and bore her steely eyes directly to Ridge with a raised eyebrow and asked, "Why has the dark one taken my daughter? Has anyone wondered why the dark one, Warrick and the demon court member Lahash wanted my daughter before?"

"Well, for starters, Warrick was using her so you wouldn't help Talon, and Lahash has a thing for Fairies or didn't you notice that?" Relic sarcastically remarked. He stood with his arms crossed staring at Selena who cast her razor-sharp eyes on Relic, locked and loaded.

"I am going to pretend that I didn't hear that, Relic. I will also pretend that you aren't the mouthy idiot that you are. Lahash may have a thing for Echo, however, he would only do what the dark one ordered for no other reason than he hates Warrick just as much as we all do. I do not worry about harm coming to the guides while in the dark realm, I worry about Luna. She draws her strength from the Fairy realm, as all fairies do." Selena continued to stare at Relic.

"Selena, I realize you are going somewhere with all of this, I do not understand what it is, please." Ridge asked kindly.

Selena tipped up her chin as she took in Ridge's words. "Well, it is like our last talk, the secrets that have been kept from all of you. Things that you do not realize about your kind. Guides may have been human at one time, but. You learned lessons on Earth. The universe sent for you and your duty is to watch over humans. To guide them with so little as your presence. It seems so simple.

All this time you all believed that you were it, there were no angels or keepers. What else do you fathom you may not know? Guides are protected by the keepers from within the hall of souls. Not that you all cannot be harmed, but it isn't the same for a fairy. We have our powers of magic, however, if we are gone too long or weak, the weakened state leaves us vulnerable to perish."

Relic sat down. "Okay, so I honestly do not know what all this means or what we can do." Relic's demeanor changed. He was sympathetic and passionate.

"Our problems continue to grow. Not only have we not solved Meridian's situation with her curse, but she has also fled to Salem. They have kidnapped my daughter along with Charity and Chance. Warrick is missing along with Farrah and Arianna.

"I find myself in unfamiliar territory, as I usually have the answers. I struggle with things I entertain for the solving of such a dilemma. Talon, I must ask you to do something you will not want to do." Selena stared at Talon whose eyes widened and his shoulders drooped with the anticipation of her request. "I need you to reveal yourself to your son." There were gasps amongst everyone and Talon made no move to respond, he had felt something like this was coming.

"Why?" Talon finally asked as though he didn't know.

"Somehow, with the help of the guides, you all need to help convince Aiden that Meridian is worth fighting for," Selena demanded.

"Selena, I want my son happy and alive. We still do not know if he and Meridian are twin souls. He will die if we are wrong," Talon protested.

Selena continued to motivate the fallen. "Talon, have you been to Earth lately? What is happening? Spirit guides are missing from their duties leaving the evil to flourish uncontrollably on Earth and the hall of souls is close to empty. There will be no more humans. The race will die out, not to mention the unrest that has already begun. What kind of life will Aiden have if we don't take a chance? He will have no life at all."

Talon turned away from everyone and rubbed his hand down his neck as he let out a sigh. "You are right. You are right. This is no life for any of us. How do you expect me to do this without scaring the life out of him?"

Within moments, Selena disappeared offering no more of her assistance. The guides and Talon arrived in Salem after a quick port from the fairy realm where they were left with few alternatives.

***

Spring and all that accompanied it flourished in the air. The birds chirped in the trees and the smell of fresh cut grass covered the town of Salem as the happy gardeners manicured their lawns. Children laughed and played in the parks, with the muffled noises of barking dogs audible while being walked with their owners.

The invisible group passed on through to the edge of town where Esmra lived with her coven. Her home ominous and frozen in time did not change despite the many seasons come and gone. No pretty flower beds adorned her house from the front view, not a shrub visible at first glance. A few steps toward the backyard showed something very different. Trees hid a beautiful, secret garden in her back yard. The house, despite its inhabitants of good witches, appeared uninviting and lonely.

Pramlee, in her innocence, could make things around her lighter with her laughter, mainly at herself. She skipped up the old wooden stairs and stood over the dated and worn mat that lay in front of the aged door with the paint peeling off. The door opened, sending out a short squeak from the aged hinges.

There stood Esmra, still the same. Long unkempt grey hair appearing as though it had never seen a pair of scissors or developed a relationship with a hairdresser that knew what they were doing. Her wrinkled lips gave way to a thin smile where her bottom teeth made a brief appearance. She was still, only staring into an empty space.

"Oh, I sensed you were coming!" Esmra exclaimed. "If I could see all of you, I would hug you!" Esmra motioned to the invisible space for everyone to move alongside her into the house. At the end of the road, watching the exchange stood two city workers repairing the massive potholes from the wear of the weather. They stood baffled and one spoke out to the other. "Did you see that? That crazy old witch was talking to herself again." The worker shook his head and continued his work while the other continued to stare for a few moments more before hesitantly moving to continue while keeping his eyes locked on the house.

Inside, the house was quiet, only Esmra was home. Esmra spent the better half of her day in her garden tending to her herbs that she loved to harvest and use for oils and healing. "Come, it is beautiful outside today. The winter up here was harsh, and I welcome the spring. Esmra pulled herself a seat from the table in the yard. "What brings you here?"

With Luna gone, this left quite the strain on the communication between the spirits and Esmra. With only her exquisite senses that alluded to their presence, she could not have a straight conversation with them as she would Luna. Pramlee was the energetic one of the group and her energy surrounded Esmra, giving ease to a connection.

Relic with Ridge offered their unspoken support, pouring an immense amount of energy through Pramlee. Esmra closed her eyes and held a large crystal quartz as she took in the message. From her silence emerged a question from the unspoken message transferring through Pramlee. "Luna is gone? You came here by request of Selena once again. The dark one in the realm, he gave you a riddle." Esmra recounted her thoughts out loud. She picked up a pen that lay on the table next to a note pad she used for making notes of things she had to tend to each day.

She picked up the yellow note pad and took out one sheet of paper and wrote down the demon's riddle. After a moment of silence, she finished writing and read the message.

"Only one Earth week to answer, or Luna is stuck in the dark realm? Oh my, this is serious." Esmra got up from the table and walked toward her garden as she stood gazing out into the horizon with her hand over her mouth. "Meridian was here, she came shortly after I left Tallulah's. I received a call from Tallulah, and she told me what happened, that Meridian thought the only way she could break the curse was to come here and have us all do another ritual again. She was very disappointed when I reminded her of Selena's words. That only Meridian could uncover the twin soul she seeks to break her curse. She did try to convince me otherwise, but I had to continue to remind her." Esmra returned to her chair and sat down. She stared into her lap and continued.

"Raina was here with her and asked me to perform another ritual and I declined. I have not seen them since, and I can only say Meridian is staying with Raina at the edge of town. I am sorry I cannot be of more help there. I have called Meridian's phone and even sent her text messages, which I do not do normally. She never responds or replies. I was thinking of going to Nevoc to find out what has happened.

Give me some time and I will do what I can to answer this riddle, at the least get Luna out of the dark realm."

***

They departed from the witch's house and in moments they were standing in front of Raina's bar. It was closed to the public, and no one was there. The guides moved through the walls and went directly to where Raina's office sat hoping to find Meridian or Raina. As they made their way in, they were disappointed to find there was no sign of either woman. Raina's desk was covered with journals, tarot cards, and a Ouija board.

Talon walked around her desk and examined the state of things strewn across the desk. "Look at this mess. It someone was in here rummaging through things and then left a big mess behind."

Pramlee stopped and stood next to Ridge. "I wish Slaten were here. I feel bad leaving him in Etheria with the way things happened. I worry what Father will do. If he were here, he could help us figure this out." Pramlee sat down on Raina's old couch in frustration.

Ridge continued to study Raina's desk and he saw a small wooden box with the Celtic symbol engraved on the top that was a witch's knot. It was not shut all the way and he could see a hint of the red velvet lining with an empty space in the middle of the box. "What do you make of this?" He pointed at the box. Talon and Pramlee shrugged their shoulders. Kieren and Relic were walking around the room looking for any hint of Meridian.

Relic could see the box from where he stood. "Who the hell knows with that crazy witch. Meridian, when we saw her in here the last time, she was in a trance of some kind and with everything that happened that night with Josh, we know Raina is keeping her under a dark spell. By the looks of this office, it seems to me that Raina has been communicating with the demon more. We still have yet to figure out this riddle. I know Esmra will do what she can but we have to really stop and think about what the demon said when Raina summoned him from Tallulah's place. In the new riddle, he mentioned a mark. Meridian has the infinity mark on her wrist, but that does not make sense. That mark would not be a hindrance. It means her mark is to show enlightenment, gifts, and purity. What mark is he talking about?" Relic continued walking around Raina's office muttering to himself over and over.

Talon peered through the window that stood next to the front door of the bar. Across the street there was another business with a sign outside that read 'Stone's Tattoo shop.' "Do any of you have any reason to believe that the word mark had any real significance? Do you think that was a trick to throw us? Why would the dark one help us? It was too easy. No demons attacked us like they did before when we went into the dark realm. There were no games, it was almost like he expected us or wanted us to be there. He didn't really hurt anyone. Why?" Talon raised a question that brought to light many things that even the guides had not thought of.

***

Across the realms back on Earth, spring break was around the corner for Aiden. He was alone in the dorm while Chris was over at his girlfriend's place seeing her off before she went away on her trip. Aiden sat on his bed with his elbows on his knees, hands clasped resting underneath his chin. The afternoon light shone through the windows brightening his blue eyes. Chris made it back to find Aiden staring at the floor where his bags set.

"Aiden, you ready?" Chris's smile left his face. He leaned his shoulder into the doorway and watched Aiden staring at his packed bag.

"I guess, I was sitting here wondering if I wanted to even go home or not. Maybe I should take a trip and be alone." Aiden stood up from his bed not breaking his eyes away from his bags.

"Look, man, you have been gloom and doom since we got back from Christmas break. I know that you care for Meridian, but the reality is, she dumped you. She took off. I have never seen you this way over a girl. Maybe it isn't meant to be, and besides all that crazy stuff that went down with Josh and let's not forget Raina. I have never in my life seen anything like that before and I never want to again." Chris's agitation with Aiden's melancholy state increased and he huffed as he turned around as if to leave the room.

Aiden broke his long stare. "Wait, wait. I know. I know you are right. I know how this must be driving you crazy. All the times you tried to get me out and even setting me up on that blind date. Which, by the way, during the date she was annoying. She wasn't Meridian. You were trying to help me, as a good friend would do," Aiden solemnly said.

"We can go home, you can visit your grandparents, you hardly even call them anymore. We can go fishing like we have been putting off. We can just be guys. It will be like old times! Me and you!" Chris slapped Aiden on his back and laughed. Aiden's face relaxed and a hint of his teeth showed through as he let out a sigh.

"Yeah man, okay. Okay. I will be all right. I just need to stay busy." Aiden reluctantly moved toward his bag, picked it up and followed Chris out to Aiden's truck to go home. "So, are you staying with us? Or what?" Aiden asked.

"Well, my parents are taking a trip to Cancun for a week, so I will come stay with you all." Chris was digging through his bag for his iPod.

"Why don't you go with them? That would be a fun trip." Aiden's face furrowed in hearing about a trip. "Why haven't you ever mentioned that before?

"Oh, no . . . this is a second honeymoon for them. Since I have been gone to school, it's like they are kids again. They need the trip alone. Besides, I will be home for summer and we have plans."

The pair continued to drive home, Aiden's heaviness returned, lingering in the truck despite Chris doing what he could to lighten up the scene.

Trying not to stare at Aiden as he drove, Chris kept shifting his head back and forth from the truck window to watching Aiden drive. "So, are you happy to be going home?"

Aiden continued to stare out of the windshield studying the scenery as they passed by the landscape full of trees in their spring bloom. Aiden drew a slow breath and sighed. "Yeah, I suppose. I miss my grandparents. I am unsure how it will go for me. This break up is unlike anything I have ever experienced. It is amazing that in such a short time I became so hung up on a girl. Just as fast as it began, it was over like it was a dream. I hope that the one place I love doesn't turn into something I dread. Going home, I mean." he paused and cut his eyes over at Chris who was listening intently. "I can't stop thinking about her. I picked up the phone to call her so many times, and I would put the phone down and stare at it. Like some fool, I was hoping I would see her number show up on my phone. I hoped that she would have changed her mind. I did text her a few weeks after everything happened, she never answered me."

Chris turned his head away to stare out the window and they continued for most of the trip in silence. After a while, Aiden stopped at the convenience store for fuel for the last stretch of the trip.

Chris went into the restroom while Aiden strolled up and down the aisle looking for something to snack on. Walking through the aisle he peeked over his shoulder as if he heard something. His eyes surveyed the space above the aisle. He turned his body toward what he thought may have been Chris who was still in the bathroom. Aiden squinted his eyes and frowned with confusion then he saw the clerk who was busy checking out another customer. Aiden continued to look at the minimal selection of mainly old stale cookies and crackers. He walked toward the drinks rubbing the back of his neck and stopped at the refrigerated selection of energy drinks. After selecting a drink, he turned to walk toward the clerk and came to a quick halt as he heard his name.

A dark voice was audible speaking in a whisper. "Aiden, don't give up."

Aiden looked around searching for where the voice came from. The hairs on the back of his neck rose and chills raced down his spine. As the chills made their way through the whole of his body, the hair on his arms stood straight up. Aiden shook, and froze in his tracks with fear.

Chris made his way out around the corner. "Hey man, so are you ready?"

Aiden, still frozen in his tracks holding his drink, didn't answer Chris right away. His eyes fluttered in confusion. Chris looked around and then back to Aiden who still had not moved. "Are you all right Aiden? What is wrong?"

"I don't know, I thought I heard a voice speaking it said my name. This is weird and it's really freaking me out." Aiden rushed his breathing. He broke his statue-like posture and brought his free hand up to his chest as he collected himself. "That is one of the strangest things that has happened."

Chris stood scratching his head in disbelief while he glimpsed the clerk and the other customers now staring at Aiden with concern. "No, the instance at Tallulah's is the strangest." Chris moved toward Aiden and put his hand behind Aiden's elbow. "Hey man, let's pay for your drink and get on the road. It's getting late." Chris ushered Aiden to the checkout.

Back in the dark realm, Luna remained in her demon-induced sleep unaware of where she was. Not far away in the same realm, a familiar face entered the great meeting room where the dark one addressed his court. He eagerly sat at the stone table with the flame in the center and watched the other members of the high demon court take their seats.

The other demons who sat in council each ruled their own legions of demons. They each had their own purpose, duties, and obligations to fulfill in return for the highly regarded position bestowed upon each one.

The other three demons, Moloch, Astaroth, and Ipos strolled in for the expected meeting the dark one called for. The familiar face last to enter, who eagerly waited for the conversation to begin was not welcomed, though tolerated not by choice. Lahash stared at the one demon in the high court that mostly was regarded as an outcast.

"Warrick. I see that you have struggled in creating the perfect solution for yourself and us. It speaks volumes that the dark one had to do your dirty work and what a debt you will pay." Lahash laughed.

"Lahash if it weren't for your lust of Echo falling victim to the fairy nymphs, the dark one would not have interfered. You failed!" Warrick shouted at the demon.

The encompassing baritone voice of the dark one shot out, fiercely through the cave. "SILENCE BOTH OF YOU! YOU FOOLS!"

The dark one shouted at the bickering demons. Both sat slumped in their chairs made of rock without so much as a peep, their heads dropped low and their eyes only flickered in panic for the anticipated verbal whipping that no doubt would come to pass.

The dark one continued. "Indeed, Warrick, I had to do your dirty work and we were lucky that Talon brought us Luna with ease. Soon the hall of souls will be depleted, and the keepers will no longer have the souls to send to Earth. The humans will die out."

Lahash sat silently drumming his long fingers slowly across the stone table. His fright slowly left, he brought his head up, locking eyes with Warrick for just a moment before he dropped his eyes once more, watching his fingers with a smirk, as he was alone in his own thoughts. Unapologetically he said, "Forgive me lord, but is it possible you have missed things. I worry that we may be short sided. It is troublesome to think humans will become extinct. What will the demons feed on if the ill-willed humans have died out? What will we do then?" Lahash got up from his chair and paced around the table full of demons.

"Lahash, our plan to diminish humanity is a necessity. The angels, the keepers of human souls have no souls to watch over after we invade the hall of souls." The dark one laughed, shaking the cave and the chairs the demons filled. "They possess the purest of energy force in the universe. It is through the angels that souls transcend. They are the conductors of the universe. With their energy for us to finally benefit from, we will no longer have a use for the humans.

Chapter 2

Orion stood guard at the Queen's door, and it was quiet in the Fairy realm. With the silence, his mind drifted as he stared through the opening to the massive garden right outside Selena's chambers. The hallway leading to Selena's quarters, dark and damp oozing with the smell of moss and the audible sounds of dripping water echoed through the halls taking Orion away to his memories of his first home.

There he stood as young Orion, childlike and innocent while he played in the river. Against his dark chocolate skin that glowed under the sunlight, made his amber eyes pop. A few feet away over a grassy knoll, his quaint home sat where he lived with his parents and siblings. As he played in the river alone, he studied the stones he found before he put them in his brown pouch to collect. As he continued to collect his stones, a tragedy was unfolding with an attack by a legion of demons sent out from the dark one, to end his kind and their existence.

Little Orion was too young to understand what was happening as he saw flames engulf his home as the demons lay waste to everything he knew. Days and nights passed, and little Orion wondered himself into exhaustion looking for his family. He traveled several miles over the course of the days he searched for his family until he could not go any further.

He lay down at the base of a tree and watched with dying eyes as the low swinging limbs brushed his small hands. His breathing was shallow and stressed, his face hollow and sunken in.

Orion later awakened to find himself in new surroundings. His clothes were removed and replaced with green, soft fabric. His hunger pacified, and he felt rested and rejuvenated. Orion could not recount the time lapse from when he went to sleep under the big tree until the moment his eyes opened.

The cool, damp air was heavy with the scent of moss. Chuckling and cackling was audible in the distance trailed with whispers. Three beautiful beings stood over little Orion watching him take in his new surroundings. From a short distance, soft footsteps came closer, revealing another beautiful being with yellow cat-like eyes and white translucent skin.

She pushed her black hair over her shoulder as she rested her hand over his forehead. "There, there, now. You are safe, no one will hurt you, little one."

Selena interrupted Orion's placid streams of memories. "Orion! Are you alright?" She put her hand on Orion's large forearm. Her face was tight with worry.

"Oh, yes, my Queen, I was daydreaming was all. I am fine." Orion moved to change the subject. "So, what news do you have to share? Are the guides going to go on your quest?"

"Oh, of course. They went back to the witch with another demon's riddle. Their entry was a little too easy and the riddle is very difficult. It may be time for the quartz sword. Come, we will go inside and you will learn its history." Selena motioned Orion inside her quarters where the fairy nymphs were seated at the grand table in the center of the room, enjoying the fairy drinks influencing their joy and laughter.

Chapter 3

Raina had awoken from just a few hours of sleep. She was in her kitchen waiting on her coffee maker to finish filling her coffee pot that needed a wash. Picking up her phone, she quickly dialed and after a brief silence on the other end, she spoke.

"Hey, it's me. So, yeah, I will need more. I am running low and the effects are wearing off. I get maybe six hours at the most. I need something stronger that lasts longer than six hours. It is getting more difficult to find ways to get Meridian to take it at the right time." Raina's voice lowered to a whisper as she walked down the hall, past the bedroom where Meridian lay asleep.

"So how fast can you have it?" Raina listened and resumed speaking after a moment. "Good, so I will meet you then, same place, same time." She hung up the phone and Meridian who had walked into the kitchen startled her.

"Oh! Meridian! You scared me! I thought you were asleep." Raina put her hand to her chest catching her breath.

Meridian was yawning and scratching her head. "Well, I thought I heard you talking to someone." Meridian nodded to Raina's hand where she still had her cell phone.

Raina looked down at her hand and back to Meridian. "Oh, yes, of course. I was talking to one of my suppliers. Checking in to let me know that he won't be able to deliver this week, that the beer I wanted is out and that he will bring it next week." Raina put her phone down and poured herself a cup of coffee. "Want some?"

"Sure, I could use caffeine." She sat down at the table. Raina's place was small but suitable enough for the two. She stared outside the bay window at the quiet street while Raina slipped off into the pantry.

"So, do you want creamer? I have a new flavor to try if you would like." Raina peeked out of the pantry at Meridian.

Meridian didn't break her stare out the window. "Sure, I am always up for something new."

Raina pulled out a bottle of blue elixir adding a few drops into Meridian's coffee. She skipped out of the pantry over to Meridian. "Here! This one is a chocolate flavor, I just love it. Ya know, it has been so awesome having you around, and with your good looks, you have certainly been good for business, huh?!" Raina smiled and nudged Meridian's arm. "The tips you are getting, no one else is that lucky in tips." Raina took a sip of her coffee.

Meridian broke her stare to watch Raina stirring her coffee. "Yeah, I have enjoyed myself here. I have met neat people in this town." Meridian sipped her coffee. "So, when do you think we could go back over and see Esmra? I know that you two don't get along that well, but remember I came here to find out about my curse. It is so odd that for all this time, Esmra is always busy or gone. Right?" Meridian said with doubt in her voice.

"Oh, you know Esmra, she goes with the wind. No telling what she is up to. Even though she doesn't approve of me, shouldn't be any reason for you not to go, I will make sure we go over there this week." Raina stood up and put her coffee mug in the sink. "How about a shower? I am sure that will help you feel better."

Raina went into the bathroom and turned on the shower and rushed back into the bedroom and dug through Meridian's purse for her phone. She read messages Meridian received from Esmra days ago. The last text from Esmra read "Meridian, are you all right? I thought you all were coming. Do I need to come to you?"

Raina quickly deleted several of Meridian's messages. A loud bang from the shower from Meridian dropping the shampoo startled Raina causing her to miss one of the last messages that Esmra had sent to Meridian. She put Meridian's phone back into her purse and walked into the bathroom.

"Meridian, I have an errand to run. Will you be all right?" Raina pulled the shower curtain back and Meridian was rinsing her hair.

"I think I will be. I feel a little dizzy again. That doctor you took me to, should we go back? I keep having my headaches. The prescription, can you get it for me?" Meridian pointed to the shelf on the wall.

"Sure." Raina pulled a prescription bottle down with Meridian's name on the label. The prescription label read Xanax. "Here, this should help you relax. Your anxiety has been worse this past couple of weeks."

Meridian left the bathroom wrapped up in a towel and sat on the end of the bed holding her head. She slowly lifted her head from her hands and stared off. Raina waved her hands in front of Meridian. "Meridian, hello?" Meridian turned and smiled at Raina.

"Hi Raina, you are playful today." Meridian giggled and lay back on the bed laughing.

Raina collected her things in anticipation of her meeting. "Well, good, everything is working out," Raina muttered to herself as she watched Meridian giggle.

Meridian sat up and said, "So, when will you be back? I will need you to take care of me, you know." Meridian flashed a smile and bit her bottom lip. Raina leaned over and gave Meridian a kiss.

"Oh, I will be back, and we will definitely take care of one another." Raina left and headed out for her meeting while Meridian passed out on the bed.

Raina dashed out of the house looking disheveled and unkempt from not sleeping with work and staying up late with Meridian. Her worries of not maintaining the lies never gave her rest. She walked into town several blocks away and went into a coffee house and sat down at a table. As she waited, she dug through her purse and pulled out the bottle that held the elixir she had been giving Meridian. As she held it up, the bottle was nearly empty. Raina placed the bottle on the table as the server arrived to take her order.

"What can I get you to drink?" The server asked Raina as she stared at the bottle. Raina moved her hand over the bottle.

"I will take coffee, black." Raina swiped the bottle back into her purse and was startled when the person she was meeting showed up.

"So, you are already out, are you?" The tall, thin, dark-headed woman dressed in a long, black, summer dress took her sunglasses off and set them on the table as she made herself comfortable. Adorned in jewelry, her fingernails were perfectly manicured with red polish. She sat with her hands clasped in her lap as she looked on Raina with a grin. "Well, I always knew you to be impetuous, but I didn't fathom you would use elixir again. When you called me the first time, I was a little surprised. This got you kicked out of Esmra's coven the first time. She has reluctantly let you back in and you are using magic on the person you were to help. Now I am curious. So, it begs the question, what are you up to?"

Raina studied the bottle, fumbled it with her fingertips and finally answered. "I need her," Raina said as she locked eyes with her friend. "Amelia, please do not give me a hard time on this one. I need her."

Amelia sat back in her chair with her arms now crossed. The server had returned with coffee and as the waitress set a cup in front of her; she lifted her hand from the cross of her arm. "None for me, thank you." Amelia looked back at Raina who was stirring sugar into her drink. "Raina, I am thinking that you have lost your way and you have forgotten what magic is about, what it is for. Every witch knows that when she uses dark magic, it comes back times three. You are in over your head." Amelia leaned forward in her chair and stared at Raina who had stopped stirring her coffee. "You will pay the price. Are you sure you want to continue down this path?"

Raina took a sip of her coffee and stared down at the bottle on the table and she didn't blink as she swallowed.

Never moving the coffee cup away from her face, she quietly said without emotion, "Yes."

Amelia picked up her purse and dug out a small black velvet bag and laid it on the table. "Very well then, here it is. This is the last I will give you. I hope you know what you are doing and what you are getting yourself into because I sure do," Amelia said as she stood up from the table and left Raina sitting and staring at the table.

Back at Raina's place, Meridian still lay asleep on the bed in a dream state. It was dark and slowly the darkness gave way to a flickering light in the distance. Meridian saw herself as she walked toward the small flickering light, dressed in white, her hair long and bright blonde. She entered a tunnel leading toward the flickering light. As she drew closer, the light became brighter, unbearable to her eyes. Blinded, she used her arms as a shield and continued her slow pace pushing onward.

She peered outward through the breaks in her arms to find her way and the silence gave way to distant cries of sobbing women. At this moment, Meridian was no longer looking at herself, but she was seeing things through her own eyes. A voice from the light spoke out to her.

"Meridian, you have come once again. I cannot see you, but I know you are near."

Meridian brought her arms down away from her face and she found she could see into the light without it hurting her eyes. Her feet dragged inches closer to the mysterious voice that echoed from deep within the light. The wind from the power of the light blew her hair back away from her face.

The voice spoke again. "Meridian, you cannot know how much I miss you. Your path has led you astray and you must find your way again and find your way back home. Remember who you are, Meridian."

Meridian threw up her hands in frustration and then threw them down just as quick, as they slapped her sides she said, "I don't understand, where is home? How do I know where to go?"

The low and familiar voice had one last message for Meridian. "Look to yourself and remember who you are, and you will find your way home. All is not lost with faith. Listen to your heart, Meridian. I sleep near the angels, but I am always with you. Remember . . . remember." The voice trailed off into a whisper and Meridian woke up startled.

She sat up in the bed and rubbed her head as she felt dizzy from the effect of the Xanax and the elixir. She got out of bed and went into the bathroom slowly, supporting herself by placing her hands on the walls in the hallway as she walked.

She flipped on the light switch and gazed into the mirror above the sink. The bright sunlight shone through the window in the bathroom and reflected off the bright white walls decorated with black and white photography. Meridian turned on the water and let it run for a few moments while her eyes adjusted to the bright room. While she watched the water run from the faucet, she thought.

That dream was so strange, and I think I have heard that voice in a dream before, but I can't recall. Why can't I remember anything? Why is everything so fuzzy all the time? Why when I check my phone, does it seem that no one has texted me? Why doesn't Esmra answer me back? Why does it seem that I do not know why I am here anymore? Why do I catch myself thinking of Aiden one day and then it is as though he hides from me? He hides from me in my mind. Maybe I am going crazy.

The tears fell down Meridian's cheek as she wrestled with her thoughts and stared at the stranger in front of her. Suddenly she heard the front door slam shut. Startled, she quickly splashed water on her face to wipe away the smeared eyeliner she never washed away along with tears. Meridian grabbed her toothbrush and began nonchalantly brushing her teeth.

"Hello! Meridian are you up, girl?" Raina strolled down the hall into the bathroom.

Meridian was still brushing and she put her finger up as she leaned over the sink to spit out a mouthful of toothpaste. "Oh, hey, Raina. Yeah, I am freshening up. So, where have you been?"

Raina stood in the doorway with her arms crossed. She pulled her hand out and examined her nails. "Oh, I had coffee with an old friend, from Esmra's."

Meridian perked up. She threw her towel down on the sink. "Yes! Esmra, when can we go see her?" Meridian was smiling and happy to hear the name.

"Oh, well, we can go now." Raina was suspect. "So why the big interest to see Esmra? I mean she hasn't returned your texts, has she?" Raina stared Meridian down.

Meridian was taken back. "Oh, I want to see her, I mean she may have forgotten to answer. So, when can we go? Who is the old friend? What about the account?" Meridian walked out of the bathroom to the bedroom to get clothes to wear. As she undressed, Raina remained quiet and came up behind her and groped her. "Why don't we spend time together?" Raina whispered in her ear.

Meridian froze and pushed Raina's hands away as she stiffened up. "Well, I want to go over to Esmra's." Meridian smiled nervously and resumed getting dressed not paying attention to Raina's reaction. Raina sat back down on the bed and huffed.

"So, what's the deal? Why are you being a cold fish?"

Meridian paused before she pulled her shirt over her head. "Cold fish? I don't think because I want to see Esmra that I am a cold fish." Meridian walked out of the bedroom and left Raina sitting on the bed. After a few moments, Raina followed Meridian and found her in the kitchen with a glass of water.

"I am so thirsty. I seem to always stay so thirsty. We need to get more to drink here, we are out of everything." Meridian opened the door to a nearly empty ice box.

Raina did not look over at the fridge. She dug through her purse and pulled out the elixir she acquired and poured a few drops into an ice coffee drink she had purchased. "Here, I was passing by a small store and they had these, you like these ice coffees." Raina handed Meridian the drink.

Meridian gulped it down. "Thanks, I wish I knew why I stay so thirsty all the time. It is strange. I mean there are moments I don't feel that way but over the past couple of weeks it has gotten worse." Meridian said as she examined the empty glass that had held the coffee.

Raina put her bag on her shoulder, "Are you ready to go to Esmra's?" With a nod from Meridian, she finished getting dressed and they got into Raina's old beat up Honda she rarely had to drive and took off.

Chapter 4

Slaten rushed down the hall of the palace. His brisk and determined walk went uninterrupted as Farrah hurried behind him to keep up urging him to calm down.

"Slaten, please it is no use. Your father will not see things any other way. You will only make things worse. Please." Farrah pulled on Slaten's arm while he tried to pull away but stopped to face her.

"Mother, I know that you have stayed here with him because you are afraid. I came back Etheria, with you in hopes to help things settle down. For what? Pramlee snuck out of here and took off. Janus and Cora are gone. According to the rumors, Charity and Chance are in the dark realm. We all know Father has connections there. Now he keeps you locked up here. Why do you put up with this?" Slaten hollered out as he raised his hands up.

"Going at it in this manner won't help. I am just playing the part without objection right now. At least Janus is all right even if they locked away her. It takes time. Please, do not do this." Farrah hugged Slaten despite he remained stiff and reluctant to return the embrace.

"Mother, what am I supposed to do? Stay here and allow Relic and Ridge to go on without my help? I need to be out there helping them! Pramlee sent word they went to the dark realm and now Luna is stuck in there. What do you think will come of that? They need her to communicate with Esmra. I feel so out of touch here and worthless!" Slaten turned his back and ran his hands through his light brown hair. Farrah's face flushed bright red through her pale skin as cried. "Mother, I am sorry. I do not think for a minute he isn't up to something. For you I won't, but for now." Slaten rushed to his quarters leaving his mother standing in the middle of the hallway. She flinched at the echo of Slaten slamming his door shut.

Farrah turned and continued her walk until she reached Warrick's quarters and she hesitated to knock when she heard voices shouting from inside. She put her hand down and leaned into the door where she could hear Warrick yelling.

"What do you mean? Brennan is a traitor! He left here after our trip to where we encountered the dark one and he told the others! I want his banishment! Now that we have Luna in the dark realm, Selena will have no other choice but to step back and leave things the way they are. The war she threatened at the council meeting is a farce and will not come to pass. I have managed to escape the trial Charity set out for me, among other things."

The other voice spoke back to Warrick. Farrah continued to strain to listen to who he was speaking with.

"Warrick, you have the dark one's support. We feel Charity, Chance, and Luna locked away with the dark one is more than enough protection. We have acquired Janus and Cora. It minimizes the threats for you. Banishing Brennan away will only go to substantiate everyone's claims. The court has already made the judgment. They cannot remain forever. You have stopped casting guides away. By doing so, the humans are slowly progressing into what we want. Their evil ways are there for the demons to continue feeding upon. As wonderful as this all is for us, it will not last. At some point we will have to face Selena and take her out. You will have your realm the way you want it when you turn over the keys to the hall so we may finish our work. This is not up for negotiation. I am just warning you. Your time grows short and our master will have what he wants."

Farrah continued to listen through the door while footsteps coming near were audible. She quickly jumped away and took a step toward the door to appear as though she had just arrived.

"What are you doing here?" Warrick snapped.

Farrah fumbled her words, "Uh, well I wanted to see if you had anything else for me to work on? I have nearly completed the writings for the next council meeting. Are we still going to have that meeting with Brennan and Charity?"

Warrick shut the door behind him. "Yes, why do you ask?" Warrick was suspicious.

Farrah stepped away from Warrick. "Oh no reason, I was wondering when?"

Warrick stared at Farrah and he had an eyebrow up. "I don't know that at this time. What else do you want?"

Farrah made an advance to open Warrick's door. "Well, I thought I would collect the journals for the meeting, you know the notes."

Warrick stepped in front of her. "You have never asked for them before, why now?"

"Well, I guess I don't need them, it is just that, it has been a while and I worry I will forget to add something to the agenda."

Warrick slid his hand down from the door slowly. "That won't be necessary." He walked away without another word, leaving her standing alone.

Etheria was quiet despite all the guides having been banned from watching over their humans leaving them to remain there in the realm. They were subdued and many guides had remained in their quarters, feeling they existed without purpose. As the humans remained without the help of their spirit guides, things on Earth were at unrest. To most humans, this showed the times they live in.

Aiden and Chris had made it home to Aiden's grandparents' house and awoke the next day to a long list of chores that Aiden's grandpa had left for them to complete while they were home for their spring break. Both were out in the pasture on four-wheelers holding bags of feed as they led the herd of cattle toward the pens.

"So, Chris, how long has it been? Are you ready to get dirty?" Aiden laughed.

Chris wasn't thrilled, staring with dread as the many cows bustled one another as they competed for the cow cake strewn through the pasture. "It has been a while, stop laughing. You know I hate doing this. You owe me a fishing trip, man!" Chris threw a rock at Aiden as he was jumping off his four-wheeler.

"Well, Grandpa wouldn't let us three do all the work, we have help to come in. Besides do you have any idea how long it would take to mark, spray and vaccinate three hundred head?" Aiden threw a rock back at Chris.

The pair stayed busy all day until the sun set. Aiden smiled more than usual, having not mentioned much about Meridian. The boys went inside to clean up and eat a meal from the grandmother who had her hands full cooking for the lot that showed up to help for the day.

The aroma from the cooking filled the house and hung right outside the screen door, teasing a hungry group.

The steaks were piled high alongside Grandmother's famous mashed potatoes. Aiden and Chris ran up the steps slugging one another and laughing to see who could get there first. As they busted through the door, a familiar voice filled the air, over the clanging of pots and pans coming from the kitchen.

"You boys better cut it out! Get in here and eat before the human garbage disposals arrive and eat more than they should!" Grandmother's voice trailed off as she went back to whistling.

Aiden and Chris collected themselves and walked into the kitchen and stood smiling ear to ear. "Grams, I smell it! Where it is? Hide it! They will come in here and I won't get any." Aiden was hunting for the cobbler, fumbling through the cupboards and lifting lids on everything that was set out in the kitchen.

Aiden's grandmother stood at the table sorting out plates and silverware and she walked over and slapped Aiden's hand as he was digging into another bowl. "Get out! Your hands are filthy, you are filthy. If you can't manage a shower first, the least you could do is wash your hands!"

Aiden giggled and walked over to the sink to wash his hands. As Aiden scrubbed, his grandmother, grinned at Chris and pointed. "You too!"

The boys eventually ate and made it upstairs to scrub off the day's hard work. They continued their light-hearted fun visiting in Aiden's room. Chris had said little to Aiden about what took place at the convenience store the night before. He glanced at Aiden, to find the best way to approach the subject, meanwhile he turned on the television while Aiden was sorting his dirty laundry.

"So last night, at the convenience store, you want to tell me what the hell that was all about?" Chris asked.

Aiden stopped sorting his laundry and sat down in the chair at his desk across from Chris. Aiden threw his head back and stared at the ceiling and swayed back and forth. His hair now grown past his shoulders hung over the chair as he swayed. "Well, I told you, I thought I heard something talking but it wasn't human or anything I could see either." Aiden stopped swiveling his chair. "Don't get that look on your face, I do not think it was anything like what Raina turned into."

"So, like a ghost or something?"

Aiden shook his head. "I don't know. I know I heard it and it said not to give up."

Chris was struggling as he scratched his head. "Look man, you have been under a lot of stress and have been upset. Are you sure you are all right? You can trust me, I wouldn't do anything that would cause you problems, you know this. I am worried. Don't take me wrong, today was the first time I have seen you smile in a long time. I want you happy. It's just that in all the years we have been friends, I have never seen you this way. So hung up on a girl. I mean in the past, you would date casually, always treated girls with respect, and somehow even at a breakup, you never acted as though it bothered you so much. I am a little jealous, I guess. I wished I could always bounce back the way you do." Chris smiled as he reminisced about some of Aiden's old breakups from prior years. "So, really, I don't know how to take you like this is all. I want everything to be okay with you."

Aiden drew a large breath followed by a slow sigh. "Yeah, I know man. I don't think I am losing it. I believe there is more to life than what we know for sure. I believe that there is something watching over us. Meridian is different, I knew it the night she came up at Stephanie's. When Eric first talked about Meridian, before I ever saw her, I had this feeling. This feeling I had to know who she was, to meet her. Something told me that I could not let the chance go by. When she walked up that night the feeling that came over me was unlike anything I could explain. I knew she was special, she had that 'something' intangible." Aiden looked back at his bed where Meridian lay the night he saved her from Raina, he smiled and continued as Chris listened. "When I looked into her eyes, it was like I knew her from somewhere, but I couldn't say where. I felt as though I was coming home, only no home I had ever been. I guess love at first sight isn't some fleeting thought or cliché. Not for me now anyway." Aiden was interrupted when Chris jumped in to point out what was on the television.

"You see that! Some lunatic went into a bank, shot everyone up and left with a lot of cash. The other day I was listening to the radio and there was some nationwide hunt for a suspected serial killer. My dad phoned and said one of our local shops got broken into and that the day before some lady went into the store going off on the owner over a refund or something. Seems lately its always bad news." Chris continued to watch the television. "My mom told me that a friend of hers that is a nurse at the hospital has seen two stillbirths. Strange."

Aiden watched the news with Chris as they both silent. After a while of watching, Aiden shut off the television. "Hey, no more gloom and doom. Let's get some shut eye. We can go fishing tomorrow, early." Aiden shut off the lights and he lay in bed, staring at the ceiling of his bedroom where his mind slowed down and it took his thoughts over by his subconscious. Meridian swam in his mind, ruling his thoughts and all he could envision was her face smiling back at him the night they met, he could almost smell her skin and feel her touch. His memories overwhelmed his mind as he thought of the last time he saw her before she left on the bus to Salem. Soon, Chris fell asleep as Aiden lay awake. After a while, Aiden rolled over and picked up his phone, pulling up Meridian's name in his address book. He began texting her.

Meridian, I hope you are doing ok. I think of you a lot. I am home and it makes it worse. I miss you.

Aiden stared at the message for a few seconds and hesitated to send it. He thought of Raina and how vile she was and how he hated her. With those thoughts, hitting send was the easiest thing he had done all day. After he hit send, he stared at his phone for a bit before he fell asleep.

Chapter 5

Pramlee, Ridge, Kieren, and Relic were still in Salem searching for any clues to find Meridian. Just as Talon had spotted the tattoo shop across the street, they all stood and watched the artist tattooing one of his clients. "Think about it. A mark, the demon said something about a mark." Talon said as he pointed in the window.

Relic stood and stared. "No, no, what about the riddle from Pyro? The night at Tallulah's house when Raina summoned, Pyro through the Ouija board? Is that his name? Really? So, does he play with fire down there in hell? That doesn't seem to be a prerequisite, or really, if that is that demon's only talent, then he isn't working to his full potential." Relic was snickering to himself as Pramlee stood glaring at him.

"Relic, don't be such an idiot!" Pramlee stood giving Relic a go to hell look as she tapped her tiny feet on the sidewalk. With a small giggle she shrugged her shoulders and stood next to Talon who was still watching the tattoo artist. "So, Talon, I know a few things about demons. So, Pyro is a high demon of course and he is the Prince of falsehoods. Think about it, if Pyro comes out over the Ouija board and whips out some riddle, then of course there will be a catch in it. Something isn't right. Selena said Meridian's twin soul would have to be something from the realm she is in. We have to remember; the Universe is the only thing that knows the answer and Meridian is the one who has to find it. So, we have to blow off Pyro, but, we will have to answer that riddle."

Relic jumped in. "Wait a minute, he said nothing of that riddle. He gave out another riddle, that is the one we answer, right? Wait, wait, wait. What if her twin soul is not in this life? What if it is one of us, but not at this time?"

Kieren appeared from around the corner. "Hey everyone, I agree with Pramlee, as much as I have struggled with this whole twin soul thing. The one phrase Pyro said stood out. Not easily tamed. It has haunted me for a while. As much as we were wild as humans, we are guides now. Being tamed isn't something that would enter in the equation. We exist to serve humans. Or before they banned us from it we were." Kieren's attention was interrupted when the mortal left the tattoo shop. "I do believe that Talon is onto something with the mark."

Relic scratched his head. "They both have tattoos, the mortal ones. Meridian went and got inked a couple of times. We need to find out if there is something to this mark reference from the riddle. In the meantime, I have no idea how to answer Pyro's riddle. I don't think there is an answer. I believe it is a trick."

Raina's home was near to her own bar she used to call home before Meridian came into her life. It was late in the evening and the air was cool and crisp with the spring on the way. Many Salem patrons were leaving the main shopping streets. They passed an herbal shop called 'Sue's' whose doors were still open despite the shop owner quickly doing her rounds to close.

"Did you hear that? The voice coming from within that store?" Relic pointed toward a shop they passed by. He turned back and walked in and there Meridian and Raina were shopping.

"Meridian, I am here, it is me Relic." Meridian stood and maintained her course as she continued to pull herbs down and examine them as she visited with Raina. Relic shrugged his shoulders. "What has happened? She acts as though we aren't here."

Ridge, just like Relic, was confused. "Meridian please answer us, we are here to help you." Meridian never batted an eye but maintained shopping and she had made her final selection hurrying to pay so that owner could close up shop.

"This is worse than what we thought. She either has closed her mind or something is closing it for her." Ridge scratched his head while he stood next to Talon with his arms crossed. "Raina has to be using her stuff on Meridian again."

Talon watched Meridian paying for her items as Raina continued to visit with the shop owner. After a short while, as Raina and Meridian were exiting the store, Talon turned and walked beside them. He motioned for the others to follow him. "This is dark magic. Meridian has to be under a spell. Remember, at Esmra's when the nymphs performed their ritual? It was then that Meridian could see us, now she can't. This is a work of dark spirits.

They continued to follow Raina and Meridian and they jumped in Raina's car and headed back to her home. The girls dashed inside the house, and it went unnoticed to Meridian they never made it over to Esmra's house. They got ready for bed and Raina was certain to get the time in to take care of Meridian as she promised earlier in the day.

The next day, time was drawing near to open the bar. Raina and Meridian emerged from the house with an invisible audience as the guides never left. The girls walked over to Raina's bar and two Raina's workers were already there setting up for the day. Raina and Meridian went back into Raina's office.

Raina left to make a plate of a quick breakfast and the guides spotted her sneaking out a bottle from her purse and put it in her pocket after having poured some contents into Meridian's water. She handed her the plate and the drink and they both ate and resumed visiting.

"I knew it!" Kieren shouted, "This is crazy, she is drugging her or something." Kieren paced around the table. His sandy blonde hair swayed with every step he took in frustration, his blue eyes remained sharp, squinting in frustration as he licked his lips quickly.

"No, Kieren, drugs alone wouldn't do this. She is under dark magic. Raina cannot pull something of this magnitude off alone. She has a supplier. A supporter of some kind," Ridge peered inside Raina's purse.

Pramlee stood and watched Meridian as she went on about her business without a sense of them being near her. She studied Meridian's mark on her wrist that remained like a regular tattoo with the infinity mark. She came closer and knelt down beside Meridian searching for any other marks or tattoos.

Nothing was visible until Meridian reached across the table for a napkin passing her arm over her cell phone. Her cropped shirt raised and Pramlee glimpsed a new tattoo she had not seen on Meridian before. "Look! Hurry! Watch when Meridian moves, her shirt lifts, revealing a new mark that I had not known her to have before. This may be what the demon was talking about. Talon! You are onto something!" Pramlee jumped up and gave Talon one of her awkward hugs again as Talon stood stiff and uncomfortable with the attention.

"I hope so, I hope I am right. But we need to see all of it and the only way that may happen is when she undresses." Talon scratched his head.

As the pair finished their plates, Meridian left the table momentarily to freshen up, and she rummaged through her purse for some lipstick. Raina seized the opportunity to take Meridian's cell phone that buzzed with a new text message. Raina took her cell phone and opened it to read the message sent from Esmra.

"Meridian, where are you?"

Raina deleted but didn't have the chance before Meridian turned around. Raina nervously jumped up from the table.

"So, if you can't find your lipstick, you can borrow mine."

Kieren and Relic were watching Raina closely. "See man, she tried to delete a message or something. I realized when her phone received a message. She is blocking Meridian from everything."

Relic had an eyebrow raised and a half-cocked grin. "So, let me pull myself together while I swallow this late breaking update," Relic said as he walked over to Pramlee who was staring at Raina shuffling Meridian out the office door.

Kieren remained antsy and paced the room, his eyes darted around. He uncrossed his arms and stomped over to Relic where he resumed his statue-like composure, arms crossed once more. "Look jackass, I am just trying to fix things. What is it with you? Take the day off, you don't have to be an asshole every day!" Kieren stomped off through the wall and followed Meridian out to the bar where she was beginning a shift.

Pramlee stopped watching Raina long enough to give Relic a side glance once more as she checked her fingernails for signs of wear as she pretended to be uninterested in the feisty exchange. "So, Relic, how much more are you going to continue to make digs at Kieren? You know, he seems to really hate you sometimes."

Relic grinned and shrugged his shoulders. "Oh, it's fun. Why does he always have to rise to the occasion? I mean, truly, Kieren is a walking trigger. Kinda like the psycho running our realm. They get so mad so easily. So, I am always up for entertainment and Kieren is entertaining. He still hasn't figure it out."

Pramlee stopped examining her nails. "Figured what out?"

Ridge who had been in and out during the exchange arrived back into the office. "What is up with Kieren? I was out checking things out with Talon and he came blowing through the bar like a hurricane. He didn't even stop, he kept going and I believe I heard him spout something off about Relic."

Relic was now laughing. "Well, of course he did! He isn't as dumb as he acts. At least he was muttering about something good."

Talon rejoined the rest of the group and dropped in. "What would that be?"

Relic took in a big breath and sighed as he pointed to himself as though he was the cat's meow. "He was talking about me, and that is always good subject matter."

Within a second, he felt a petite hand slap him across the back of the head. Pramlee zoomed by. "Will you please put a sock in it! Look at Raina!"

Raina was alone in her office and she hung her head out the door and shouted to Meridian. "I will be out shortly; I have some paperwork to do and I will be out."

Raina then walked back over to her desk and pulled out the brown box with the Celtic symbol on top. She opened it and placed a bottle from her pocket inside the box and shut it. She put the box back in her hiding space and walked back over to her office door and quietly locked it.

In the space above the shelf that hid her box of elixir was a cabinet with double doors. She reached up and opened the cabinet and pulled out a bigger box and reached inside to pull out a black cloth with a bright orange pentagram embroidered into the cloth. She strategically placed the top point of the star facing south and the two opposing end points pointing north. She once more reached into the box and removed a Ouija board, some black candles, and a red satchel with incense she promptly lit before lighting her black candles.

After Raina completed her setup, she pulled out a necklace with a pendant made of silver with a sigil mark engraved into the talisman. Below the engraving was the name Ipos.

> *"Oh, dark one, hear my call*
> *Appear to me and let me know all.*
> *Pyro I beckon to thee,*
> *Bestow your wisdom upon me."*

The flames on the candles gave a soft flicker simultaneously. The smoke from the incense that lingered through the air formed together slowly creating a soft moving funnel over the Ouija board. Raina opened her eyes to the empty space above the board fill with smoke creating the funnel showing a face from within the smoke. The demon's eyes were closed, and his face blended in with the smoke until he opened his eyes where a bonze iridescent light emerged from his face, expressionless and still. Raina bowed her head to the demon. Her head remained bowed until the demon spoke.

> *"Dark sister, you have summoned me.*
> *It is my wisdom you shall receive.*
> *From which you seek, you will know all,*
> *What token will you return large or small?"*

"Pyro, it is with much appreciation you have answered my summon and I am in dire need of your help once more. I realize that my requests are not infinite and that I have yet to return the gratitude. I have made contact to request assistance in my spells with the Elixir. It grows short, making it more difficult to maintain the effects needed to keep Meridian."

Pyro watched intently as the dark witch spoke with her request. "Dark sister, you will have all you need to fulfill your task. Keeping Meridian with you was your task and return of favor, however an additional request of demon powers will cost you. I will require more of your help on Earth. You must kill Esmra. This is a demand. Esmra gone and Luna in the dark realm will make communications difficult for the guides. I am ordering you to kill the psychic. This is the only way I can guarantee your protection from the dark one's descent upon the humans."

Raina's eyes grew large as plates as her bottom jaw dropped open. "Lord, I have never taken a life. I do not know that I can do such a task."

"You will have demonic power as you once again submit your soul. You will be unstoppable in your task. Kill Esmra and I will return. You will have what you need to keep Meridian subdued. And if you are lucky, a union with the demon you worship, Ipos. Do this and you will please him, do it not and you will remain."

Pyro vanished from sight leaving the smoke lingering in the empty space above the Ouija board and Raina beside herself with the demand. In all her days of summoning a demon, she had never had a request of this magnitude.

The guides swiftly left Salem and headed out to Tallulah's sending a warning of what was on the horizon.

Chapter 6

Aiden and Chris were a couple of days into spring break and as they discussed, the pair had left out for a much-needed fishing trip together. Chris was all smiles as he ran down the bank of the fishing hole they always used. "Man, this is just like old times, isn't it?" Chris shouted up to Aiden who was grabbing his gear out of his truck.

"Yeah, in some ways it seems like yesterday we were here. Time moves too fast." Aiden made his way down the bank and sat as he fumbled through his lures for the perfect bait. After a few moments he cast his line and reeled in. "I texted Meridian last night, and I haven't heard back. I can't shake this feeling that there is something wrong."

Chris let out a snicker. "Yeah man, she dumped you, that is what is wrong."

Aiden pulled his line in to re-cast and he paused. "No smart ass, I really feel like something is wrong. I can't shake it." Aiden cast his line and went silent with his thoughts.

Chris feeling awkward for his statement sat silent for a while before he spoke up again, "Hey, I am sorry. I get it. Maybe we could go up to Salem and try to find her? Maybe find closure for you?"

Aiden raised an eyebrow but offered no response. He continued to stay silent during their fishing expedition. After a couple of hours, they loaded up and left to go back to Aiden's. As they were pulling down the old dirt driveway, Aiden ran through his memories of his first date with Meridian and the night that the pair met each other at Stephanie's bar. Aiden finally broke his silence, "You mean that? Go to Salem?"

Chris turned and smiled at Aiden. "Of course, I am here for you."

Aiden put his truck in park and the two jumped out. "I think we need to go by Tallulah's. I have questions before we do something like that."

The best friends cleaned up and drove over, turning down Hieber Lane, where Tallulah's house and Stephanie's bar were. As they got out of the truck, they were noticed first by Talon and the guides who had arrived at Tallulah's looking for her moments before.

"Look! It's Aiden. Maybe something has happened?" Pramlee said to Talon.

Talon put his hand up to Pramlee as he watched his son walk to the front door to knock. "I don't think so. I think my son took my hint. Maybe he will go after Meridian."

Aiden knocked but there was no answer, however, Stephanie's bar was heating up for the night. Aiden quickly nudged Chris and he pointed to Stephanie's. "Over there, I bet she is there. Her car is still here. Let's go." The pair walked across the street and encountered B.F.D., who was the main bouncer for her bar. When Aiden was spotted, B.F.D. gave them a nod as Chris and Aiden passed by. They headed toward the back where Stephanie's office was and they were greeted by Stephanie and Tallulah.

"Aiden! Oh my! It is so good to see you." Tallulah reached up to hug Aiden as she was overjoyed with excitement to see him. "Oh, young man, you and I need to talk." Tallulah tugged on Aiden's arm through the bar leaving Stephanie behind.

Aiden willfully followed Tallulah despite her death grip on his hand as she trotted through the crowd of people in Stephanie's establishment. All three made it inside to Tallulah's where the guys took a seat at her old kitchen table.

Talon despite all his own rules to keep far from his son decided that he could no longer do so to ensure that Tallulah understood the danger she was in. Talon moved swiftly before the guides even noticed and was one of the rare times Talon would stand this close to Aiden.

"Tallulah, I know we are amidst spring but a person could hang meat in here." Aiden said as he crossed his arms over his chest and rubbed his arms up and down with his hands to warm himself.

Tallulah paused as she was putting her purse on the table and reached for the pot to make warm water for tea. "You are cold? That is odd, I have not even turned the air conditioner on yet," Tallulah said. "Oh my, that is a draft. We have company. The guides are here, and I am sure that is Talon."

Aiden frowned and pulled his head back with confusion. "Talon? My father?"

Tallulah stood silent for a moment, "Aiden, we need to talk, and this is not something I am sure that Chris will need to hear just yet. Chris, can you give us a few moments?"

Chris stood up and smiled. "Sure Mrs. T, no problem." Aiden handed Chris his keys to his truck and Chris left the pair alone to visit.

Tallulah parked herself at the table and before she could begin, Aiden's active mind propelled him to start.

"When I came you explained who Meridian was before she took off. We never got into anything else. I barely got the story of her parents in Etheria and, of course, my father. Quite honestly, I could not wrap my head around who Meridian truly is. The only thing that gives credence to what you said, is her behavior and the small things that most people do or talk about. Meridian always seemed tense during those exchanges, like she was holding back," Aiden said.

Tallulah sipped her tea and made sure that Aiden had a cup for himself. "Listen, there is an entire world you do not know a lot about. There is so much that you need to know, but I am not sure if it is the right time." Tallulah stopped and looked around the room, distracted.

Aiden watched Tallulah stare at the space in front of her. "Tallulah? Are you, all right? What is it?"

"The guides, they are here. You don't know full well, but they are communicating with me right now. It is Meridian, they are telling me she is in danger. With Raina. They are telling me that Esmra is in danger and that Luna has been kidnapped." Tallulah paused from her explanations from Aiden.

Aiden's confusion was rising, "Who is Luna?" Aiden asked shaking his head.

Tallulah gasped to herself, "Oh my. Oh my. We have to leave at once." Tallulah grabbed Aiden's hand that was rested on the table. "I can't explain this right now, you need to trust me, we are leaving for Salem. You cannot bring Chris with you. He is not ready for what you will learn." Tallulah jumped up from the table and headed toward the stairs.

"What? Where are you going?" Aiden chased after Tallulah.

She paused as she had one foot on the step. "Aiden, go back and pack a bag and meet me in an hour. Go now." Tallulah continued upstairs and Aiden to text Chris so he could come back and pick him up.

Once they arrived, Aiden spent little time with explanations to anyone, even Chris who was puzzled, although supportive of Aiden.

Relic and Talon followed Aiden back, while Pramlee, Kieren and Ridge remained behind with Tallulah.

Talon was full of tension as he spoke. "Aiden senses I am around. He is gifted, more than I anticipated. I don't understand why he does not sense you all."

Pramlee shook her head, "Maybe because you are his father, did you ever think of that?" She smirked at the fallen one, who himself was amused with her observations.

As Aiden went inside to pack, the pair stood outside in the driveway could see him going back and forth in front of the window. He frantically packed and could be seen explaining what he could to Chris.

"Who is to say that he doesn't sense us? He sensed Meridian up the road by the oak tree," Relic said as he nodded toward the famous tree where many things had transpired between Earth and Etheria.

Talon examined the old tree that was at quite a distance from where they stood. "Yes, I remember. I felt as though it was more to do with Meridian and Aiden's connection than anything else. Maybe you are right. I never notice him respond much to any of the other guides."

Talon looked back up to Aiden's window where his light shut off and he ran downstairs. "Chris, I am sorry, man. Just run me over to Tallulah's. You can keep my truck and use it. Feel free to stay here." Chris and Aiden jumped in his truck and left once more.

Once Aiden arrived back at Tallulah's, he found her already standing outside her car having just thrown a bag in the back seat. Aiden jumped out of his truck to accompany Tallulah back to Salem.

It would be a long car ride back up north, with plenty of time to speak of the many things that Aiden did not know. Talon and the guides disappeared together and, in a snap, had arrived at Esmra's house, and they marched right in to find her in her usual place.

Esmra sat quietly at her kitchen table reading with her usual cup of herbal tea.

"I know you are here. I know Tallulah comes and that I am in danger from Raina. She picked up on that much and told me with her phone call. I have to say it doesn't surprise me. Raina consorts with demons and I know that she must have been up to something after Amelia dropped by here and told me that Raina requested more powder. The sacred blue powder that can make elixir."

Esmra stood up from her table as she held the book in her hand. She continued to read from the book as she shuffled over to her sink to get a glass of water to drink. She made her way back to the table, barely making a break from the book with her eyes to find her seat again. Her eyes were droopy.

The guides and Talon watched the good witch as she continued her research. They were quiet in her company, mostly with concern and sympathy. With Luna captured in the dark realm, it would strain communications until Tallulah arrived.

Talon paced back and forth from the kitchen to the living room.

Kieren noticed Talon's increasing tension. "What is it now?"

Talon stopped and looked at everyone, "If I have to, I will. I will do it."

Pramlee shrugged her shoulders and Relic's face showed doubt, however not without a one-liner for the moment, "You mean you will go demon hulk on Raina?"

Talon continued his pace. "Yes, I will protect Esmra or Tallulah from Raina, if it comes to that. There is nothing that limits me from harming a human. For you all it is against your laws." Talon left the house and went outside to think.

***

In the fairy realm, things were heating up. Selena grew impatient waiting for news back from the guides on any updates. She paced back and forth as Orion stood silent. Rising from her seat, she brushed her long green dress away from the quick and short motions of her swift gait.

"I am finished waiting around. It has been too long to wait. My daughter is in danger, and it is time I take care of this myself!" Selena shouted at Orion.

Orion did not respond or engage, as he maintained his usual composure, he watched Selena continue until the door swung open.

There stood all five fairy nymphs, with ease and control, they strode in. Karma at her leisure poured herself a glass of the famous fairy-kooliade, as Relic referred to the drink of the fairies. She took a long sip as her eyes glazed over the top of the glass watching the other nymphs file into the room and gather.

Selena stopped pacing as she quietly moved toward Orion. She snapped her head around at Venus who had taken a seat next to the Selena's empty chair.

"How is it you all are this calm!" Selena shouted.

Siren who had maintained standing closest to the door spoke up, "Selena, it is not that we are calm so much as we have never witnessed you in such a state. You are usually so controlled. We are unsure what we should do."

Selena let out a sigh, her shoulders dropped down and her arms collapsed at her sides. She dropped her chin and scanned the room of nymph spectators.

"I never mastered the skill of being a calm mother. It is taking too long to hear anything. I will tell you what we will all do and that is portal to Earth. It is time for an intervention. Riddle or no riddle from the dark one, it's time," she said.

Siren and Karma shrugged their shoulders. Karma walked toward Selena who regained composure and seated her herself in her chair. "No offense Selena, but when is the last time you went to Earth? Last I knew, you rarely travel there anymore."

Selena darted her amber eyes upward, staring at Karma. Her tension radiated through her scowl, and she drummed her fingers are the arm of the chair. Her long nails tapped, slowly. "Why not? Why should it matter that it has been a long time? I worry about Luna, I cannot take losing her once more." She quickly lifted her head up. "We will all go. This situation with Warrick, these games must stop. Maybe Relic was right about the meeting Warrick called, we should have ended him then. But with the way things were going, especially with Meridian, I did not believe it was the right time."

Selena left her chair and motioned for Orion and the nymphs to accompany her. Orion circled his large and long arms and, the portal laced with fire formed. Just on the other side was Earth. Without a pause or a glance over her shoulders, the regal fairy stepped through, accompanied by Orion and the nymphs.

A few yards from Esmra's house, the ground gave away to a shake, the water-like appearance of the landscape grew in splendor from just a small floating bubble. Now large enough for all to pass, in all their magnificence the fairies graced the glum surroundings of a barren field across from Esmra's house. Their glowing appearance and striking eyes stood out in the dark horizon. The group appeared to float across the ground as they walked.

As the fairies approached Esmra's house, the guides immediately spotted them. Esmra jumped to her feet from her book to greet the fairies.

Siren and Venus were the first ones to approach Esmra.

"Hello, Esmra, it is good to see you again...You know why we are here." Siren nodded to Selena who made her way toward Esmra followed by her trusted advisor, Orion.

"Yes, we need not waste any time. Good to see you here, Selena. Your trips to Earth are rare. I have been working here with the guides on this riddle, and during this time I received a frantic call from Tallulah. She said she and Aiden were on their way here. She knows that Luna has been kidnapped, that Raina has an arrangement with Pyro. Raina has been instructed to kill both Tallulah and me by this demon. I guess to bring favor to her."

"I am aware of Raina and her ways, strangely though, fairies usually sense most things. Unless of course the evil influences come from a stronger demon, we may not. This is disturbing news my daughter is kidnapped, again in the dark realm and this human, a dark witch. The guides did tell me of the demon riddle from the dark one. Now that we are all here. Let's put things together."

Everyone followed Esmra back to her table where she had been reading and attempting to understand the variables of the riddles that Pyro put out before Meridian left, and the most recent riddle from the dark one.

"It has been a couple of days and the dark one wants this riddle answered soon. As a witch and like many, I recognize astrological references when I see or hear them." Esmra pointed to the riddle she had written down on paper.

"The deceiver arrived in the time of new. Well, that may mean a birth or an actual arrival, possibly. Or it may represent a season. That would be the spring, in the time of new. So, I wrote all the signs are of spring. They are Aries, Taurus and Gemini. The riddle stated, 'the sign is a part of a word.' For example, Aries is the ram. Taurus is the bull and Gemini represents twins.

So, I went around and around with words that could be worked into the signs. 'Symbols run to and fro,' Esmra continued, "What threw me was 'which way will margana go?' I was stumped until I got the call from Tallulah telling me about Raina. So, it hit me." Esmra shuffled through her papers, "Raina runs the bar, and the name is an anagram, a reverse one. I sold her that bar years ago. I named it. Nevoc spelled backwards is Coven." Esmra pointed out all the writing she had been doing to uncover the riddle, "Margana is the word anagram spelled backwards. But the demon said, 'which way will margana go.' Well, anagrams can go any which way, at least I think they can. Now, another point is here, take her name and rearrange the letters. The letters in her name can also spell 'Arian' or Aries which is a ram. See the word anagram. The last three letters are ram. It is Raina. Her birthday is in April, spring, the time of new. The sign for Aries is the ram."

Relic and Kieren stood at the table listening as Ridge and Talon whispered amongst themselves putting together what they could.

Ridge was taken back but relieved, "Well, that is complicated but makes perfect sense."

Relic jabbed Kieren in the side, "Wow, the old crazy witch pulled it off!"

Pramlee, who always could be counted on to put Relic in his place, slapped him over the head. "Really? Be glad she can't hear you saying those things!"

Ridge scratched his head and right along with him, Kieren's look was that he was lost. The fairies remained silent as the humans worked out the riddle.

Siren said to Ridge, "Ridge, I we all do not know you that well, that we all just saw one another at Warrick's meeting he called last. I couldn't help but notice you look confused. Is there something you think Esmra has miscalculated?"

Ridge nodded as Siren spoke, "Yes, not the riddle. I do not understand when Kieren, Relic and the rest made their trip to the dark realm, why would the dark one help? Give us a riddle we or someone else could answer. It makes little sense."

Karma knew exactly what the reasoning was along with the other fairies and said, "So, Ridge, you understand that the dark one made it easy. He hoped that you all would come and bring Luna along. That way he could kidnap her and inspire Selena to not aid you all and turn the fallen ones back to their original form of being spirit guides like yourself. That is why it was so easy."

"Why have you all come? I mean I am not complaining you are here." Relic was googly eyed over Lotus who sat quietly and shyly behind Echo.

Selena interrupted the conversation and said, "Relic we will ensure the return of my daughter and to expedite all communications between the fairies and Esmra. Now we have the answer to the riddle, you all must leave and go to the dark realm. I am sending Orion and the nymphs. I fully expect that Raina will soon make her appearance and do as Pyro has instructed. Although, she will be possessed by a demon, she will not be herself."

Kieren interrupted, "What do you mean possession?"

Venus made her way through the group to speak. "She will be possessed. Have you all not been paying attention to what is happening here on Earth?"

Talon said, "Yes, Lahash spoke of it. The first night I met him, he spoke of all they will make the tales of possession a reality if the dark one was to find out that things were not going the way that he and Warrick had planned out. I am assuming this is the beginning?"

Venus nodded, "Yes, this is the start. Soon the human possessions will begin and Earth will be in chaos. However, we have some other pressing issues to tend to as well as get Luna, but first Karma has a message for all of you."

Venus stepped aside as everyone gathered around Karma.

"As you all know, we are elemental fairy nymphs and we are the fairies of desire, temptation and lust. Now that is not all we are good for." Karma smiled in amusement hearing her own words and watching the faces of the guides and Talon.

"We use those powers to get things we want, and it usually works. Each one of us rules an element and that element gives us our own unique ways we use our power. Much like the elements we rule, those elements make us who we are and shape our personalities, much like birth signs of humans. Air rules Venus; her planet ruler is actually Venus which rules love. Yes, we influence love, but that is more Venus's area. She rules true love. She has come to help

Meridian in her challenge of finding her twin soul. Not any of us would see who this is, and we realize that she is under a dark and evil spell from Raina, who must get this level of power from the dark realm. For me, I am Karma and I am not ruled by any element, however I have my own uses. Selena will tell you our plans."

"As I said, Orion will accompany the guides back to the dark realm. Siren and Lotus will make the journey as well. With Siren's fire element in opposition of Lotus in her water element will be protection in the face of the dark one when you deliver his answer to the riddle. An answer he will not expect you to have guessed, or even come close. He will not be happy, and I can't foresee what will come of that realization." Selena cut her eyes back to the guides. "Karma and Echo must make their own journey to gain the quartz sword. This sword is made of the purest of Quartz and it is the only thing that can kill a demon and can kill Warrick. Quartz comes from the Earth, however blessed by the keepers, the angels that live in the hall of souls."

Relic was amazed at the many more new things he was learning about his own realm, that had been kept in secrecy. "Where is it? Why have we never heard of it? Why were the keepers keeping a secret?"

Talon who had been at the other end of Warrick's deception understood and said, "Relic think about it. Warrick is obsessed with power and control. He will destroy families and lives to keep the illusion he was in power. Many religions believe that there is a supreme being or beings. A higher power. Warrick couldn't stand the thought of it not being him. He is a demon, full of deceit and disguise and we believed what they taught us when we left our human lives for this existence. They taught us in the essence of doing right and for the good of humans we watch over, that we were it. That there were no other beings in the Universe that would see that prayers were answered, lives were saved, or peace could be made."

Talon looked down toward the ground while softening his speech, "The humans we watch over believe in that higher power as we did once long ago when we were human. Guides are simply the evolved souls of many lives that learned many lessons and made the choice to help humans. With every soul that evolves, it is with the hope that through that evolution humankind would evolve to such a state of enlightenment and for the betterment of themselves. It makes sense that Warrick would cast away guides who were good. It was meant to stop the continual evolution of humans. We do not live forever. We were meant to die a guide death and return to the hall where our souls could transcend again to a new life that is brought into the world. If he stopped that, then what would be left for demons to feed from? Nothing!"

Selena's careful eyes studied the guides' reaction to the words Talon shared and said, "They cannot exist without the downtrodden, the vile, and the greed of man. Nothing stops with you all as guides. It begins with you! It is like a human parent who when they bring a child into the world, want that child to be better than they were. Have a better life in some ways. Spirit guides are the hub of humankind. The keepers, the Angels that have been locked away and hidden from you, that reside in the hall are the source of the Universe's power. It is from the angels' source of power in the Universe that souls are created, nowhere else."

Tears rolled down Pramlee's cheeks as she listened to a fallen and a fairy speak of such things she never knew. The one being who stood at the bitter end of Warrick's vile ways, see things so clearly. To explain something as grand as this was humbling to know that who they were truly were remained so small in the grand scheme of things.

Relic asked, "Ok, where do the fairies fit into this?"

Selena said, "We don't fit into this. We are the beings who were not good enough to be an angel but not bad enough to be a demon. Some fairies help humans pass over to the next life when they are lost, like a ghost. We exist to serve humans, just in a different way than you do. You all will have to trust that Karma and Echo will make the journey back to Etheria for the angel's blessing and from there the search for the quartz sword will commence. It will certainly come with challenges and that is getting past Warrick."

Pramlee was jumpy and fidgety as usual, but this time it was different. She was politely holding back what she wanted to say until after Selena finished. "What about the rest of the riddle? The mark? I saw Meridian had a tattoo under her shirt, but I couldn't make out exactly what it was. Don't we need to find that before we do anything?"

Selena remained puzzled for a moment but then her words illustrated that she saw Pramlee's point. "Of course, yes. Knowing who the deceitful one is wasn't that hard to figure out, but this mark has something to it."

Pramlee jumped up and clapped her hands with joy as she tightened her whole body and slipped toward Relic. "Ok, now we have to find out what this mark is. I will do it. By now Meridian has to be done with her shift. Let's go."

Chapter 7

Pramlee accompanied by her support group made their way back to Meridian finished with her shift and went home. The pair were doing their usual nightly routine. Relic had a lofty grin upon his face, beaming with the thoughts of seeing Meridian. Pramlee's excitement dwindled as she slapped Relic.

"Ow! What was that for? Geez, you are turning into Meridian. She was always slapping me!"

Pramlee was shuffling her hands together back and forth as though she completed a dirty job, slapping the grunge off. "Well, apparently she didn't do it enough, you are still a jackass." she smugly walked past Kieren who stood in amusement with the scene.

"Yep, can't lie. I sure enjoy someone else knocking you back into place." Kieren was laughing as the group walked into Raina's home. It was decorated in black and white throughout, like the bathroom. The smell of the burning incense came on strong from the living area. The light flickering from the candles burning lightened up the bottles of her collection of essential oils that rested on the windowsill of the kitchen. Magazines, books and papers cluttered her shelves, leaving the kitchen ill-equipped for cooking, not a typical kitchen of a human at all. Her countertop had one plant, an ivy that had been setting a while. The vine had made its way across the countertop to the light that shone through the window in the mornings.

Her cupboards were full of glass bottles, and inside the bottles were an array of herbs and other spell casting assistants such as salt and lavender.

"This place gives me the creeps. It feels like an institution." Relic spouted off as he rubbed his own arms up and down as if he were cold.

"Yes, and you certainly would know what an institution would feel like, yeah?" Talon had reemerged from the spare room speaking to Relic as he dashed across the hall. He made sure to turn his head and directly face Relic as he spoke. He disappeared again.

"What the hell is he doing? Now all of a sudden, he goes from serious to 'Mr. Light and Fluffy.' Please." Relic shrugged his shoulders with the cutting sarcasm that left his lips as though he was entitled to dish it out.

Ridge shook his head and hissed a little. "Oh, Relic. Calm down. You are still head peacock of the dumb ass peacock society. By the way the head peacock called, he wants his swagger back." Ridge disappeared through the wall as he spoke his last word. There stood Relic alone and all he could hear were Pramlee's giggles coming from behind him.

"Aren't we here to see Meridian get naked?" Relic was pissy.

"Oh, chill out, pissy pants. You won't be getting your peep show tonight. Girls only. Get out and wait outside. No walking through the walls either! I am going into the bedroom. I can hear Raina and Meridian talking." Pramlee gave Relic one more slap as she walked by.

Relic was rubbing his head and frowning at the petite powerhouse. "How is it you are that short and manage to hit me in the head?"

Pramlee made no response as she hummed to herself a song that sounded as though it came from another time. I'm confessing that I love you, was the song she sang." She moved with a pep in her step and her own swagger as her mind echoed the thoughts to the guides all around that she was content. It had been a long time since she and her best friend were of the same realm, on the same page and Pramlee was overjoyed to find Meridian on her way back home, or so Pramlee believed.

The boys of the group, as Pramlee referred stepped back into the living room as Pramlee went into Raina's room.

There Raina sat on the edge of the bed, quiet as Meridian was digging through the dresser drawer for a change of clothes.

"What gives?" Meridian said as she shoved the tidbits of clothes back into the drawer. She had a red T-shirt in her hand and she sat next to Raina.

"What? Oh, nothing, I am tired." Raina was trying to pass it off. "I have some things I need to take care of this evening. Nothing major, I just need to get paid on an account that is past due. It is frustrating."

Meridian left the bed side and undressed. Pramlee was perched on the chair next to the bed watching the pair have their discussion. "So how long will you be?"

Raina stood up from the bed and pulled open a drawer in the nightstand. She fumbled around a bit before she stopped and put something into her purse that was sitting on the floor in front of the nightstand. "Oh, an hour maybe?" Raina returned to give Meridian and gave her a kiss. "I'll be back soon." Raina left.

Meridian took off her shirt and Pramlee got as close as she could to examine her left side. There from below her arm pit down her side was a large and different looking tattoo. Pramlee struggled to put together what it was, but she would make notes in her head so the others would read her thoughts and pick up on what she was seeing.

It was a tattoo in the shape of a circle with letters at the four points of the circle. I P O S. Inside the circle was another circle. The lines ran very close to the outside line. On the inside two lines ran north and south and across from one another. Toward the top the lines appeared to get closer together. At the top of each line the shape appeared to be a backwards letter, B. From the top to the bottom of the two lines were five lines that ran down and as they descended, they grew shorter in length. The top line had two circles at the top and the remaining lines ended with a short line that ran north and south. Inside and at the center another smaller circle that sat atop of a singular line that ran through the middle. Pramlee studied the marking but could not understand what it meant.

Meridian continued to dress and get ready for bed. Pramlee left the room and went outside to find the others with glum faces. "What, why the sad faces?" Pramlee was confused.

Ridge was shaking his head as he stared at Pramlee. "Pramlee, that is not a tattoo really. It is a demon sigil. It is the sigil of a very powerful demon, Ipos. He rules many legions and he can foretell the future and he knows the past and how to find treasure," Talon explained with doubt in his own voice. "Why would she go and get a tattoo of a sigil? Ipos of all demons?"

Ridge's face furrowed, "I do not know. This is a question for Selena. It must have been during a time we were not around Meridian."

***

Meridian walked into the bathroom to brush her teeth. She was thinking about the dream she had. When she finished brushing, she had turned the water off in time to hear a noise. It was a loud beeping coming from the bedroom. It beeped a couple of times and stopped. Meridian stood still in thought trying to piece together the familiar tone. She scratched her head and made her way into the bedroom toward the closet where Raina kept her things. She heard the beeping again. She pulled a shoe box out and opened it and there was a phone. Meridian's phone. Meridian was even more confused.

I thought that I left my phone in my purse? Why would it be in here? I don't remember leaving my phone in a shoe box, and it needs to be charged.

There were a few messages she didn't recall receiving and one text message that had just came through. One text was from Esmra from earlier that day. It read,

"Meridian, I have been calling you and texting. What has happened?"

The next text was from Aiden, this text was a few days old. Meridian stared at her phone, then she surveyed the room and once again back to her phone.

"Meridian, I hope you are doing ok. I think of you a lot. I am home and it makes it worse. I miss you."

Meridian was struggling to put things together. Things that Raina saw fit to keep from her. Meridian stumbled backwards to the bed and sat down. She could not always remember people, places and things. It was becoming obvious there were pieces to her day she couldn't recall and even worse, she couldn't understand why she never thought about why. Her heart was racing, and her breathing was ragged. Reading Aiden's message was a wake-up call to her. An awakening she had not known she was missing. After all these months he was contacting her to say that he was at home with his grandparents. Little did she know that he was getting close to Esmra's house on his trip with Tallulah.

Meridian got up off the bed and put on clothes and set out on foot to Esmra's house to discover what was going on. She flew out of the front door with her phone in her hand and she jogged frantically toward Esmra's house.

What is going on? Aiden, Aiden, Aiden.

Her mind was swimming in his name and as she ran down the street, she thought of their first encounter at the bar. She stopped for air and then proceeded at a slow pace and her mind was going back to the day she left Aiden at the bus stop. As she drew closer to Esmra's house, she saw the lights on and Raina's car parked out front. Next to Raina's car, there sat Tallulah's car. It sat empty with the driver's and passenger's doors open. She picked up her pace and ran toward the house and she stopped in her tracks when she heard screaming. Then, with little time, Raina came flying through the front door of the house, in suspension through the air and something flung her into a tree and dropped to the ground.

Tallulah came running outside, "What in the hell was that? Esmra what on Earth have you been communing with? I thought you practiced only white magic!"

Esmra came busting through and ran out to Raina where she lay barely breathing. The guides swarmed the scene in shock. Except for Relic.

"I love it when he does that! Talon, can you do that again!" Relic was running around Esmra's house in the dark looking for Talon who was in hiding as he struggled to calm himself.

The last human to stumble through the doorway and stood frozen on the porch away from the grotesque scene. Certainly a sight for Meridian's sore eyes. With only the moonlight from the sky to give a hint to who he was, the slight breeze in the air danced through his hair. His silhouette moved as he pushed wisps of hair from his face and stood with one hand on his hip. He then rubbed the back of his neck looking around in confusion.

Meridian immediately recognized him. "Aiden!" she yelled and ran as fast as she could down Esmra's driveway.

He jerked his head back toward the road and squinted his eyes to the girl running toward him in the dark. "Meridian?" He took off running from the porch and the pair continued to run toward one another, until they made contact and a long overdue embrace they both needed and had been denied for so long.

Pramlee showed up still with a pep in her step, as she slid past Relic who had been out in the yard searching for Talon. She breezed by as she bumped into Relic still singing to herself as she watched Aiden and Meridian hugging.

Relic was glaring at Pramlee. "What the hell are you singing, you are so annoying!"

Pramlee stopped and smiled smugly. "Well, just because you live as though you left your last life in the time of 80s hair doesn't mean the rest of us don't know a thing or two about music! One human I watched over many years ago, listened to the song 'I'm confessing that I love you.' I loved that song and that time. It was so fun to watch the glamour in the women, the hair, the clothes." Pramlee was nostalgic.

Relic stood with a smirk on his face. He never thought to ever ask Pramlee about her days watching over humans. She had such a youthful approach to things; it was hard to accept her as a guide that far into her guide years. She continued to sing to herself as she pranced up the stairs leaving the mess for the humans and everyone else to deal with. As she pranced and examined her perfect nails, she hummed the words to her favorite song.

Kieren and Ridge walked over toward Relic who was still hunting Talon. "What gives? Is she out of touch or what? Every time things get crazy, she always has this air of don't care about her, or oblivious," Ridge said as he watched Pramlee.

Kieren said, "Maybe she doesn't care, but in the worst of times she seems to always have an answer and never lets too much get to her."

Talon reemerged from behind the house. "Oh, I think it's because of the two humans we care about," he said as he nodded to Meridian and Aiden walking toward Esmra and Tallulah as they stood over Raina who was still passed out.

Chapter 8

Lahash had returned from his moment with Echo whom he fancied very much and unbeknownst to him, he was sinking further into her fairy spell. He sat in the room alone, in the rock chairs, cold and dark grey. He watched the flickering flame that burned without a source in the center of the table. Two demons interrupted his quiet thoughts when they appeared standing behind the empty chairs at the table.

"Lahash, you are never early to these things. Why so glum? Huh? Are you riding the cusp of fairy trouble? Ha, ha!" The demon pranced as he walked and ran his long hands across the backs of the chairs as he made his way over to Lahash. You should try your luck with mortal witches! I seem to have no trouble getting what I want to appease the dark one!" Pyro bragged to a somber Lahash.

The other demon that accompanied Pyro stood quietly with his hands clasped behind his back. He made no motion with his body or his cold face. He stood and watched the exchange take place. Lahash looked up from the table to the mysterious demon, ignoring Pyro.

"Ipos, what brings you here? I mean aren't these meetings beneath you?" Lahash gave a slight grin as he insulted the demon.

Ipos took notice of Lahash's remarks and maintained his composure. "I wouldn't go that far, Lahash, after all it would seem that these meetings are below your standards. After all, you push the boundaries with the dark one, bordering on not doing what is requested. He has summoned me from my duties to attend. It seems a mortal witch, thanks to Pyro, has marked the 'one' with my sigil which puts me in quite the precarious predicament, wouldn't you agree?"

Lahash stood up from his chair and flung his arm up and waved it around dismissing the Duke of Hell. "Oh whatever. Humans get tattoos all the time, marks of the beast they believe. It does nothing. Let the dark witch believe that with her marks she can access your powers of knowing the future, uncovering the past. It won't work, we have seen this before." Lahash continued to mutter as he walked away from the two demons.

Ipos followed Lahash and stood behind him as Lahash kept his back to the powerful Duke of Hell. "Lahash, you are allowing the fairy tricks to work on you. I need your assistance on this one. Raina has placed my mark on Meridian. She is the one, the one who will take over Etheria if we do not remedy this situation. If Raina evokes the mark, it will summon me through it, I will possess her. It all sounds like a great thing, to possess a human. However, she is pure, if I am pulled through, it will destroy me. Furthermore, your fairy friend is on her way with Karma to Etheria for the keepers' blessing to acquire the quartz sword. The ultimate destroyer of our kind. Will you do yourself a favor and snap out of it!"

Lahash with his back turned had been holding himself up leaning on the great rock wall that held the massive burning fireplace. He took a paused from the words he heard and peered over his shoulder. "Why would I help you? Why should I care if it destroys you? Why should I care if Warrick goes down or even you, Pyro!" Lahash pointed across the room at giddy Pyro.

"You should care, Lahash. The very demons you look down upon feed off the very ones who give rise to the politicians you feed from. Without my command of those demons, without their influence in breaking laws, there would be no need for your kind of humans and no need for you. Deal with it and move on. Things will be much easier for you." Ipos walked away, hands still clasped behind his back.

Pyro was bouncing in his chair and laughed. "Man, Lahash, this maverick attitude will land you on the dark one's bad side. We all need each other, even if you hate us."

Lahash flung his hand away from the wall and muttered under his breath pacing the room. The other demons summoned to the meeting arrived and took their seats, this included Warrick. As they all took their seats,

Lahash continued his pacing and muttering to himself while he glared at Ipos as he approached the table.

Lahash jerked the stone chair as he pulled it away to the table to sit down once again. He leaned his forehead into his hand, as his elbow rested on the arm of the chair. Lahash made no eye contact with the rest of the demons.

Warrick sat in silence watching Lahash in minor amusement. After a careful study of the steaming demon, he could not resist a manipulation of the situation.

"Lahash, you are in rare form. So, what gives? Ipos really got under your skin, did he? He is the Duke here, I am unsure exactly what your position is here in the dark realm."

Before Lahash could fire a round of a host of insults to Warrick, the dark one's voice penetrated the room. His baritone clashed down among the demons of the high court and it humbled them, a scene that was a rarity.

"Lahash, I am disappointed in you. I appreciate your independence amongst your own kind, however I struggle to understand the merit in which you operate. Explain to all of us why you have not one concern for all of us? Ipos is one of my Dukes. He commands a great legion, the majority of humanity. Without his demons' influences, your favorite humans you keep company with would become obsolete. So would you. Do tell."

Lahash rubbed his fingers into his large and penetrating eyes in his hesitance to answer to his master. He pulled his hand away from his face and kept his eyes to the dark floor.

"I do not ask for a lot here, lord. I do not want to be expected to care for the others. We are all equally evil and the influences that drive us within humanity cannot be appreciated amongst us all. Why should it matter?"

There was a brief silence in the room and once the dark one spoke, Lahash fell out of his chair holding his chest, writhing in pain, unable to speak. He only grunted in pain as he curled into a ball on the floor.

The dark one made his demand. "You will exit the dark realm, Lahash. You will find Echo and Karma. You will follow them once the keepers give them their blessing and you will destroy Karma. If Karma retrieves the quartz sword, it will be a death sentence for us all. You will intercept with Warrick's support. I will not yield on this one. If you look to Earth, there have already been priests reporting possession. The Vatican has responded to these reports. Ipos's demons are slowly conquering. Our plan to invade the hall of souls is within our grasp. The next sign we wait for is the human stillborn deaths. The evolution of human souls to the hall are decreasing, leaving newborns vulnerable. As our possessions progress, our plan will come to fruition.

There will be no tolerance of resistance. Do not disappoint me."

Lahash stopped grabbing himself and regained his composure as he resumed his seated position at the table. Ipos had steadily watched Lahash. His eyes were large and soft.

"Lahash, please do not make this harder on yourself. I will assist you from afar with my legion. This will not be difficult if you do not resist." He arose from his chair and approached Lahash. "You must resist Echo. All of us at one point in our existence have encountered the fairy nymphs. They are as hypnotic as they are ruthless, and they too are our weakness. You have to fight it. Echo has already succeeded in weakening you. Allow her to believe that you are under her spell, and in the moment of weakness, you must destroy her." Ipos walked away from Lahash and exited the room following Pyro.

Chapter 9

Meridian was shaking with excitement as Aiden held her tightly. They had not managed to break their embrace as they continued to walk toward Tallulah and Esmra. A tear rolled down Meridian's face and disappeared into Aiden's shirt, while she kept her head snug into his chest. She breathed in deeply, taking in his smell that she did not realize until that moment she had been missing. Aiden stroked her head softly and kissed the top of her head while he pulled her chin away to make her look him in the eye. It was as though he couldn't believe he was holding her once more.

They stopped walking. "Meridian, I have been trying to get ahold of you. How did you know I was here? What happened? Why haven't you answered me?" Aiden was shaking, and his breathing was ragged as he peppered Meridian with questions. They stopped walking.

"Aiden, I don't know what is happening. I don't remember things. I lose track of time. One minute I am thinking something and the next I am somewhere, and I don't even know how I got there. I am so confused. There are messages on my phone I didn't even realize I had until tonight. I have been with Raina, but I have no sense of time." Meridian saw Raina who was lying in the yard. She then looked back to Aiden who stood scratching his head.

"I came with Tallulah." Aiden paused as he continued to scratch his head. "To find you, Meridian." Aiden looked into Meridian's concerned eyes. She continued to stare at Aiden, in surprise. She pulled away from Aiden and folded her arms.

"So, you came with Tallulah to find me. Why?" Meridian's voice though low, was full of delight.

Aiden stood in place not moving but locked his eyes on Meridian. "Meridian, the last time I saw you was months ago, after Christmas break. You took off with Raina." Aiden nodded over toward Esmra and Tallulah where they still stood looking over Raina while she remained knocked out. "Raina did all these terrible things to you. You seemed to be mad at her, wanted nothing to do with her after what you found out she was doing to you. You kept pushing me away. I finally find you getting on the same bus as she was and I told you that Tallulah told me about your secret. I know who you are, I found out then. You pushed me away, you left. After all that I went back to school and tried to keep my mind off of you. Here we are again, I am on another school break. So much has happened. After I came home for break, I couldn't help myself. I texted you and didn't get an answer. So, I went to see Tallulah. She grabbed me and told me everything, and I mean everything. We had a long drive here with just the two of us. She enlightened me on the many things I thought were folk tales. I have had my own experiences with hearing voices and other things I do not understand. If you and I are meant to be and I believe that everything that has happened, then that changes a lot. All the things that I was raised to believe, going to church has some truths to it, but I have more questions now. But first, I have to know, even if you thought by running away from me was the answer. Why with her, with Raina?"

Meridian stood barely able to look at Aiden. Her guilt for causing his pain stifled her empathetic responses she knew he deserved. She didn't feel with all she had done that she deserved Aiden. "Aiden, I left because that curse, the curse I still have could hurt you. I didn't want to hurt you. I don't want to hurt anyone anymore. I thought all those months of living with Tallulah that when I was with those men, it meant something. I didn't understand what it meant to a human man. To me it made me feel alive, it filled something missing. I felt what I thought was love. Later, I discovered who I was through the fairy nymphs. I met you. I had been searching for you for a while. I couldn't tell you the truth. That was too big for any human to understand. I believe when I was a spirit guide, that day you were born in the hospital, C. Heyworth Medical Center, I chose you. My memory of being a guide is still very distant and I can't remember everything. When I was cast away, all I could remember was your name and Talon's. Now with the help of the guides after the nymphs helped expose the creator of the curse, I was able to connect with them for a little information. But ever since I left for Salem, I can't hear them anymore. I think they abandoned me or something. I didn't leave with Raina that day. I ran into her at the bus stop. We happened to be on the same bus to leave. I thought if Raina could connect to the dark ones, she could find a way to break the curse."

Tallulah and Esmra picked Raina up and shuffled to get her inside, but not before noticing the couple they so desperately wanted to see together. Talon remained in the shadows even after he had turned back to what was his normal self. The remainder of the unseen but always present stood at a distance from Meridian and Aiden as they were talking. Aiden and Meridian both watched Raina being carried in. Meridian's mouth dropped open while shaking her head. She then looked to Aiden.

"Don't ask me, we just got here, we went up to the house to make sure Esmra was okay. We saw Raina's car, and we ran inside, before we made it all the way in, Raina came flying out of the house," Aiden said.

Aiden sighed and cut his eyes back toward Meridian who was staring at the house. "And now, I guess without a question I know who must have hurled Raina out. My father, Talon."

Talon perked up and emerged from the shadows. In all of Aiden's life he had never heard Aiden talk much of his father and never until this moment heard Aiden acknowledge him as his father. "Tallulah told me that my father was a spirit guide at one time. That is why my mother never could introduce him to my grandparents. Makes sense now. Tallulah told me that he was cast away as a fallen. That is all I got to know, except he is close to me, I just can't see him. I know about the fairies, the other guides. It is so overwhelming and nearly impossible to believe it. After the things I watched happen with Raina, I am a believer now." Aiden hugged Meridian briefly. He opened up the distance between them and looked into her eyes. "I know all now, Meridian. I am still here. I want to be a part of your life, I want to help you. Please, don't push me away again."

Aiden's soulful and deep eyes were hard for Meridian to resist. She uncrossed her arms and embraced Aiden and they stood holding one another for several minutes. After the embrace broke apart Meridian opened up more about herself.

"I didn't want to be with Raina, Okay? I never wanted to be with her. She did horrible things to me. I ran into her at the bus stop that day, on my way to go to Esmra's. Running into her, I thought she was the way for me to break the curse. I thought staying with Esmra would help. But lately, I can't remember things. I feel like we talk about seeing Esmra, and then suddenly, I realize days have passed and we don't get there. Raina seems to always be taking care of me,

I thought she was really falling in love with me at one point. But things aren't making sense. I ended up here because she said she was leaving to get paid on an account. So, I was getting ready for bed and I heard my phone. I found it hidden in our closet. I guess she had been taking my phone and keeping things from me. You and Esmra both had been trying to get ahold of me. Had she not left and I didn't hear the beeping, I wouldn't have made it here." Meridian walked toward the house. "Let's find out what is going on."

Chapter 10

Selena was quiet with her thoughts of Luna and how she hoped that things would resolve, and her daughter would come home once again. Orion who stood quietly in the doorway of her quarters as he remained in watch over his Queen. She broke the silence amongst the group. "Orion, I would like to have a word with you, please."

Orion quickly turned to face Selena as he walked into her quarters. "Yes."

"Orion, you and I did not finish having a conversation. Do you recall when we discussed in part why you are immune to iron?" Selena was drumming her fingers slowly on her glass of fairy potion she indulged in.

"Yes, Yes I do. We never finished. Do you wish to finish now?" Orion patiently asked.

"Well, I want to know why if you are of fairy blood, why is it you remain resistant to the effects of iron?" Selena seemed impatient for the answer as she shifted forward in her seat.

"My Queen, I am not of fairy blood. You rescued me in my youth. I thought you knew some of what I was. I am not exactly the same as you and the others." It puzzled Orion.

"Yes, I rescued you while you were young, the difference is noticeable. You are quite larger than the other fairies indeed. You have no wings, you tower over us in height and stature. I guess for the longest time, I never thought much of it. Not until Warrick came at me with his sword in the night club on Earth. Please, explain." Selena pushed more.

"Well, I am an Ifrit. Many cultures on Earth see me differently. However, most agree that my kind is a sort of demon. This is not true. Have I done something wrong?" Orion asked.

"No, of course not. I see you as a child of my own. I thought when I found you, you were more like me and Luna. As you grew, I knew you were different, but that never gave me any reason to be concerned. I ask, if you are immune to the iron, I need you to fight against Warrick. Are there any other gifts you have?"

Orion moved closer to the queen. "Well, I am an Ifrit. My kind can go either way good or bad. I would hope you realize that I am good. My powers if any are not anything special. I can be called upon in a similar manner like the demons, but I am not usually called upon unless it is by you. My strength lies in protection and carrying out the commands of the one who oversees me, which is you. "I am here for whatever you need."

The exchange was broken apart when Venus chimed in. "I hate to interrupt, but the guides have made it over to Esmra's. Meridian has been reunited with Aiden who has traveled with Tallulah. Raina has been possessed by Ipos. With Karma and Echo on their way to Etheria, I think we should portal back to Esmra's instead of waiting. Or at the least, give me permission to go back. I want to help Meridian. I may not have all the answers to the curse, but I can surely help Meridian in finding her twin soul. Let me go now with Orion so he can go with the rest to the dark realm for the riddle." Selena nodded and Orion and Venus swiftly left and ported back to Salem.

Meanwhile, Karma and Echo had successfully ported back to Etheria. Warrick had left the dark realm after the dark one's meeting had adjourned. Karma and Echo arrived a short distance from the castle that sat up on the hill that overlooked Etheria. The town although with many guides shuffling around, seemed quiet with low energy and, happiness. Many guides kept their heads down as they walked, barely making eye contact with one another. Many were seated in places to rest or study. As the fairy nymphs journeyed through the realm, they caught admiring glances of the guides as they stared. The fairies stood out amongst the guides with their vibrant wings and life force.

Karma gazed out amongst the guides. "Wow, this place is not what I thought it would be. Every guide here looks sad and depressed."

"Wouldn't you be? They can't tend to their humans. They exist knowing all the chaos that is taking place on Earth and they can do nothing to stop it with the demons taking over. While we were at Esmra's, she had left her television on. The news was horrible. Drug use has increased, more wars are being reported globally and crimes have been at an all-time high. You can't look at the guides and pretend to not understand." Echo remarked.

"I guess you are right. I didn't stop to think of it that way." Karma said as she stopped at the castle that stood in front of them. "When Warrick sees us, he will not hand over the key to the hall of souls. We are in for a battle. You up for it?"

Echo gave out a sly grin she put her hands on her hips. "Up for it? I was born for this. I put one demon under my spell, Warrick will be no different."

"What if he is different? He knows about us, what we do, how we work. He will have a heightened sense to resist us and he may not let his lust get to him like Lahash did." Karma questioned her partner in crime.

"Please, I got this. You watch my back. If my element doesn't work, we can always call for help. Siren and

Lotus will back us up, just be ready." The fairy pair walked right into the palace without invitation and with grins ear to ear without apologies.

As they emerged, the guards of the palace were immediately alerted. So was their lust and desire as Echo strode across the grand room. She spread her wings and put her arms out as she whispered her spell. As the guards all became distracted, Karma zoomed past the guards in their trance and fled down the hall headed toward the great room where Caius's trial was held when he was cast away. Karma waved her arms and the large doors opened with her command and she walked in. Across the room were the second set of large double doors that led to the hall of souls.

It was quiet, not a being in sight. The room was dark with only the light coming from the lighted torches that illuminated the great doors to the hall of souls. Karma searched for the key and as and was startled by a voice.

"Looking for these?" There stood Warrick holding the sacred key to the doors. He held the key between his thumb and his index finger and jingled it up high where Karma could see.

"Warrick!" Karma charged toward him.

Warrick smiled with delight as he drew his iron sword from his hip. Relishing in his inner monologue. He rushed forward toward Karma. Karma shot straight up into the air and hovered over Etheria's hated leader. Warrick looked up and laughed as Karma hurled herself straight down toward Warrick, holding a ball of fire.

As she drew within a few feet of his face, he thrust his sword straight up and knocked Karma down onto the ground, evading the heated ball of fury she carried for him. As he lunged toward the fairy he swung and lashed her leg. As her leg singed with the lash from the sword, she fell back to the ground screaming. As Karma struggled to her feet, Warrick was in full run toward her once more.

She put both hands in the air over her head and cupped the bottom of her hands together. In the empty space between her hands, a spinning silver ball appeared. As the ball continued to spin, it grew in size. With little time to spare, Karma hurled it into Warrick's chest. It blew him back into the wall next to the doors to enter the great room. Leaving a crater in his chest. No blood left Warrick's body, only smoke encircled the crater left in his chest from the ball. The stench was unimaginable. It was combined sulphur and demon filth.

Warrick jumped to his feet. "You fairy hag! You will not make it out of here with your life!"

The doors to enter the great room swung open and a voice shouted over the commotion. "Father! Stop it!" There stood Slaten alongside his mother Farrah. Trailing behind came Echo who rushed in to protect Karma.

"Father STOP!" Slaten yelled at his father again. Warrick did not slow down and Karma was at it again, this time her silver glowing ball was bigger and full of force. She drew back and hurled the ball of light at Warrick, this time knocking him to the ground from which he could not recover so easily. As he lay there injured an unable to move, Slaten and Farrah approached. "What are you doing? You are no match for her!" Slaten pointed to Karma.

As Warrick lay still, with burning demon flesh, unable to move, Karma quickly searched the area for the key knocked out of Warrick's possession during the feisty exchange. She found the key not too far from the doors.

"Slaten, it is okay. My magic will hold him for a bit more time. If you will hold everyone back with the help of Echo, I am going in, I will get the blessing of the keepers to find the quartz sword." Karma said as she walked up the stairs to the doors.

Slaten stood in silence as his eyes widened while he studied the mesmerizing fairy take charge and open the great doors. "What is happening?" Slaten had not been present when Selena shared all the secrets that had been kept from them.

"Slaten, do not worry. In time you will learn of the many secrets that have been kept away from you. You must trust me and allow me to enter, alone. I am here to help you and Etheria. We are here to stop all of this." Karma turned back toward the door. She held up the key, large and lengthy and was made of gold. At the top of the key was a quartz in the shape of a perfect sphere and solid all the way through. She carefully put the key into the hidden keyhole and turned it. The lock clicked, echoing throughout the great gathering room, the doors unlocked and slowly opened for Karma.

Warrick could not resist, he used his elbows to rake his smoke-filled body across the floor toward the entrance to the hall.

As the doors came open, the light from within was nearly impossible to look at. Everyone in the room covered their eyes to shield from the immense brightness. As Karma stood in front of the doorway, she was nearly invisible from the light engulfing her.

Warrick, within inches of the door and the powerful light reached one last time toward the entrance, dropping his hand in the path of the exuberant light. In a moment, it revealed his lack of purity when his hand as it singed and blistered in the light. He jerked his hand back away and tucked it into his body as he rolled into a ball shrieking in pain.

Karma glanced back; without words she gave a cool grin before she turned to enter the coveted place where all pure souls rest. As she moved into the light, her body became a silhouette briefly before she disappeared, and the doors closed behind her.

Chapter 11

After the demons meeting, Lahash was at unrest. His ego was driven by being the dark one's favorite. Raina imposing a mark on Meridian to call Ipos would render him useless and potentially perish without having the evil within politicians to feed from.

Near to within his thoughts, Echo the fairy nymph that he wanted more of, continued to wreak havoc on his demon mind. Giving no care he was under her spell, he liked it. Lahash remained in the dark realm to himself staring at the same place he had kidnapped and kept Luna before the fairy nymphs bestowed their fairy nymph glamour on him. He smiled as he reminisced about his experience with the nymphs and relished in the memory of the nymphs' who subdued him.

Struggling with what he was meant to do and what he wanted to do, he hastily left the dark realm for Earth, to seek the one human that had thrown a kink in his plan. The dark witch who played with Pyro for answers, the dark witch who now sought to use the powers of Ipos for her gain.

Lahash created his portal with aggression, his determination to have what he wanted fueled his lustful desire. Such an irony, he liked feeling subdued and welcomed

Echo to be the one to do it. His arm quickly moved in circles and created an opening for the portal, and he made it back to the graveyard. The same place where his favorite fairy nymph departed for the blessing of the keepers for the quartz sword. Once in Salem, he took in the quaint town and all it offered a human. The streets were quiet at the evening hour, most were asleep in their beds.

As he approached Esmra's house he saw her front door was wide open, voices were audible and clear from the road. Lahash moved closer to see Esmra and Tallulah stood over Raina. Raina stumbled on her words with noticeable discomfort. She rubbed her sunken head that hung down between her legs as the angered witches admonished her.

Talon and the guides noticed the approaching demon. It had been a since the meeting Warrick called, last they saw one another.

"Lahash, what brings you here, of all places?" Talon charged toward the demon. Lahash stopped in his tracks as he continued to work out what was happening inside the house.

"Why are you here?" Lahash locked eyes with Talon.

"You should know that, Lahash. You yourself questioned the irony of what I do and who for. Isn't coming here below your standards?"

"My business here is none of your concern." Lahash sharply dismissed Talon.

"If you plan on harming anyone in that house, then yes, it is my business." Talon quickly moved in front of Lahash to stop him.

"Oh, now Talon, you mustn't get in such a fuss here. I wish no harm on anyone in that house, except maybe one. The witch. She is my business now to take care of. Step away." Lahash moved past Talon, up the steps to Esmra's house where there was quite a turmoil built up between the humans.

Talon moved from Lahash's path, but his curiosity wouldn't let him be. "Lahash, wait!"

Lahash stopped in his tracks but did not offer to turn around. He kept his eyes on Raina who he could see sitting still inside the house. "What is it you want, Talon? I wish no harm on your son or the others. I want Raina."

"Why? Not that we would stop you for what she has done, but why the interest in her. Please." Talon's demeanor changed, he was humbled in need for understanding.

Lahash slowly turned around and faced Talon who now was accompanied by the guides as they were curious about what the exchange would bring.

"I am not accustomed to sharing need to know basis information with a fallen and a bunch of guides. You know I like none of you. But Echo is fond of you all for some reason. So, I will share something. Raina has been possessed by Pyro to instigate what has transpired here tonight. By the way of it, she doesn't seem to know what happened. Pyro is the demon she summons through her Ouija board. Pyro has no loyalties to anything, he also loves riddles like the dark one. However, her summoning Pyro has opened her to more and more. Her soul is writing checks her body can't cash. It is time to pay the piper. She has crossed the line in the way of who she summons, and I am here to put a stop to it." Lahash nodded in snobbery as he tilted his head toward the house, allowing his penetrating eyes to fall to ground, hiding the one thing that the guides sought, the answer to the tattoo on Meridian.

Pramlee had lost her giggles and no longer reminisced about lyrics of the past, instead she lurched toward Lahash. Kieren grabbed her arm, but Pramlee continued to move closer.

"What do you know, Lahash? If Raina has been possessed, then that would mean that what you told Talon back at the club months ago has already come to pass. The possessions you spoke of, the human possessions."

Lahash looked to Pramlee in surprise. His eyes widened and his face lightened with a cocky grin.

"Possessions. Yes, that is the way of it. That is why I am here, so I can possess her. That would sound so simple wouldn't it? I hate to disappoint you, but no. She isn't being possessed because we are pulling our deals off the table with Warrick, not yet anyway. Right now, Raina will have to come with me. I will stop her from what she is doing, for now, as long as it suits me."

Lahash tuned away from the group and he paused once more. "Do not take this as I am offering some assistance to you, know this . . . whatever I do, I do for me and me only. Count yourselves lucky that you will receive a benefit from my doings." Lahash walked through the doorway into the house. The guides followed to watch over the humans while Talon stayed on the other side of the wall, watching to make sure that his son was unharmed by whatever Lahash was about to do.

A loud clap emerged shaking the ground and then appeared the nymphs.

Relic spotted the one he was falling for, Lotus. As the fairies strode through the grass, their skin glistened in the moonlight and their presence left a trail of lavender aroma in their path.

"What is going on here?" Siren pointed to Lahash. "Why is a demon from the court here? Lahash of all of them?"

Talon shook his head. "Well, he is here for Raina, and he was cryptic, but promised no harm to the others. Raina came here and tried to kill Esmra, she was possessed according to Lahash. Possessed by Pyro."

"Pyro? The trickster of court?" Siren crossed her arms and softly drummed her fingers across the fold of her elbow as she raised an eyebrow.

"What would he want with Raina?" Venus pushed through the group trying to find Meridian.

"This is interesting. He is not being forthcoming. We can't trust Lahash, but if he will take care of Raina." Someone interrupted Siren.

"Hey, we still have to go back and answer the dark one's riddle," Ridge quietly said.

Before anyone could say any more, the commotion from within the house increased.

Tallulah lost her temper and yelled at Esmra. "What in the hell has gone on here? I get a call from you about Raina, we show up here, she is lying out in the yard. Meridian doesn't seem to have a clue what is going on. I thought Meridian came here to stay with you? I told you I could not get ahold of her, that she won't return my calls or messages."

"Tallulah calm down. I never got ahold of Meridian or answered my messages either. The guides came here, I could not always communicate with them without Luna! The dark one has kidnapped Luna. He has put out another riddle to answer in order for her release!" Esmra was frantic, her voice ragged and her breathing rushed, she put her hand over her chest. "I have managed to work out, as I told you that the person responsible for much of the problem, is Raina! She showed up here, unannounced, spoke in Latin, just as she did back at your place. I was frozen and could not move. She came at me with this." Esmra handed her a knife.

"Oh my! This is crazy! She tried to kill you?" Tallulah gasped.

"Yes! She also said she was coming after you! All of a sudden, a cold draft moved through, something hurled her outside. You and Aiden showed up, then suddenly Meridian came running down the driveway. This has grown to such a situation. Some of the fairy nymphs are outside, I can see them. I also sense another dark presence and it's not Talon, it is something else! What if it is this demon that has taken Raina over, the one she summons?!" Esmra was running to the kitchen to get her salts, to protect the house.

The fairy nymphs approached Esmra. Lahash who remained in the house spotted Venus and was disarmed, he immediately looked for Echo who was still in Etheria. "She isn't here, so stop it." Venus lectured Lahash.

The nymphs moved to comfort Esmra to calm her and let her know there was no more harm to come.

Raina stood up and collected herself. "I do not know how I got here, honestly but yes I do call on Pyro. He wanted you both dead. He is my lord and I will do what I have to do in order to please him." Raina was as somber and straight faced as she could be.

Meridian clung to Aiden. "Meridian is mine. She will come with me. Now!" Raina's voice suddenly turned dark and raspy.

Aiden moved in front of Meridian, keeping his arm tightly around her as she pressed her face into his back.

"Get out of my way you fool!" Raina flung her arms up and Aiden was pushed up into the air, slammed him back into the ground and knocked him out. Meridian rushed to his side and had a flashback of the time she was in the dark realm. Flashes of Aiden raced in her mind while experienced déjà vu, living out what her visions were when they went to the dark realm for the fairy book.

Aiden woke up and screamed in pain reaching for Meridian barely able to move, and his voice stifled.

"Stop! What are you doing! You are hurting him!" Meridian jumped to her feet and went head on toward Raina. Raina put both hands up in the air and pushed them out with force and Meridian stopped in her tracks, flew into the wall and was knocked unconscious. She brought down the many decorations that filled Esmra's wall, tumbling on top of her head and her body, she fell over lifeless.

Talon rushed in and passed Lahash who stood by and watched the exchange happen. He lifted Raina and threw her back outside again, screaming a spine shivering shriek as he clasped his large hands and razor-sharp claws around Raina's neck and choked while he shook her.

Esmra and Tallulah were chanting protection spells and Venus alongside the guides rushed out into the yard as Talon was slowly squeezing the life out of her. Raina grabbed into the empty space in front of her, fighting a ghost that in appearance was trying to kill her.

Lahash smugly and slowly made his way down the steps and arrived standing over Talon who was in full rage. He unclasped his hands he held behind his back to place on Talon's shoulder.

"Now there, Talon. You are wasting your energy. Allow me." Talon peered over his shoulder in confusion, staring at Lahash's hand to ensure that what he heard was real. Lahash gave a tight grin with a nod followed by a quick pat once again on his shoulder. "Yes, allow my indulgence."

Talon moved away from Raina who was coughing and grabbing her throat. Lahash knelt down in front of the witch.

"Okay, Pyro, you have made your point. Now we have all gotten a show here, it is time to come out. Come out where ever you are. You have some explaining to do." Lahash arose from his squatted posture. There he stood staring at Raina who stopped choking and looked right up to Lahash with an evil grin.

"NO! She sold her soul to me! I will have her. She works for the dark one." Raina's voice was dark and frothy.

"Pyro, you don't own Raina. Release her, she will be no use to you this way. You know this. Instructing her to kill two human women will provide nothing, so give it up!"

Pyro would not let go easily. "Back off Lahash, you want her so you can stop her from summoning Ipos. You only want to stop this for your own selfish wants!"

Lahash laughed. "And you don't? Look at you. If she manages to summon Ipos, it would destroy him, and you would love being next in line for more authority with the court. I can't exist without Ipos and the legions he commands. He was right, I need the demons he commands. I need them, they keep my humans busy making laws and politics. So what? I like what I do and where I go." Lahash remained smug.

"If Ipos is summoned, the girl goes, we get what we want!" Pyro said.

Lahash stuck Raina hoping Pyro would leave. Pyro laughed. Lahash stuck again, this time knocking Raina out once more.

Blood ran down Raina's face from all the blunt force trauma. Pyro exited her body and stood momentarily looking at Lahash. Before another word could be said, Pyro vanished, leaving Lahash to explain to all who witnessed the events.

Esmra and Tallulah walked down the steps back into the front yard where Raina was lying once more, chanting their spell as they approached Raina. The guides were on the women's heels as they approached Raina and the invisible Lahash.

Talon made a move toward Lahash to further inquire about what all that was about, but before he could ask, a loud thunderclap snapped the ears of all that stood around. A flash of light shot through Raina, before she and Lahash disappeared from everyone's sight.

Chapter 12

As Karma entered the hall of souls, she was nearly blinded by the great light that engulfed her body. Her wings reflected the lights exhibiting all colors of the rainbow. She cowered in her posture, using her arms to cover her eyes, and even then, she still looked magnificent.

As her eyes adjusted to the blinding light, she brought her head back up where her eyes looked high up at the grand ceiling. The grand walls were pristine white and sparkled with the crystal quartz embedded into them. The hall seemed to run endlessly, there were doors on each side lined with gold. Each door had a keyhole in the center. The only dark image in the hall of souls; each keyhole was the color black.

Karma continued to walk and moved at a slow pace taking in the beautiful setting. After some time of an endless pace and procession of gold doors, she stopped when a distant voice carried in what seemed from all directions from within the hall of souls.

"Who enters the hall of souls?" The voice sounded to be a woman's voice.

Karma stopped. "It is Karma. I am a fairy nymph. I came to ask for the blessing to find the quartz sword."

There was silence for only a few moments. Still no appearance of anything that Karma could see with her own eyes.

"The quartz sword is only used by the keepers. Why do you come for the sword?" The voice asked.

"The demons have grown too powerful and Etheria has been taken over by a demon named Warrick. There are possessions on Earth, the sprit guides have been banned from looking over their humans. I have come for your blessing to stop it, to stop the demons." Karma said.

"Do not fear me. I am one of the keepers, the protectors of the precious souls. We know what is happening beyond the doors of the great hall and that this day would come. The demons will come for us, to attain our source of power and strength in the Universe."

As the voice trailed off a large presence emerged, bright as the sun. The silhouette continued to become clearer to Karma as she stared, hardly blinking to make sure she missed nothing. The silhouette revealed a womanly shape, with grand wings that stretched upwards to the ceiling as she approached. Her wings were solid white, and the angel's hair was long, platinum white giving it a silvery shimmer. Her skin, equally luminous and translucent. Karma dropped to her knees and bowed her head afraid to look at the beautiful angel that stood over her.

"Please, Karma, stand before me. You have no reason to fear me. I am Laila, one of the many angels that reside here. I must ask you, how did you pass Warrick and why would the guides send a fairy here?"

Karma rose to her feet. "There is not anyone else to do this job. I bring karma and I draw my power from the Universe as do the angels; I am the deliverer of karmic debt and karmic lessons for humans so they learn before evolving to the next life or coming here to be a spirit guide. I have come to protect the humans and see to it that the karmic debt the demons have earned is delivered." Karma looked back to her feet that glistened in the bright light.

"Karma, the only one who can use the sword to protect Etheria is either one of us, the keepers or it is one from Etheria. Etheria's chosen one. A fairy could never be the one to use the sword."

"We believe that the chosen one has been cast away, she is lost and succumbed to the dark power and spells. The fairy Queen sent me here, for your blessing to retrieve the sword. We must have your blessing to use the sword to defeat the demons."

The angel's light voice turned stern. "The keepers will never approve of the sword to be used by any other being than an Etherian. You have our blessing to find and retrieve the sword, but you must deliver it to the chosen one of

Etheria, or it will render the sword useless." The angel's voice faded away and she disappeared leaving Karma standing alone.

Chapter 13

There stood Tallulah and Esmra confounded from witnessing the shocking event with Raina who had now disappeared before their eyes. They stood in Esmra's front yard staring down at the empty space, holding one another. Inside the house, Aiden kneeled down, tending to Meridian who was still knocked out from the blow to her head from being hurled into the wall.

Talon once more disappeared hiding himself away from the eyes of the spirit guides. Relic stood next to Pramlee waiting to see if she would sing the song that previously got on his nerves. They watched Ridge go into the house where he first saw the fairies who had stood by not lifting a finger to help the situation.

"Where were you? Why didn't you step in? You watched everything happen and did nothing!" Ridge shouted.

Selena stood idle during the entire exchange while Lahash took Raina.

"Ridge, calm yourself please. Did it ever occur to you we were helping? Not all protection comes in the same form as what Talon would do. Lahash arrived to take care of the one person who is stifling our successes. Your biggest worry right now should be your trip to the dark realm to answer the riddle that hangs."

The other guides made their way inside the house right behind Esmra and Tallulah who were helping Aiden tend to Meridian. Ridge did not respond to Selena and he turned away and headed to the space where Raina disappeared with Lahash.

Talon joined Ridge to create the portal to the dark realm.

"I am going. You all will need me." Pramlee tried to remain bubbly despite the look of terror in her eyes. She turned her petite chin toward Relic who was visibly shaking just thinking about returning to the place that nearly had him trapped the first time. Orion, Siren and Lotus stood with confidence next to Talon as the portal opened and shot out a brisk bolt of hot air. The heat slapped them across their faces and knocked them back with a ferocious gale force wind.

"I sure wish Slaten were here!" Pramlee bellowed over the roar of the portal. She squinted her eyes as she continued to speak over the magnitude of the portal roar. "We can do this!" Pramlee shouted, forcing the much-needed confidence to take on the demon realm.

Relic and Kieren locked eyes as Pramlee looked at the pair smitten for Meridian. They both gave a forced smile but their eyes didn't change. Their bodies stiff, their hands clenched into fists ready for the dark forces they were soon to face.

"Okay! It is like before! Remember, anything goes. Keep your wits! Listen to your hearts! The dark one won't expect us to have the answer. We have Orion and the nymphs. Stay positive!" Talon shouted over the noise of the portal.

Flames brushed the opening that lead to a bright red tunnel of heat and ash. Talon motioned them to move forward and one by one the guides, the fairies and Talon walked through disappearing into the flames.

Selena watched from afar, as they disappeared to find her daughter, leaving behind silt and ashes in the air from the portal. Her daunting eyes glowed in the dark and her face even brighter, reflected the full moon's light.

On the other side of the dark realm's portal, Pramlee walked confidently next to Talon who scouted the path for any signs of demons. She stayed close to him allowing herself to brush his arm with hers as they walked in sync. Relic and Kieren were much the same as they remained shoulder to shoulder. Sometimes, Relic would drift a step or two behind so he could watch Lotus who kept her head down most of way as she stayed tucked in with her sister, Siren. Their wings dragged the hard and cracked ground, leaving behind a small flutter of dust with each step.

Orion and Ridge stayed in the back to watch over everyone. The scenery was all the same, dark red with the foul odor that most often accompanied demons. The sulphur in the air thick and heavy, and the wind from the dark realm had quieted but still strong enough to give cause for their eyes to squint while the grit brushed their faces.

As they continued to push through, a low hissing surrounded the realm with no indication of the source. Everyone moved together while Talon put his hands up as if to guard his friends.

"Remember, it is mind tricks. The demons, they are here." Talon overhead and pointed to the red atmosphere, where silhouettes of demons floated above.

"What is happening? Why aren't they attacking?" Relic whispered.

Talon's eyes widened. "Where is Ridge? What happened to Orion?"

Suddenly, the silhouettes came down like daggers flying into the group driving them to the ground.

Relic jumped up and threw his fists up in the air shaking them all while dodging the incoming fury. "C'mon! C'mon! You think you can take us! You can't! Bring it!"

Relic screamed as loud as he could, sweat pouring from his forehead, his jaw tight and his face red accompanied by the veins that bulged under his skin.

Pramlee crawled over to Siren. "Siren, I am scared! This didn't happen before." Pramlee's words drifted into silence despite her mouth still moving but seemed to be in slow motion. Her face strained as she clawed her fingers into the hardened demon dirt they dragged her on.

Siren jumped to her feet and opened her mouth to let out her demon hated shrill that singed the ears of the dark filth that roamed the realm. Without as much as a hesitation, the dark shadow emerged and took Pramlee by her ankles and dragged her away and she disappeared.

Siren stunned at the magnitude and speed of the demons, she quickly ran to Lotus who stood with a death grip on Relic. Before she could make it, a demon shot down from above and knocked Siren to her knees. Relic and Lotus ducked at the incoming shadows filled with vengeance and rage.

"What in the hell is happening?!" Kieren shouted as he ran toward Relic. Both he and Lotus were too distracted helping Siren to her feet. As they created a tight circle to be ready for the next assault, the demons were gone and the attacks stopped.

Ridge and Orion were gone and all that was left were the two fairy nymphs, Talon, Kieren and Relic. Talon exhausted with the fighting stood unable to speak.

Relic paced back and forth, frantically running his fingers through his hair. He stopped his hands at both sides of his head and he bent over as if in pain. He let out a growl, a guttural rage he could not quell as he fisted his own hair in anger.

"AHHH! What do you want! We came here to answer your stupid riddles and you take more of what does not belong to you!"

The nymphs were arm in arm holding one another. Kieren stood frozen with fear having never seen this side of Relic. Talon dragged himself toward Relic as he held his side from his injuries.

"Relic, please. Stop." Talon's breaths were ragged as he fell down. Relic's angered face softened, his brows lifted as he dropped to Talon's side.

A low and deep voice spoke out, ringing through the realm. "So, you return with your answers? Well, do tell Relic, my jester. Do tell." The dark one went quiet.

Talon whispered to Relic. "Relic, do not screw this up. You have to answer his riddles. This is not a joke. He is playing for keeps. Answer him," Talon quietly begged.

"Why? Why should I answer him? He stole my wife, he has toyed with answers about Meridian's curse, now more are missing. Then what will it be? More riddles to rescue all of them? When does it stop? How can we be sure he will release Luna? Charity, Farrah and maybe Chance? We are losing here, and I am sick and tired of the GAMES!" Relic looked upward and threw his hands up.

The dark one laughed followed by a hiss. "Let's take a trip down memory lane."

Within moments the scenery changed, and everyone now stood in Tallulah's house the night that Raina called Pyro through the Ouija board to aid Tallulah. The scene played out in front of them as though it was happening all over again. They saw Raina setting out her upside-down pentagram, then onto Pyro where he exposed his face in the empty space above the board. Then Pyro answered Raina's question.

"The being whose work is dark can only be stopped with the twin soul.
The being you seek is hard to hold.
Spirit guides who engage with a mortal are not pure of heart in that act,
but in the face of true love all remains intact.
Meridian does not trust herself in her choice.
She will not listen to her inner voice.
So many can enter her mind,
her greatest challenge in the true find."

As soon as Pyro finished his riddle, the group suddenly stood once again back in the dark realm, but his time there was Raina in the center of a pentagram carved into the dirt. Still and flat on her back, her eyes were open but black and lifeless.

"What is going on!" Siren shouted. "This is the witch from the ceremony, the witch who had Meridian. Lahash took her. What is happening?"

The dark one spoke again, this time his voice was short, quick and with conviction. "This witch calls on my demon Pyro for her own selfish wants. She seeks Meridian for her own uses of power. She sold her soul to Pyro." The dark one let out a guttural laugh that shook the atmosphere. Demons swarmed though the air like snakes as they danced around the pentagram.

Lotus shut her eyes. "Don't look at them! Do not look at them! Close your eyes!" Everyone closed their eyes as the swimming demons entwined their bodies in and around the nymphs and the guides.

The dark one continued to speak, "She, like the nymphs are just causing a little too much trouble." ANSWER THE RIDDLE!" Relic fell to the ground writhing in pain holding himself as he rolled around on the ground. Talon ran to assist him, and everyone's eyes were forced open with the shock.

"What do you want from us?" Talon paced back and forth, "We came to answer the riddles!"

Nothing more was said, but once again they were transported back to a scene on Earth, the night that Raina confronted Meridian on the street outside Stephanie's bar. They stood and watched Meridian after she left Stephanie's for the night. Raina approached her while she chanted one of her dark spells and Meridian collapsed in the street. After a few moments she stood back up on her feet and Raina took her to get the tattoo of the sigil. Then suddenly, the scene was gone and they were back in the dark realm.

"The answer to the riddle is no one. We cannot foresee who the twin soul is. Only Meridian knows!" Relic struggled to his feet, out of breath and in pain. "Please, please." Relic put his hands up in submission. "Please," he whispered. "There is no answer. Me and Kieren. We both wanted it to be us. Meridian must choose. Please." Relic fell to the ground.

"Is that your answer, Relic? The selfish guide who would not obey his own leader, who only cares for himself. Who always has an answer for everything, for everyone . . . you resign yourself to being there is no answer? After Selena told you who it may be, you will risk all, for there is no answer?"

Relic stood up without hesitation, "Yes! There is not an answer from us. The answer comes from Meridian. I don't care, kill me, keep me, hurt me. It doesn't matter anymore. What else do you want?"

It was quiet, only the sound of their breathing was audible throughout the realm. The demons disappeared and shortly after footsteps were audible through the realm as if they were on solid flooring. The steps drew closer and a silhouette emerged from the smoky crimson atmosphere. He was slow in pace as if in no hurry to approach, his swagger he carried was like no other and he tucked his hands behind his back as if he kept small secrets.

As the crimson gave way to his face, Lahash appeared with his lip slightly upturned as he strode by Raina. He gave her a sideways glance and a quick smirk and tucked his chin as though he may be ashamed at the trophy laying in the center of the pentagram.

"Lahash! What are you doing here?"

"What am I doing here? Oh now, Relic, what rhetorical questions you ask. Do I need to answer that for you? Where do you think I come from? Last I checked, a church maybe where I live?" Lahash stopped and locked on to Relic who stood silent with his eyes squinted not giving any more away.

Talon stepped between the two. "Lahash, what is going on?"

Lahash stood unwavering and smug., "Well, for starters, try asking the right questions. Something like oh, Lahash, what a pleasure it is to see you. We appreciate you taking that psycho witch off our hands. What can we do for you?" Lahash softly drummed his long fingers across his tie as if he were studying it for the first time. He kept his head down still studying his tie and let out a small grin, where his lower teeth emerged accompanied by a raised eyebrow.

Relic let out a sigh. "Oh sure, church. Yeah, you sure dress like you are going to church. Nah, I can't say we appreciate that you did anything with ol' darky over there. She is the idiot that sold her soul to the devil, so I would say your job was mediocre at best. Before I would go bragging about what a good job I did, I would look at the odds. It isn't like you had to possess her, she did so willingly, and another demon did it. Please. I mean you certainly aren't going to do anything to get your suit dirty." Relic's usual cocky attitude reemerged with minimal provocation.

"Now, now Relic. Careful." Lahash grinned as he waved his index finger to Relic in warning. "Now that we have cleared the air about what a wonderful help I was to you, I was wondering if you would be in the spirit of returning favors." Lahash dropped his hands slowly behind his back and walked toward the nymphs who looked disgusted.

"Now, you wait, Lahash, your charms do not work on us. Now, I know that you can't get enough of us, or your favorite Echo. But we will have to pass for now." Siren stood with her hands on her hips. "Or would you like us to work our magic on you now?" Lotus laughed.

Lahash passed by them and continued to pace the circle, watching Raina. "What will it be? You answered the first riddle. Now all that is left is answer the second riddle and your wishes come true." Lahash grinned, "What is the answer to the second riddle? Spill it." Lahash stood on the other side of the pentagram staring them all down. His smile left his face and his eyes darkened. He leaned in over the pentagram and awaited the answer.

Talon was directly on the opposing side of the pentagram. What a scene it was for the guides. Within the dark realm, a fallen and a demon of the high court stood at odds while the witch who sold her soul lay lifeless in the center of the pentagram.

Talon stood stiff, his fists clenched, and arms locked. His head lowered as he stared at Lahash, eyes squint tight and his breathing deep, but quick. "No more games. Enough of this. Why did you collect Raina? Why did you bring her here? Why don't you answer this stupid riddle?"

Lahash dropped his eyes toward Raina, his face softened for a moment. He closed his eyes and held them closed. "ANSWER THE RIDDLE!"

No one moved, the guides were frozen with fear as the scene grew in tension. The fairy nymphs were the only two beings that moved toward Talon. Lotus softly placed her hand on Talon and closed her eyes. Talon changed his defensive composure, his eyes opened larger as he focused on Raina. Lotus whispered in Talon's ear in a language that not he or the spirit guides had ever heard. A foreign language Talon somehow understood as he broke his stare from Raina and looked into Lotus's big and soft turquois eyes.

Chapter 14

Meridian remained asleep, in the same bed Esmra put her in the first day they met. Tallulah had awoken to a messy house from the previous night's frantic horror as she made her way down the creaky wooden stairs. The only sounds beyond the creaking of the stairs, were the birds chirping and playing in the garden as they gobbled up the seeds that Esmra left for them.

Esmra, already awake ahead of anyone else, was downstairs, seated in her favorite chair remained quiet with her thoughts as she slowly sipped a cup of tea. Tallulah walked into the kitchen and waited for a few moments before she spoke while she leaned on the doorway. Her eyes were tired, sunken in from lying awake all night. She stared at the floor and let out a large sigh.

Esmra turned to see her friend slouched over. "Good morning, Tallulah. Words aren't needed, you are exhausted." Esmra stood from her chair and walked over to her old 1950s style stove and took the old teapot that was still steaming with hot water. She poured Tallulah a cup of tea and she shuffled back over to the table and set it down. She winked at Tallulah with an upturn of her lip as she sat back down in her chair.

Tallulah came away from the doorway that appeared to be holding her up. The sounds of her house shoes scraped the kitchen floor as she slowly walked to the table and took her seat. The pair sat quietly without words, looking out the window watching the birds squabble over their food in the garden. Every once in a while, a soft breeze would tickle the wind chimes hanging outside the big picture window in the kitchen softening the ominous feeling the two shared without words.

Meanwhile, upstairs Meridian and Aiden still lay asleep. Meridian was tucked under the soft white quilt that adorned the bed, on her back with her arms relaxed at her side and her face turned toward Aiden. Aiden lay on his left side facing Meridian deep in his own slumber with rapid eye movement that fluttered his lids.

Aiden drifted into his continuous dream that never seemed to move forward or have an ending. As he drifted into his recurring dream, he once again in his mind's eye could see his own self in the hospital he was born where his mother lost her life, giving Aiden his. There Aiden lay on the couch in the hospital asleep and once again, he awakened and walked down the hall of the hospital where the nurses and doctors were quickly moving in and out of the room he walked towards.

He placed his hand up on the door to push it open, and for the first time, the dream progressed further. Aiden took a few steps into the room, and instantly he no longer saw himself in his mind's eye, but now he is seeing through his own eyes. He looked around the room and his view was obstructed by the frantic movement of the staff around the bed of the person who lay in it. The more he struggled to see who lay in the bed, the more obstructed and blurrier the scene became.

Looking around the room for other clues, he saw two people standing at the foot of the bed, but unable to make out who they were. No sound, no talking and the two people who stood at the foot of the bed didn't move as the staff hurried around the room caring for the person who lay still in it.

Aiden could see three golden floating orbs hovering away from the bed. Behind him, five bright illuminating beings with silhouettes of people, stood quietly.

Startled from what he saw, Aiden tried to move quickly and push his way through to the bed. The harder he tried to move, the harder moving became as though something put him in slow motion. He screamed in the dream as he fought to get to the bed out of reach. No one in the room noticed him or his fearful screams as he frantically lurched for the bed. He fell down and he rolled over onto his back and saw a glowing apparition that floated above him.

Aiden jolted and awoke from his recurring dream now turned into a nightmare. He sat straight up in the bed, his breathing rushed, his face white with sweat beads. Meridian, who was unphased by his sudden movement that shook the bed remained asleep. His face still covered with shock, he maintained a stare on Meridian.

As Aiden regained his senses, a soft smile emerged as he brought his hand up to Meridian's head and stroked her hair softly. The minutes passed into an hour as he watched Meridian sleep and listened to the soft sounds she made as she would breathe. Slowly, Meridian opened her eyes and her lips that were once still and quiet gave way to a smile as her eyes fixed on Aiden's face.

Aiden's face was soft but full of concern as he watched Meridian wake up. "Good morning, how are you feeling?"

Meridian tried to move and she struggled from the slam into the wall from the previous night's events that left her with a massive headache and a sore body. Her eyes winced in pain as he tried to move. "Oh, my head!" Meridian grumbled lifting her hand to her forehead. "What happened? Did I drink again?" Meridian sounded disgusted.

Aiden snickered a little at the sarcasm. "No, or I don't think you had been drinking when I saw you. You don't remember?"

Meridian's face was blank, and then her eyes widened, showing a spark of recognition. "Oh, yeah, I remember. I was at Raina's, I found my phone hidden in her closet, I ran to Esmra's and found you. Raina was already there and she was throwing you around, flying in the air. What happened after?"

"Well, for starters, you were thrown too, hence your headache. Can you get out of the bed? I don't know if Tallulah and Esmra are awake. I think we should all talk together about what has happened." Aiden got out of bed and put his T-shirt back on from the night before. Meridian followed suit and the pair jogged down the stairs, not stopping to see the disarray Esmra's house was in. They stepped over debris in the floor and rushed to the kitchen where they found Esmra and Tallulah seated at the table.

The two women quickly turned around to see the pair walk in together.

"Look who is up! Come over here and sit down, we have been waiting for the both of you. How are you both feeling?" Esmra smiled as she brushed her hands over Aiden and Meridian's arms.

"Well, we both have headaches, that is all I think we have," Aiden said as he pulled out a chair for Meridian to sit in.

Meridian took her seat and began a round of inquiries. "What is happening?"

Tallulah broke her silence. "Meridian, why don't you start first and tell us what has been happening with you?"

"I have been staying at Raina's, but really I don't know why." Meridian's voice lowered, she crossed her arms. "When I left for Salem, I had it in my mind to come find Esmra. I ran into Raina, and I decided that maybe she could help me. I can't understand it, I can't remember how I made it here." Meridian scratched her head while she recalled fuzzy memories.

"I don't know why I would be with Raina. I never intended to stay with her. I thought that maybe, if I went along with her on some things that she would help me find a way to break my curse." Meridian threw her hands up. "I arrive here and there is so much that I can't recall, and a lot seems so fuzzy to me. I had a lot of anxiety, so Raina took me to a doctor and he prescribed medicine. And I stay thirsty a lot, but . . ." Meridian paused as she put things together. "She is always there with something to drink, and once again I feel there are massive time gaps in my memory. I thought I was losing my mind." Meridian walked the floor, her eyes shifty. "She must be putting something in my drinks. Then last night, Raina said she had to go do something for work. I heard beeping coming from the closet, I found my phone and some messages that I didn't see that I had before. I remember sending messages to Esmra and it always seemed she didn't answer." Meridian was growing frantic as she shared what she could remember.

Meridian took a ragged breath and a tear rolled down her pale face from her unique green eyes.

Aiden put his arm around her. "Hey, it will be okay, no matter what, I am not leaving you and I won't let you push me away." Aiden grinned as he put his hand under her chin and tilted her head up to make eye contact, bringing that smile back to her face that Aiden loved to see.

Tallulah continued to stir her tea with one of Esmra's dated and old silver spoons from decades past.

"Meridian, since you have been away, Esmra and I both have tried to contact you. Now it is clear why you didn't return our messages, we need to find out what Raina has truly become involved with, and more important, why she has become so fixated on you." Tallulah let out a huff as she finally pulled her spoon out of her tea to take a sip.

Meridian watched Tallulah and her mind drifted back to the day they first met. It was then she looked into Tallulah's soulful eyes, the same eyes Meridian connected with when she found her again.

"Tallulah, I want to say how sorry I am." Meridian stood from her seat and kneeled down next to Tallulah.

Meridian's long black hair was swept over her shoulders, messy and unkempt. She pulled her hair back away from her face and brought herself close to Tallulah.

Tallulah brushed her hand over the top of Meridian's head and down her high cheek bones where her hand stopped and held Meridian's chin. "Meridian, you do not have to be sorry. I know that I can be a bit overbearing. At the time, you had gone through so much and discovered some unbelievable things about yourself, along with a horrible curse, that you still carry around. I can't blame you for running here. I am sure you were just trying to protect all of us and find answers. Who could blame you for that?"

Esmra rose from her seat to clear off the table while she kept a concerned eye on Meridian. She quickly wiped down the place mats with dribbles of tea from the morning's long session. "That is right Meridian. No one can blame you. I have seen some strange things in my life as a witch, but nothing compares to what I have seen in Raina. I owe you an apology for exposing you to her. If it weren't for me, you may not be in this shape." Esmra turned her back, walked toward the sink and turned on the water to hide her tears. "I am so sorry." She grabbed a towel from the countertop to wipe her hands and tears. She put away the old towel and took a deep breath with a quick turn to face Meridian. "Can you forgive me?" Her eyes reddened, her face flushed and resembled how much emotion she tried to hold back.

Meridian rose from her squatted position and dashed over to Esmra. "Esmra, you do not owe me an apology. None of this is your fault. You tried to save me. Help me. Please, do not beat yourself up over this." Meridian hugged Esmra tightly. "I love you."

Esmra slowly wrapped her arms tightly around Meridian and squinted her eyes fighting more tears. She finally let out a bit of a cry as Meridian held on tightly. As they released their embrace, Meridian turned to Aiden and Tallulah. "I love all of you. You are the only family I have since being here on Earth. I can barely remember the guides that at one time I used to see, and now I can't since being here with Raina in Salem. I have these crazy dreams but, in the dreams, I feel safe and I don't want to wake up, I feel like I am home, but no home I ever could recall. You all in my waking new life give me hope and reason."

Meridian sat back down at the chair and looked down at her lap. "I never wanted to hurt anyone. I felt that this was something I had to find out on my own. In breaking my curse. I never fathomed things would get so out of control. I am truly at a loss as to what to do."

Aiden smiled at everyone and said, "One thing is for sure, this is something we can all do together. No more being apart. I have learned a lot about who I am, the strangest thing is, I have learned more about me and my past from what was a total stranger."

"We spent a lot of time talking on the drive up here to Esmra's. It has been overwhelming for me to finally have the knowledge of who my father was or is. To know that he was someone of your world, Meridian. My father was like your parents at one time before Warrick cast him away, like you. I know he is around and that means so much to me. I feel like I want to call home and tell my grandparents, but they would think I had lost my mind. I have all of you wonderful women in my life I can share my secret with and be understood. I am here for anything any of you may need. I am not anyone special, but I do what I can." Aiden's face flushed as he peered up at Tallulah with his bright piercing blue eyes. They seemed to turn green matching the color of his shirt.

Tallulah smiled and leaned over and gave Aiden a hug. "Well, I am glad we are all okay. Now what are we going to do about Raina? How in the world are we ever going to figure out what she was up to? We do not understand what happened to her after she vanished from outside. Something tells me, we haven't heard the last from Raina."

Chapter 15

Warrick, even with a momentary defeat in his own backyard, was steamed with the intrusion of the fairy nymphs. He was no match for Echo as she fought him and his guards off while Karma entered the hall of souls.

He had barely collected himself and stood toe to toe with Echo ready to go at it again. "Give it up Warrick, your guards won't even protect you against us. You are no match for the nymphs or any fairy or that matter. You are weak and a poor excuse for any being to live in this Universe!"

Before Warrick could respond with an attack or another verbal sparring with the feisty fairy nymph, Karma walked out from within the hall of souls. As she emerged, she carried the large and sacred key to the door firmly in her grasp. "Don't waste your time with that baboon, he is not worth our time."

"Don't worry Echo, we are going to go get the sword that no doubt will put an end to Warrick's tyranny." Karma marched right past Warrick who was seething with rage. She smirked as she approached Echo. "Let's go."

"You won't get away with this! I have Luna! With Luna, even your precious Selena won't fight against me!"

Warrick continued to shout as the nymphs as they left the palace.

"She will have no choice but to turn the stone and the book over to me! The dark one will make sure of it." Warrick's words fell into an empty room that at one time was a room where guides came to gather and support one another and a place for council meetings.

The nymphs found a quiet place to portal from arriving back in Selena's company, who slowly had lost her patience for the news.

The fairy's wicked eyes met. "Karma! What news do you have?"

"Selena, we made it to Etheria. I made it into the hall of souls, and I managed to find the key." Karma handed the key over to Selena. "I spoke with the angel Laila." Karma took measure of Selena's reaction.

Selena carefully studied the key, the great and powerful key, to the hall of souls. She stopped and broke her amber, cat-like yellow eyes away from the key and locked them on Karma.

"You . . . you spoke to one of the angels? One of the keepers?"

Selena remained doubtful, as though it was unbelievable that something such as a conversation with an angel was a farce. She backed up and away from the nymphs and fell back on her chair as she remained in shock. "I believe you; it is just that the angels do not speak to anyone, especially to our kind. What was it!? What did the angel say?"

"It was an angel, Laila was her name. She was uncertain of why it was I who came into the hall of souls. It was not expected that a fairy would show up. The keepers were expecting an Etherian to come and request the blessing for the quartz sword, which is, by the way, is Gabriel's sword. I have received the blessing to recover the sword, however if it is used against the demons by anyone other than the chosen one of Etheria, it will render the sword useless. Only the chosen one can use the quartz sword and be the savior of Etheria, and the protection of humanity."

"So, it is true then. With everything that has come to pass, it has to be for certain that Meridian is the rightful leader and salvation of Etheria. Her soul was born of her realm, from two people's souls who were born of Etheria. A long line of succession of pure and enlighten souls that transcended through the ages of human lives." Selena sat in thought. "I do not know how we can achieve getting Meridian's curse broken so that she can join all of us to conquer Warrick. How? How are we going to do this? Meridian lost her way for a bit, but now that she has found Aiden and he knows the whole of his story and there is hope. It is up to Venus to help Aiden and Meridian come together."

"Selena, I know that Venus can do this, she rules love and lust. The decision, it still lies in Meridian's hands. The one thing that the we have not given attention to is that even if we "break" the curse. What does that imply? That she returns to Etheria? She remains a human? Did anyone ever consider this?" Karma moved toward Selena and leaned on the arm of Selena's great chair was seated in. The pair locked eyes in silence with new thoughts around what would it bring if the curse was actually broken.

***

Meanwhile, in the dark realm, fireworks were in full bloom fueled by quarrelsome demons. Lahash, the demon of the high court waited for Talon to answer the riddle.

"What is it going to be Talon? Are you going to answer the riddle and set yourself free? Set your friends free? The answer is on the tip of your tongue," Lahash lectured as he salivated with the desire to hear the answer.

"How can I be sure that Charity and the others will be set free? How do I know you will release Luna? Why should I believe you? If you are so motivated to answer the riddle, why don't you do it yourself? You, after all were the one who brought Raina here to begin with." Talon had not changed his composure and alike, Lahash remained unwavering.

Relic stood in silence taking in the exchange that unfolded, while Pramlee's who returned from the demon dragging her away, showed ponder and concern. She quickly moved toward the pentagram and whispered to Talon.

"There is a reason he won't answer the riddle, there is a reason he wants this riddle answered by us. Why? What is in it for him? This has something to do with Raina." Pramlee remained nervous. "I know never trust a demon but this, it is different. He is too hasty. So many have disappeared from us, have been taken. I am afraid of answering the riddle and what that would entail. Think about it, he knows the answer. We know the answer. What is in it for us if we answer this riddle here and now?" Pramlee stood stiff and close to Talon, hiding herself from Lahash who had zoned in on Pramlee's whispers.

"I don't want them to drag me away again. I still do not see Ridge or Orion." Pramlee looked around.

Lahash moved, but this time when he did, it wasn't with his own two feet. He hovered above the pentagram and as his feet dangled above Raina, he stopped and allowed himself to descend onto the hard and crusty ground of the dark realm and said, "This witch, she likes to play with tarot cards, does she? Well, allow me."

Lahash brought both his long arms up in the air and in the empty space above Raina, tarot cards appeared and floated in the space all spread out. Taking on the position of the querent, he waved his hands back and forth several times and with each passing of his hands one card would separate from the spread. The isolated card hovered alone, until he chose the next card.

After he chose eight tarot cards the remaining cards disappeared from sight. He was the only one who could see what he had chosen. The back side of the cards were the only thing that Talon, the guides and the nymphs could see.

Siren joined Talon and Pramlee where they stood. "Do not play this game. Do not read the cards," Siren urged, her voice strained.

Pramlee turned to Siren and said, "Why? What is he doing?"

"This is not a game you will win. He is challenging you because you refuse to answer the riddle. He will benefit from whatever this is. He will gain something or maintain something if you utter the one name that is the answer to this riddle."

Siren ascended above the center of the pentagram while Lahash's dark eyes followed the fairy nymph. An evil smile emerged, and his lips curled with pleasure. "You can't help them. This is not your fight," Lahash said.

Siren drew a breath to speak, but she was interrupted with the all too familiar baritone voice of evil and deceit. A voice without a face.

"What is this? Why do you all come once again to my abode, without so much as an offering of gifts? You have the answer to the riddle that was set before you. Answer the riddle or all of you will remain here with us for eternity."

Relic had his fill of the dark one and his long and drawn out games. "NO! We will not answer your stupid riddle! We have had no benefit in doing anything by answering these riddles!"

The ground violently shook once more and Raina who still lay in the middle of the pentagram, was pulled back and forth from the shaking.

Lotus quickly went into action and flew toward Relic who seemed to not have a care for what his remarks would bring. The ground beneath his feet opened up, hot flames shot from the break while the dirt dissipated from his feet. In a matter of moments, Relic fell within the canyon that formed.

Lotus flew to rescue Relic who descended into the fire pits of the dark realm. His arms waved frantically in a backwards motion, his eyes wide with horror while his scream echoed throughout the realm. Falling faster and faster, he nearly vanished from Lotus's sight.

Her wings extended and grew in length, as they propelled shockwaves through the sulfurous air. He fell as though something were clutching onto him pulling him further and further into the sweltering pit.

As they both continued their dissention, the heat took its toll and Relic suffocated. No longer audible, his scream halted while bouts of pulsating heat slammed into Lotus. With one wave after another, the pulsating heat knocked her further back.

Siren unlocked her stare on Lahash who stood with humor with the eruption of events. Siren took to the air to help Lotus, and through the seemingly endless pit of fire, she closed the gap quickly.

"Stop, I will save him! You are out of your element here. Lotus! He will need you when I catch him!"

Lotus stopped her downward spiral to save Relic who had now gone into a trance. He was silent as he fell, his arms limp and his body lifeless. Lotus reluctantly turned herself around to escape the canyon that was closing.

As Siren flew further into the pit of hell, her skin heated and her face flushed. The very fire within the burning pit fed her fire element and she grew stronger as she drew closer to the massive fire. As she moved closer to Relic, it engulfed her body in flames. From within the burning flames that swallowed her body, her arms stretched before her and opened wide as she embraced Relic in time before he reached the fire pit.

She quickly ascended but the opening to the fire pit was quickly closing. Lotus barely made it out, and she and the guides peered over the gaping canyon of heat, helpless and watching Siren fly upward toward the opening.

"She won't make it! She won't make it!" Pramlee was frantic as she clung to Talon.

The dark one laughed his evil laugh as the gaping hole had completely closed. Siren cradled Relic who was still unconscious and unaware as she sped up toward the space that now had completely closed. She twisted in a spiral as she flew straight away. With increased speed, it completely engulfed her and Relic in a blur of smoke and fire.

As they burst through the hardened ground that was meant to trap them for eternity, debris from the breakage spread beyond the guides who were blown backward with the bursting bullet of a fairy nymph. The debris continued to disburse and reached the pentagram where Lahash stood.

A moment after Siren broke through the trap she appeared as a grand ball of light where she hovered as though the scene played out in surreal slow motion. The guides, Talon, and even Lahash put their arms in front of their eyes for protection from the blinding light.

Her spin slowed, the light faded away and her silhouette emerged through the blaring light. She softly lowered herself to the ground whilst she held Relic who remained in his trance.

Lotus, quick to Relic's aid, kneeled beside him. She placed her hands over his face, closed her eyes and spread her wings as if to protect him. "Move away!"

Everyone backed away quickly, with confusion. She reached into a small pocket hidden within her stocking on her leg. In her hand she held a round crystal quartz. She stood up beside Relic and walked around him in a circle and slowly began her ascension into the air.

As she circled over him, her flying quickened, accompanied by a large cloud. The heavy cloud burst with lightning and clapped with thunder releasing a heavy mist. From the mist, the rain poured down and turned to a flood. The hardened ground of the dark realm was no longer gritty, but now slick with runoff.

Invisible to the eye, a barrier formed around Relic in a circle, holding the water inside where it flooded around him, until he was submerged. Lotus hovered beneath the dark cloud and tossed the crystal quartz up in the air where each quartz burst into thousands of tiny fragments, falling into the water changing color to an emerald green, giving the appearance of a sparkling pool of magical waters.

Fairy Nymphs & the Demon Court

As Relic lay submerged in the magical water, Lahash, still awaiting the answer to the dark one's riddle, rushed over and appeared standing next to Karma he looked up at Lotus with a devious smile full of lust and admiration.

Lahash leaned in and whispered in Karma's ear. "So, enjoying the fairy glamour, are you? I realize many are taken with the fairy nymphs, myself included. But for different reasons."

Karma's stare broke, and she drew in a long breath as she crossed her arms and cut her eyes up at Lahash.

"I would appreciate it if you wouldn't ruin the moment here. Lotus and Siren have something good to offer others, unlike yourself." Karma shoved Lahash out of her way.

Lahash's eyes widened along with his sly grin followed by a chuckle. He was in awe of spunky Karma.

"Oh, here now. I have good things to offer. I took the witch off your hands, didn't I?" Lahash questioned Karma as he followed her toward Relic who was now awakened from within the emerald water.

Everyone remained in suspension as they awaited the results of the fairy nymphs' work. Talon walked away from the scene and headed toward a loud rumble just over the pentagram, coming from another hall from within the dark realm. The rumble grew louder into a full crescendo. The guides left the nymphs by Relic's side and dashed over to follow Talon.

Hollering filled the air, followed by two demons who were being hurled out into the open. The demons ejected from within the mysterious hallway that lead to somewhere else, collected themselves and quick to their feet.

The demons looked at one another and then back at the cave and another demon lurched through the air flying without grace, stumbling in his landing. The dark one's voice rang out.

"How dare you! How dare you assault those of the high court! You will pay for this!"

Within seconds a large dark-skinned being zoomed out of the cave, with a rapid pace, leaving a blur in his tracks. Once again, he streaked around the three demons in a circle as they pleaded for it to stop. The being came to a standstill, and those around discerned who the creature was.

There he stood, eight feet tall, muscular and he stared past the guides with blood-red eyes. His head was large and his mouth was full of sharp teeth. His stare was on the being who approached and stopped in the flooded area where Relic was submerged.

"Oh my, Orion. Orion, your truth. You said in time your truth would be revealed for Luna. Here you are. How did I not know? How could I not have seen who you were, when you were resistant to the iron the night Warrick came at me with his sword." Selena continued to approach the creature that Orion had become. She quickened her pace toward him, one hand was on her heart and the other covering her mouth. As she drew closer, Orion knelt down.

"My Queen, I am sorry for you to see me this way." Orion kept his eyes to the ground, hiding his eyes. He slumped over as if to make himself appear smaller.

Selena kneeled beside Orion, put her hand under his wide chin and pulled it towards her. Their eyes met and there was silence for many moments as Selena gazed into his eyes.

"You are an Ifrit," Selena said.

Orion softly pulled away from his queen. "My Queen, when you rescued me as a young one, I thought you knew. As time went on, I became unsure. Some believe that we are all evil, few see my kind as good as I said before. I always stood with the conviction I was benevolent. I try to do right, but in the face of those I care for, I would allow my true colors to come through. I hope I am not a disappointment."

Selena helped the large Ifrit to his feet. "I could never be disappointed in you. I always thought that an Ifrit stayed in this form, you always looked like one of us. I guess when you told me, I just did not imagine this part of you. Of course, you are so much larger. I didn't ever entertain why. We love you, Orion. Please do not think of yourself as though you are different. You are one of the fairies and always will be."

Selena noticed Ridge who appeared in the dark realm after she recognized Orion. Ridge was stilling rubbing his throat laced with deep scratches, his blue blood telling of his injuries. Straggling behind were Pramlee and Luna. Relic interrupted the moment of realizations and momentary confusion.

"So, yeah, I realize we are in hell. I know I was getting hot and all. I fell! Did you see how tattered my threads are? Don't tell me; knocked out? I thought only humans threw water on each other to be wakened. What gives?" Relic was pulling his shirt away from his body checking out the green tint in his clothes. "Is this Fairy Kool-aide? I don't remember it being green. It is usually purple. So, Selena is here. Have you been holding out on a new recipe?"

Everyone rolled their eyes, but Orion couldn't help but laugh, even when they were all stuck in hell. "Ahhh, haaa!" Orion continued to laugh. "Oh Relic, you are never short of commentary at all the wrong times."

The ground shook once more. "Well, not everyone seems to have a sense of humor, look!" Ridge stopped rubbing his neck, grabbed Pramlee and hit the ground.

Scores of demons in the form of shadows came flying, darting downward into the guides with aggression. Relic let go of his shirt and his smile quickly changed. His eyes widened, his face devoid of humor and was now filled with shock. He took Lotus by the hand to climb to a rocky ledge that stood away from the rock wall high into the realm.

Orion, though, in his rare form of Ifrit, went into action. He noticed the hundreds of shadows swirling toward them, hissing and growling. He shot up into the air and found himself to not just be in company of several demons, but Talon with gallant speed, burst through the air to fight off the demons as they swirled in and out attacking the fighting duo.

Still on the ground, Selena and the remaining Fairy nymphs created a storm all their own. Selena lifted her hands and hovering over her slender palms were balls of fluorescent green poison in each hand.

"Look out!" Lahash warned Selena of a two-headed demon in the form of a snake coming toward her with its jaws wide open with fangs oozing with poison.

Selena lurched toward the demon and hurled her spheres of punishment to the slithering demon. As they penetrated the demon's two heads, in the nick of time the demon was destroyed.

The dark one's voice began a violent speech in Latin cursing everyone. A guttural laugh filled the dark realm, sending the fairy nymphs into flight, where once more, a funnel cloud dragged the shadowy demons into the fairy driven tornado. One by one they were sucked in, making an appearance each time the funnel made a revolution. Their faces stuck out from the enormous funnel, gruesome mouths open with fright as they screamed, their eyes widened in horrific outrage.

Pramlee and Ridge still staggering with their own injuries, stood close holding each other in their arms as they watched the demon show take place within the fairy storm.

"Look! You can barely make out their faces!" Pramlee pointed to a couple of demons rearing their ugly heads.

"Yes! I see! Their arms are flailing out of the funnel. They are afraid!" Ridge shouted over the hurling wind.

Lotus dropped Relic down with Ridge and Pramlee and once more she jetted back up over the funnel and offered her assistance to her sisters. All fairies moved at a rapid pace as the funnel continued to suck the demons up like rag dolls. Slowly the many faces of the demons disappeared.

"Where are they?" Relic was pointing up at the funnel.

Talon came back down from battling and stood next to Relic. He pointed upward. "Look."

There above the tornado and above the four elemental fairy nymphs was Karma. She hovered quietly above the storm and clasped her hands together above her head. Her hair blew back from the winds, her eyes changed colors, to a transparent golden tint. Her pupils widened in the shape of a cat's pupil, growing larger until the iris of her eye had nearly disappeared.

Karma unclasped her hands and she stretched out her arms away from her body with her palms faced downward into the funnel. Her red stoned necklace glowed and with the passage of the moments, the light from the necklace blinked. The four elemental fairy nymphs slowed their pace and continued to circle above the funnel in a slow ascension until they were just an arm's length from Karma.

The nymphs now hovered, and each lit up and shot a ray of light which pulsated away from their bodies and merged connecting in a perfect circle.

The funnel froze and no longer did the vicious funnel cloud spin, locking the demons in tightly. The fairies' statuesque formation, regal and uncompromising successfully trapped the demons.

For a moment, time stopped for the dark realm. No longer could anyone hear the dark one admonishing the unwelcomed visitors. The last shattering ray of light formed from the center of the circle the nymphs created with their rays. With a loud and violent clap, the final ray shot straight up into Karma's hands. Her bright red stone necklace pulsated with every beat of her heart.

Once more, the cloud moved in slow motion, and the vile creatures violently spun into the funnel that moved up and through the connected rays of the fairy nymphs. Slowly the funnel grew smaller and smaller, and finally the funnel picked up warp speed and shot straight up into the single ray of light absorbed by Karma's hands.

In a blink of an eye, Karma commanded the demon cloud up and into her hands and it disappeared forever. With a loud and echoing thunderclap, the demons were gone.

Karma gently floated to the ground to be greeted by everyone while Relic ran to Lotus's side and Talon straggled in behind, careful not to lose sight of Lahash who never lent a hand to the demons. Raina still unconscious through the escapade, lay still in the center of the pentagram. Kieren could not tear his eyes away from Lahash, his body stiff.

Lahash made his way to the group with a soft and swaggering stroll, his hands behind his back. He turned his head toward the dark witch with a soft but mischievous smile.

"So, fairies. I am impressed. Here we are in the dark lord's realm and you have surpassed a few members of his army of demon soldiers." Lahash stopped walking and brought his hands forward with a slow-motion, insulting clap of his hands.

Kieren still locked on to Lahash lunged toward the arrogant demon. "Cool it, Lahash!" Kieren's eyes were red with rage.

"Oh boy, now really. Do you challenge me?" Lahash snickered under his breath.

"Challenge? Look at you! Disgusting! I wouldn't lower myself to your standards." Kieren popped off.

Pramlee took advantage of the situation. "Lahash, why didn't you help the demons? Why did you warn Selena? I saw that."

"Please, I wouldn't sink to that level to do the soldiers' bidding. They serve the dark lord and they answer to Ipos who is protecting himself. I need not be involved." Lahash moved away, turned his back, and walked back over toward Raina.

"What are you speaking of demon?" Orion, still in his Ifrit form, was on Lahash's heels.

Lahash stopped moving. While he kept his back turned toward everyone, he turned his head slightly. "That is none of your concern. You should be grateful that I have taken the witch off your hands and that I warned Selena. You should be grateful that I have not unleashed hell on any of you!" Lahash turned swiftly with his head lowered and his eyes glowed red. His mouth was slightly open, baring his teeth as his breathing picked up with his anger. "Now, we have unfinished business. Answer the riddle!"

Ridge pushed his way through the group. "Lahash, now this has become out of hand. Why is it so important that we answer the riddle? You know the answer. We know the answer. Why must we be the ones to say the name?"

Selena broke her silence. "He cannot answer the riddle. Only the ones that originally had the question posed to them can. One of you that was in the dark realm at the time of the question may answer the riddle. Now, who was here the first time?"

Pramlee recounted it. "Well, I was here, Relic, Talon, Luna and Kieren. One of us has to answer the riddle."

"Well, that leaves Pramlee, Relic or Kieren that can answer this riddle. But first, what is it that you will gain if we answer the riddle? What is the guarantee that my daughter will be set free? That Charity, Chance and the others will be released?" Selena said.

Lahash walked right up to Selena, just inches from her face. "You are right, I cannot answer the riddle. If you do answer it, we will release Luna. The dark one will have no other choice but to do so."

Selena was not convinced. "Why? Why would the dark one have to do so?"

"Well, if he doesn't, it will weaken all demons' powers, including myself and the members of the high court. It is a double-edged sword in getting the answer from you. Once you answer the riddle, we will set Luna and Raina free."

Talon became hysterical. "What?! How? Why!? Why would you take her in the first place? You admitted you weren't doing anyone any favors. Why did you take her to begin with?"

Lahash's face grew serious, he would not reveal his selfish agenda, in ensuring that they met his needs. "Answer the riddle, Luna will be set free and I will tell you."

Ridge jumped in. "I don't believe him! Something is not right."

Selena locked eyes on the demon with mistrust and concern. "Lahash, no more games. We will answer the riddle. If it is meant to be that Raina returns to Earth, then so be it. The fairies will protect Meridian." Selena turned toward the guides. "I give you my word. We will guard her with our own lives."

Relic's mouth dropped open in disbelief. The group banded together and moved toward Lahash. Relic decided this was the moment, he knew he could trust Selena. He felt it.

"The answer to the riddle is Raina."

Slowly the tarot cards that hovered over Raina in the pentagram disappeared. Raina awakened and grumbled, disoriented and confused.

Lahash looked back over his shoulder toward Raina and then back at the group that all stared at him, waiting. "There is another aspect to the riddle. You may have the answer. However, only in part."

Lahash recounted the riddle.

"Answer the dark one's riddle and soon you will find the solace you seek is hindered by a mark entwined. Which direction will margana go? Symbols and letters scramble to and fro. The deceiver arrived in the time of new, the birth sign is a part of a word, finding the word is your clue."

"You managed to get your clue, that brought you to the correct answer who the deceiver is. Raina. However, you overlooked one small detail. Hindered by a mark entwined. The mark is the thing that could lend itself to a few outcomes."

Before Lahash could utter another syllable, Pramlee's face lit up. "I know this! Remember! The night that Raina took Meridian from the street! She took her to a tattoo parlor. Remember? That tattoo is a sigil for calling upon a demon, Ipos!"

Ridge's face softened with recognition. "Yes, Ipos. That is the mark. It is a tattoo of a demon sigil. What does this mark mean?"

Everyone's attention became redirected when quiet but deliberate footsteps drew closer.

"What is that? I hear footsteps, I can't see anything?" Relic paced until Talon grabbed him by the arm.

"Look." Talon pointed toward the space next to Raina.

Suddenly the empty space was now filled with another demon. Tall, handsome and regal. Very similar to Lahash. He dressed as though he was from another time. Like a duke from the eighteenth century, he was adorned with elegant attire and stockings creating a vision of formal dress.

The demon approached slowly with conviction in his eyes. "I am Ipos. You are correct. That mark hinted the riddle is a sigil used to summon me."

Talon pushed Lahash out of his way. "What does it mean? What does it mean that Meridian carries your mark?"

Ipos did not answer Talon and avoided eye contact while Lahash smiled, not trying terribly hard to hide it.

"If Raina summons Ipos through the mark Meridian carries, then he will perish. Meridian is pure and without regard she is a human, she will perish."

Relic was grinning. "Awesome, so we can take Raina and she can do her work, and at least one demon is taken care of."

Pramlee shook her head and her face was furrowed. "Shut up! That isn't good at all. Did you not hear what he said? Lahash would benefit from this or he wouldn't be grinning, and he said Meridian would perish."

Talon raised his voice at Lahash. "What is in it for you?"

Lahash drew a cocky breath, "Well, if Ipos should perish, that would not be a benefit for me. He commands a legion of demons that feed on the downtrodden of Earth. Those downtrodden humans give rise and reason for the very humans I draw my power from. Lawmakers and politicians. Without Ipos commanding his legion of demons, the symbiotic relationship between those humans will not exist. The demons can't feed on what isn't there and the humans won't give power to demons to feed on. There isn't a clear answer as to how bad it would be. But the humans under my legion, the law makers would not have reason to make laws or continue corruption. My future would be uncertain."

Relic laughed. "Okay, well, this is perfect! I say let Raina do it! Take 'em all out!"

Selena was the one to take the wind out of Relic's sails. "Relic, we can't let this happen."

Relic threw his hand up. "Why?"

"Because if Ipos is summoned through Meridian, it may destroy her. She may survive something like this, I don't know." Selena stared at Lahash.

The group grew quiet recounting their thoughts on what would become of Meridian if she endured such a summoning. Then they realized what would happen if they didn't answer the riddle.

Pramlee rushed to Selena's side like a small child in fear. "Selena, can the demons keep Raina here like this? I mean she is a human and she isn't dead. So, they couldn't hold her here forever anyway, right? We can deal with Raina if she ever is free once more." Pramlee stood close to Selena, hiding herself from the cutting eyes of Lahash.

In a blink of an eye, as though they had never gone to the dark realm, the fairies, Talon, and the guides found themselves in front of Esmra's house. They all looked around in confusion when they saw Aiden, Meridian, Tallulah and Esmra come out of the front door.

Chapter 16

Days passed while the wild exchange took its course in the dark realm. Aiden and Meridian waited patiently with Esmra and Tallulah for answers. Suddenly their waiting was finished. The nymphs, Selena, Talon, Orion and the other guides arrived back on Earth.

Esmra spotted the fairies, but her eyes took her past Selena and the nymphs toward the end of the long driveway, where Luna stood.

Selena studied the witch's face and with a slow head turn to see what had Esmra's attention. "Luna!" Selena ran to her daughter with her arms open wide. Luna stood confused even after Selena embraced her with gushed affection.

"Mother!" Luna exclaimed. All the deep resentment and frustration seemed to leave her after such a long spell away from her mother. "Oh Mother, what happened? I was in the dark realm, that is all I can remember. How did we arrive here?"

Everyone ran to catch up with Selena and Luna. "Luna, are you okay?" Relic asked, in relief to see Luna was okay.

Aiden and Meridian hand in hand followed Esmra to find out what the fuss was about. "Selena, you all answered the riddle? The dark one let her go, what is the catch?"

"Well, Relic answered the riddle and it appears that the dark one did let Luna go but we do not know about the others. Raina was there, unconscious. It was terrible. Ridge, Orion and Pramlee were kidnapped for a short while. According to Lahash, Raina will be set free, that can only mean she will be back for Meridian. Echo and Karma made it to the hall of souls and Karma received the blessing to retrieve the quartz sword. However, only the chosen one of Etheria may use the sword against demons," Selena said as she stared at Meridian.

"What is going on?" Aiden whispered to Esmra.

"Meridian is listening to Selena." Tallulah answered for her.

Aiden stood quietly, he couldn't see his father, the guides, or the fairies.

"Please tell my son that I watch over him. That someday I hope he can see me and in a better place." Talon's voice full of urgency and concern.

Luna broke away from the group and her mother's embrace to recite Talon's words.

Esmra smiled and turned toward Aiden. "I forget, you can't see or hear the fairies. Your father is near. He wants you to know that he hopes someday you will see him in a different form."

Aiden smiled big but dropped his head and kicked a loose rock in the road. The blush in his cheeks were visible, when he lifted his head back up and make eye contact with Esmra.

"It feels strange now. So strange. All my life I didn't know who my father was or where he was. All these grand things that I learned so quickly has me taken back a little. I am so unsure what to say. All I know is that I feel joy to know that my father is close, even though I cannot see him. I can't wait for that day either." Aiden put his arm around Meridian with a hint of blush that still lingered on his face.

"Raina more than likely is free and she will return, in what form I have no idea. Meridian, you must go with the fairies to retrieve the quartz sword. Can you see the guides?"

Meridian looked around. "No, I can hear and communicate with them. All I see are the fairies." Meridian stared at the space in front of her. "Where is the quartz sword located?"

Esmra walked back to her house with all in tow and as everyone followed her she recounted the message from

Karma. "The quartz sword is in a quartz cave known as 'Swords' Cave'."

"Meridian has to go to Mexico to a cave to retrieve a sword? What?" Tallulah hollered out franticly. "She can't go to another country to get what? A sword? No, someone else like Karma to get the sword. She got the blessing, let her do it."

After a moment, Esmra approached and took her by the hand helping her find her seat in the couch. "Tallulah, I understand why you are concerned. Karma got the blessing, but Meridian needs to retrieve it. I'm sorry, the sword cannot be used by any other being. We are not for sure that Meridian is the 'chosen one,' however I think we can all agree that we believe she is. We know she was once a spirit, we all know she has a horrible curse placed on her and all that leads to telling me Meridian has to be important enough for Warrick to do such a thing."

Esmra sat next to Tallulah while she remained in her stare at the floor in disbelief on what Esmra was telling her. Luna heard this for the first time and did her best to catch up on all the lost time. Relic took time to regard his once wife and he took her aside to tell her what everyone went through for her.

As the pair were still off talking, the fairies accompanied Selena and stood next to Esmra as she comforted Tallulah. Selena put her hand on Esmra's shoulder.

"Tell her Meridian will be protected. I will send the nymphs along with Orion. I can't risk my daughter anymore so we will go back to the fairy realm. I know that the guides will be with her and that Aiden would not want to leave her side. "

Esmra recounted the words from Selena. Tallulah shook her head. I can't let her go, I can't. She is too naïve to things."

Meridian broke away from Aiden, "Tallulah, I can see that you are worried for me. Aiden doesn't even know the half of it yet, I am sure he will see things the same way, but I will have protection. Don't you want all this to stop? Raina to stop? What is it?" Meridian down on her knees, looked up into Tallulah's eyes.

Tallulah found herself in unfamiliar territory with the emotions that flooded her, never having had a daughter- like friend in her life, Tallulah for the first time felt the real threat of a potential loss of a child.

Tallulah put her hand over her mouth and tried to keep the sobs in and the words at bay. "I can't lose you. I can't lose you." Tallulah threw herself onto Meridian as she cried. Meridian froze with surprise while she stood and held her. Without giving Meridian any time to respond, Tallulah broke her embrace with Meridian and ran off into the house and to her room and shut the door.

Esmra stood up and headed toward the staircase. "Meridian, visit with Selena and the others to find out what the best plan is. I am going to check on Tallulah."

Esmra disappeared upstairs leaving the group alone to put together everything.

There stood Meridian, staring at the vacant staircase. Aiden leaned into Meridian as he put his arms around her while he moved behind her without unlocking his embrace. She relaxed as she allowed her head to lean back into his chest. He nuzzled his nose into her hair and Aiden gave her a kiss.

Kieren and Relic watched Aiden hold Meridian in his arms.

Relic shook his legs back and forth as he fidgeted with his shirt still stained from the dark realm.

"C'mon, Selena will take care of speaking with Meridian." Lotus took Relic by the hand and escorted him away from Esmra's house.

Before they could exit Kieren was in a fluster as he hurled himself away from everyone and disappeared.

"Kieren, wait!" Ridge shouted.

It did not matter, Kieren was gone away from everyone. Ridge remained in Esmra's front yard staring into an empty space. He let out a loud sigh and dropped his eyes to the ground.

Pramlee snuck up behind him and reached her arm up and tapped him on the shoulder with her small fingers. "Kieren needs a break, he is still struggling to accept the way of things with Meridian and now Aiden. Let him be."

Ridge turned around and softly smiled at Pramlee. "You are right. Funny how that works with you."

Meanwhile, back in Esmra's house, the remaining fairy nymphs and Orion took Meridian aside to tell her about the journey to acquire the sword. There Meridian stood by herself with the appearance of talking to thin air.

"This is so great I can see all of you. For the longest time, I guess I was under Raina's spell. So much is a fog. My memory is still hazy with the most recent past. I remember things from when I was a spirit guide. The strangest thing is at one time I was able to see the spirit guides. I remember seeing Pramlee and Kieren that day after the very first ritual. Now I can't see any of them. Why?" Meridian asked Karma.

"Meridian, we are not sure why you can see us but not the others. We realize so much has happened to you and we can't pretend to understand. I don't mean to add to your troubles, however I need to catch you up on some things."

Karma moved close to Meridian and put her hand on her leg. "This curse that Warrick cast upon you, you struggle with knowing who your twin soul is. A fairy cannot break this for you, however, we believe that Venus can help you."

"She rules love. Despite the fact that we rule lust and we use those traits in other beings against them, we also lend a hand from time to time in areas of love. Venus is different and we believe that she can guide you to uncover your twin soul. I raised the question to Selena that even if you broke this curse, what would happen? Really, would you die a human death and go back to Etheria? Would you pass and live another human life? Would you be a ghost and lost?"

Meridian slumped in her chair and her long hair draped over her shoulders, covering her solemn face. Even as she sat still, her shirt quivered with every racing beat of her heart while she thought of what would really come of her if she ever broke the curse.

"What if I never broke it? I mean, even if I did, there is no hard evidence I am the one to take over Etheria as the chosen one. I have a life here, I finally have Aiden, even if it isn't the way I would really want it. I feel like I have a family with Tallulah and Esmra. I can barely recall anything about my life as a spirit. What if I don't want things to change?"

Venus studied Meridian while she still sat slumped over, still hidden by her own hair.

Echo's eyes softened, hesitant, she kneeled down in front of Meridian, "Meridian, listen. Things have been so hard and must have taken a toll on you. Raina coming after you, lying to you, and now there is this curse that follows you like a dark cloud. I know all this is hard to take and you are right, we do not have hard proof you are the chosen one. Think about it, even if you were not the chosen one, do you really want to go on living this way? Not finding out what your existence is meant to be? Holding back from true love because of a curse or because of fear or lack of faith in yourself? Your tattoo, it is not just any tattoo that Raina had put on you. Not all sigils are bad, however, this particular one summons a demon, Ipos."

Meridian sat in silence pondering the wise words from the Earth Fairy. She broke her hands apart from their clasped position and turned her wrist over to examine her infinity tattoo.

"A demon sigil?" Meridian pulled her shirt up to examine the tattoo and pointed toward the demon sigil. "This? This tattoo?"

Karma nodded.

Meridian dropped her shirt down and let out a large huff, "Well, I can get it removed, right?"

"I don't know, I mean we do not know how a tattooed sigil would respond to a removal, on you anyway."

The moment was grim, and Meridian's face flushed as it always did when she became upset. "Where are the guides, I want to talk to them." Meridian stormed away from the nymphs marching through the living room area and slammed the front door.

Meridian jogged off the steps of the front porch looking upward and around for her invisible support.

"Pramlee?! Relic?! Are you here? Please, I need to talk to you." Meridian paced back and forth at the edge of the yard.

"We are here, Meridian. We don't go far. Are you all right?" Pramlee asked.

"No, I am not all right. The nymphs talked to me about the curse, then jolted me with the news of my tattoo. Is it true?" Meridian held her hands up.

Pramlee's voice was shaky, "Yes Meridian, it is true."

Meridian's anger fired up a few more notches. "How can this be? Why in the hell would Raina put something . . . a tattoo of something so evil on me? Why would she need me?"

Orion heard all the fussing from Meridian. "Meridian, please do calm yourself. You are a very special being. You were once a realm-born spirit guide and you have gifts. Raina seeks the dark side of things, she welcomes it and she wants to be of it. She wanted to use you for summoning demons, to bring her power here on Earth."

Meridian stopped pacing and crossed her arms, "Why? Why would it need to be me? She can call demons through her magic and Ouija board. It doesn't make sense. If I am or was once from a place that is for the betterment of humankind, then how could anyone reason that using me would give her any benefit?"

Orion reached his long arm out and placed his hand on Meridian's shoulder. His eyes were large, kind and full of care. "Meridian, she wants to destroy you. Raina has not figured out that summoning Ipos won't do anything for her. She has fallen prey to the whims of another demon, Pyro. Things would go back to the way they were . . . minus you in existence."

"Destroy me? This whole time. She has been pushing herself on me out of lust, greed, and for power? This is disgusting! She is wretched!" Meridian paced again back and forth, "Take me to the dark realm! I have been there once before. Take me back, I want to speak to Ipos!"

The fairy nymphs stood back while witnessing the exchange between the Ifrit and Meridian.

Lotus approached Meridian. "Meridian, calm yourself. Going to the dark realm to face demons will not solve anything. We need to focus on getting the quartz sword, that is your answer."

Meridian remained flustered, "I am going in, I need some space to talk to Aiden." Meridian stomped back off into the house where she found Aiden sitting at the foot of the staircase slumped over with his elbows on his knees holding his phone in both hands. At the moment he tore his eyes away, he saw Meridian standing in the room watching him.

"So, what is going on? I feel a little left out here," he said with a smile. "I can't see these fairies like you. Esmra is still with Tallulah. Why the glum face?"

Meridian smiled as she nodded toward upstairs. "C'mon, you and I need to talk. Let's go."

Meridian and Aiden jogged up the stairs and went into the room where they had been staying since the incident with Raina. Aiden walked in behind Meridian and closed the door while she took a seat on the bed.

"Meridian, before you say anything, I have to get back to school, spring break is over for me in a day. I am actually supposed to be going back now. Chris texted me asking what has happened and asked when I will be back. He has my truck and I told him to go on without me and I would figure it out," Aiden said.

"I know, I know you have to get back. I wished you didn't have to go. I have to go to Mexico." Meridian winced as she spoke the words.

"Mexico!? What? Why? Is that what all that was about with the fairies? Mexico? I don't understand." Aiden ran his hands through his hair.

"Well, I know Tallulah caught you up. The hall of souls is where all souls journey to go to when all lives have lived and reached the point of enlightenment. It is where the spirit guides go until the angels or the keepers release the soul again for a newborn. According to Selena, all the guides have been lied to by Warrick and he allowed no one to know of the keepers." Meridian paused when Aiden stopped pacing and sat down next to her.

Aiden stared into Meridian's eyes with wonder and surprise with his mouth open. Barely breathing with the wash of information coming through, he anticipated more.

"Go on, go on. Tell me."

"Well, there are several keepers, but the one that Karma spoke to was Laila. Echo and Karma went to Etheria and entered the hall of souls where the keeper told Karma that the only way to defeat Warrick or any demon is with a hidden sword in a cave somewhere. They believe I am the chosen one of Etheria, or they want to believe, meaning I need to go."

Aiden became frantic. "Well, why do you have to go get it? Why can't they journey to get it? Why can't you come with me? Or go with Tallulah and stay with her? Please, don't go, Meridian."

"Aiden, I don't want to go either, I would rather stay with you. I don't even know if I want things to change. They are unsure of what will come of me if we break it. Like, will I go back to Etheria, or will I pass on as a ghost and be lost? Or will nothing happen, I stay a human?" Meridian put her arms around Aiden.

Aiden held Meridian in his arms and he nestled his chin in her shoulder. "So, when do you have to go?"

They pair broke contact and Meridian stared out the window where she saw the Fairies outside talking to one another.

"I would think now. I would hope that Esmra and Tallulah would go with me. I wanted to give you this news now, in private."

Aiden jumped up off the bed and stood in front of Meridian. "I am going with you. I will tell Chris for sure. I will email my instructors at school I have had an emergency. I am going."

Without giving Meridian a second to respond, he took her by the hand and pulled her along downstairs to find Esmra and Tallulah in the living room speaking.

"So, I take it you know? I sense you will be coming along?" Esmra smiled at Aiden. She turned to Tallulah, whose face still swollen from crying. "I guess we are all going! I will make the arrangements, but first we have to go back to Tallulah's place so she can collect a few things."

Talon stood away in the room listening to the conversation and with the relief of the good news of Aiden going along, he let the others know. "They are all going with Meridian. She will be well cared for," Talon said as he smiled.

Chapter 17

Warrick maintained a low profile, not even taking any time to visit the dark realm. Hidden away in his chambers in Etheria healing from the invasive wounds of Karma, his coup of supporters grew thin. Brennan had not returned to the realm at all after the trip with Warrick to the dark realm. He had gone missing, just as the others had disappeared. Arianna, Charity, Janus, Cora and Chance were still missing, but not much of a sign on where sneaky Warrick stashed them away.

Warrick, who was seated at his large gathering table, turned his attention toward the audible footsteps approaching from his secret pathway out of Etheria into the dark realm.

"Ah, Warrick. You must be truly busy these days." Lahash appeared with his sly grin.

Lahash walked around Warrick's table and positioned himself across the table where he was in direct line with Warrick. He leaned over one chair while using his arms to hold himself up.

"What do you want!" Warrick stood up from his chair and shouted.

Lahash maintained his posture with ease and a half-cocked grin to boot. "Oh, I want a lot actually. But life isn't fair, we all can't have what we want, now can we? Something you are growing familiar with, don't you think? Ahh, the reality of how things are setting in. I don't think I like this look on you Warrick. It is just so . . ." Lahash peered down his nose at Warrick. "Well, unbecoming. You just don't seem yourself these days."

Warrick left his table and turned his back on Lahash. "What do you want?"

"Well, we had quite the meeting in the dark realm you missed out on. Everyone was there. I was so disappointed that you didn't come to the event." Lahash let out a chuckle.

"Well, I don't recall receiving an invitation. So why don't you quit wasting my time and tell me why you are here." Warrick turned around to face Lahash, his jaw locked tight, and his dark eyes narrowed.

Lahash moved away from the chair at the table and casually strolled over toward Warrick. On his way by he wondered and his eyes surveyed Warrick's chambers.

"Quite dim here. You like the dark, don't you? Well, I guess I could share with you, after all you look like you are about to burst." Lahash gave a tight smile as he coolly folded his hands behind his back.

"Well, the fairies showed up along with the guides and oh, yes, Orion who turned out to be an Ifrit. Interesting, huh? So, I did what I always have to do and took the witch to the dark realm with me . . . of course helping the guides no less. Well, when they returned to the realm to answer the dark one's riddle, we were quite disappointed that they even could answer it." Lahash was now being stared at by Warrick.

As Lahash strode by the table he allowed his index finger to run across the table. He pulled his hand up toward his face and he examined the tip of his finger. "Wow, you really know how to keep a place clean. I can't say that I see any dirt and you may pass the white glove test indeed, however, it leaves me feeling, well… filthy. Anything come to mind?"

Warrick paced as he pretended to be concerned with other important matters than Lahash's head games. "I am not wasting my time with you, Lahash. Either you spill it or get out. So, you have the witch, great. So now she can't summon Ipos through Meridian. I don't care about all that. Luna is there, so I am safe. Selena will have no choice but to back down.

Lahash softly laughed. "Oh, I just love irony, don't you? Well, when the guides unexpectedly answered the dark one's riddle, he had no other choice but to set Luna free . . . and of course Raina. I am sure she won't waste time embracing another possession by Pyro or any other demon she calls on. She will eventually find Meridian and summon Ipos."

Warrick was incredulous. "What! Someone set Luna free! Why? The dark one did not mention that he had any plans on releasing her. What is going on?"

"Oh, Warrick, please. Being here pretending to be a goody-goody has weakened your demon common sense. Our master is notorious for not exactly doing what he says. Why do you think he fears the fairies? They are in many ways like we are. Anyway, you are surely about to bust at the seams. Calm yourself, there is good news."

Lahash pulled up a seat at the table that Warrick had abandoned for the moment. "Now with Raina on the loose, the potential of Meridian being caught by her and Ipos summoned, may indeed leave her mildly exposed to many possibilities. Maybe Meridian wouldn't live through such an ordeal. So where do you fathom someone like Meridian would go if she perished from such an unfortunate event?" Lahash smiled as he drummed his fingers on the table.

Warrick was quiet with thought. He did not answer Lahash too quick. He remained subdued. "I wouldn't know. Why don't you enlighten me since you seem to know everything?"

"Well, if Meridian passes away, does she have a soul? A human can't exist without a soul, now can they? What of Meridian's soul?"

"Lahash, what you are getting at, but I have other things to be worried with now. Slaten remains here and only for his mother, Farrah. He has not left her side for fear of me. I have much damage control to attend too. Meridian's soul will never make it back here, she was cursed as a fallen, it doesn't matter that the curse didn't work out exactly the way I planned, but a fallen . . ." Warrick's eyes widened, he stopped as he worked things out for himself. They can turn be turned back by the fairies." Warrick's mouth hung open in shock.

"Oh Warrick, this is much fun. I like these games! So now we are on the same page. I guess you realize something I have known and it wouldn't appear that anyone else has thought of. All this time everyone running around trying to help Meridian find her twin soul, to break a curse you put on her. Not one person raised the question I have. So why haven't they figured it out?" Lahash inquired.

"Okay Lahash, what do you want?" Warrick seated himself at the table across from Lahash.

"Well, it is good to know that you are coming around. So now the nymphs have got past you into the hall of souls, and they have met one keeper. Now they are on their way to get the quartz sword. I suppose, you know, to take you, and I guess the rest of us out. So, what would happen if we remove Meridian, by say Raina summoning Ipos. She kicks the ol' human bucket, never having had the chance to get the sword, you remain in your position here, shall I say your fake position here. Sound good?" Lahash smiled as he got up from his chair and adjusted his cuffs. "Then my existence can go back to what I would rather be doing."

Warrick cocked his eyebrow up, his voice telling of disbelief. "Really? More like who you would like to be doing. Don't pretend for a second I don't realize you are in it for yourself. You have fallen prey to Echo, having seduced you, and you are in trouble. You would love nothing more than to have her, and control over Ipos's legion of demons when he perishes." Warrick said.

"Well, you are right, I am in it for myself. However, you will benefit. So, we have an agreement, you make sure that Meridian and Raina connect once more and quickly before Selena figures anything out and before they get to the quartz sword. Besides, you should want all this to work out. If it doesn't you are out of a job and our master won't be thrilled to have you at court." Lahash adjusted his tie and glanced at his wrist to an invisible watch. In moments he was gone.

Chapter 18

Meridian left Aiden to talk with Tallulah. He sat alone firing off texts to Chris, urging him to drive back to school alone, without him. Aiden's eyes were telling of the lack of sleep and exhaustion with the whirlwind events that put a kink in his schedule in returning to school.

Aiden sat on the edge of the bed staring at the screen on his phone, anxiously waiting for a message from Chris. His boot heel gave an anchor from which he dangled his foot off the bed side railing. His other foot rested on the wood floor but did not stay still as his leg continued to jiggle. His hand appeared to be just as jumpy as it swayed and jumped with the jiggling of his leg. Still staring at his phone quietly resting in his right hand, his eyes widened when Chris responded to his message. His still face gave way to a smile, his tired eyes lifted with a sigh. Chris's message read.

"Ok man, I sure don't know what you are involved with, but I will pick up anything needed from your instructors. I hope they don't ask me too many questions. I am just going to tell them you have the flu. That should give you at least a week."

Aiden finished the message and with his relief his simple reply read:

"Cool man, I owe you one. I'll explain later."

Aiden stopped jiggling his leg and he took in a deep breath and let out a longer sigh. With the room quiet and the sun close to meeting the horizon, evening drew closer. Aiden's slump gave way to a fall back on the bed, and he lay there still, and his cell phone slid out of his hand onto the bed. He stared at the ceiling and recounted everything that had come to pass.

I can't believe all this. I can't believe, that I can't believe it all. I have Meridian back; at least I think I do. What happens if she gets spooked again? According to Grams that seems to be something girls do too. Meridian isn't a normal girl. What if this curse thing is too much for her and she runs away? Surely not? Would she run back to with that psychopath Raina? Where is Raina anyway? I would stay with Meridian no matter what, but that fact seems to keep her guarded. Trip . . . trip. I haven't thought of what I would tell my grandparents. I can't tell them I have the flu . . . they wouldn't believe it, anyway. I hardly get sick. I guess I can tell them I am helping a friend? Not a total lie, Meridian is a friend.

Aiden fell asleep in a matter of seconds and his exhaustion was so much, that he fell into a deep sleep. Once again, his recurring dream played out just like before.

Aiden could see himself on the couch of the hospital where he was born, he awakens and then to walk down a busy hall full of doctors and nurses, many of which were walking in and out of the room he was headed for.

Then just as he was about to push the door open to the room he was entering, he could no longer see himself, but now he was seeing through his own eyes in his dream. He pushed the door open, there was a person in the bed, but again his view was obstructed from where he stood. The nurses and the doctors were quick in their pace around the bed. There again, stood two people at the end of the bed, watching the person who lay still.

Aiden tried to move forward to reach the end of the bed to see who was there, but the more he attempted to get to the bed, the harder it became for him to progress. He screamed for the attention of the two persons standing at the foot of the bed, where they never moved or gave notice to Aiden.

The three golden floating lights in the room's corner are still in the dream, but this time they moved over toward the bed and ascended, hovered over the mystery patient. Aiden fell to the ground just like before, the same five glowing apparitions with silhouettes as humans appeared in front of him.

From within the glowing light an arm of one apparition pointed at the stranger in the bed. Finally, the dream progressed further, and a voice spoke out to Aiden.

"Would you die for her?" the voice said.

Aiden stopped moving, frozen still with shock and surprise. He stared with his mouth open at the five illuminated beings that stood at his feet. There was no other sound in the room except Aiden's beating heart until he finally took in a deep breath.

He rushed the release of his breath "What? Would I die for who?" Aiden tried to move against the invisible force that held him on the floor.

The voice spoke out again, "Would you die for her?"

Aiden could no longer hear his own heartbeat, but now he only heard the shallow sound of his own breathing. The force that kept him immobile lifted and he could sit up. He remained seated on the floor but turned so he could see the heart monitor on the mysterious person he struggled to see. He leaned forward a bit more and for an instant he could see a long blonde nape of hair that hung off the side of the bed where the woman rested her head.

Aiden slowly pushed himself from the floor and as he did so, the voice spoke out again.

"She risked much for you," the voice sunk to a whisper.

The five beings were gone from sight and the three floating orbs that hovered over the bed vanished and Aiden woke up startled.

Meridian stood over Aiden in the bedroom as he opened his eyes and jumped. He lifted his hand to wipe the sweat from his brow as he sat upright.

"Aiden, what is wrong? You were moaning in your sleep. It sounded like you were saying, 'mom.' But I couldn't tell. Are you all right?" Meridian brought a rag for Aiden.

"I don't know, I keep having this recurring dream and I am in the hospital where I was born. Where my mother passed away giving birth to me. There are spirits, angels or something in the room. Every time I have the dream, I cannot see who lay in the bed until now. I saw her hair. It was blonde. My mother was a blonde. There were voices, one asked me if I would die for her. I don't know why I keep having this dream." Aiden looked deeply into Meridian's concerned eyes while he used the wet rag to remove the sweat from his forehead.

"I understand. I have a recurring dream and I hear a voice speaking to me. I have no idea where I am, but it tells me to wake up, or remember. I just guessed that it may have something to do with when I was a spirit guide. I don't know. Maybe your dream is deep down you feel guilt or loss for your mother. Do you think about it a lot?" Meridian ran her hands through Aiden's hair, studying its length while she pushed it back away from his face.

"Well, sometimes. I don't know if it is guilt I feel, maybe I do. Maybe it is buried in my subconscious. I wished I knew where she went. Tallulah and I talked a lot on the way up here and she told me that humans live five lives. If at the end of the fifth life they learned all their lessons, it gives them the choice to reincarnate to live another life or to go on as a spirit guide. I don't know, she said is what Esmra told her and Luna passed that information. Fairies are tricksters, right?" Aiden rubbed his head as he stared back down at his lap.

"Well, according to Esmra, yes they play tricks. I know that Luna and her mother have had their differences because of tricks. Luna now I can see her strikes me to be different. I think she has a good heart." Meridian said as she rubbed Aiden's leg and smiled.

Aiden pulled himself to the end of the bed and faced Meridian. "Well, after all the crazy stuff I have seen, I would believe it. I wonder if my mother was on her last life, or if not, where did she go?"

"I don't know, the fairies nor the spirit guides have shared any of the information." Meridian leaned forward and put her head on Aiden's shoulder.

"I would like to know, maybe. I don't know. So, what were you doing while I was up here?" Aiden played with Meridian's hair while she kept her head on his shoulder.

"Well, I was talking to Esmra and Tallulah about some things you were wondering about. They were telling me more about being a spirit guide. They want me to ask more about my life as a spirit guide. They believe that it may help spark my memory more. We also talked about the curse, this tattoo that no one seems to think I should try to have removed. We talked about you." Meridian lifted her head up off Aiden's shoulder to see his reaction.

"Oh, really? What about the curse? We haven't had a second to talk about anything with all that has happened. I want you to know, that no matter what, I am not leaving your side. I don't care about the curse. I don't want you to run away from me again."

Meridian glanced at Aiden's hands that were rested on her legs. Her face lost the smile and her mood shifted. "Well, I am glad you feel that way, but at the same time, I am not even sure how long it will take to break the curse and I don't even know if you are my twin soul. What if you aren't the one?" Meridian got up and walked to the window. With the sunset, purples and violets streaked the sky. She stared at the few stars in the sky peeking through the clouds.

Aiden walked across the room and turned on a lamp that set on the dresser. "Look Meridian, I am one that believes that things will work out the way it's supposed to. We have no idea what the answers are in this life or in the next. All I know is how is what is in here," he pointed to his chest, "For me, I believe you are the one. You are it for me. If something happens and it turns out I am not for whatever reason, I can accept that. But I will not run away from you because of the unknown."

Aiden walked over to the window where Meridian stood, with her head leaning on the wall, peering out of the window at the moon. Aiden took Meridian by the hand and pulled her back over to the bed as he sat back down. "I don't run away or scare that easily. With you, I believe that we are meant to be. I can't answer if it is this life or the next, but you and I have crossed paths because of something bigger, a higher purpose. I am not going to let anything stand in the way of that, until I see for sure, without a shred of doubt you are the one."

Aiden leaned in and gave Meridian a kiss. The pair locked lips barely moving. Aiden slowly brought his arms up and wrapped them around Meridian, bringing her as close as he could.

Meridian stretched her arms and locked them around his neck and returned the embrace. After a long moment, they released their kiss and Aiden tilted his forehead where it met Meridian's. He stared at her and smiled. After a few seconds Meridian put her chin over his shoulder and hugged Aiden tighter.

Aiden rubbed Meridian's back up and down several strokes. He stopped and gave more strength to his embrace and said, "I mean that, I am not going anywhere, not unless the Universe tells me different. Even if I am not the one, it would be hard for me to believe. You are a part of I my heart and no matter what happens, you will always have a place there. I can't shake it. We are meant for one another." He released his tight embrace and created space between the two. His face lit up with a big smile. "By the way, that tattoo I can't blame you for wanting to get rid of it, though, not easy to do. It can take several times with a laser. Time we do not seem to have." Aiden winked at Meridian and leaned in for another kiss.

Downstairs, Tallulah and Esmra were preparing for the trip. Esmra contacted her fellow witches in the coven and had them over to watch over her house while she was away.

"Esmra, are you sure you can go, and this not be any trouble?" Tallulah was throwing her belongings in her suitcase.

Esmra left the coven members, shutting the door behind her leaving them alone. "Oh, I don't see how. I don't have a lot going on right now, and with something of this much importance, I can't just stay here. Besides, they are happy to be here and help." Esmra nodded back toward the door she closed behind her. "Once we get back to your house, you can tend to what you need to, and we can leave for the trip." Esmra handed Tallulah a bag of stones.

"What's this?" Tallulah pulled open the pouch to examine the contents.

"Oh, I meant to give those to you a while back, but with everything that has gone on, I got a little sidetracked." Esmra quickly changed the subject to what was on her mind. "I am still worried about Raina. No sign of her. Not even the members of my own coven have seen her around town, not even at her bar. They said it has been closed down." Esmra walked on, toward her kitchen for water for her plants.

Tallulah stopped packing and put the pouch in her purse and walked back into the living room area where Esmra stood over her many ivy plants. "Esmra, do you think we will be okay? I mean what she did that time at my house, with that boy Josh. I have never been so afraid in all my life."

"We will be okay, Tallulah. Remember, we now have the protection of the fairies and now an Ifrit. Which that is new to me." Esmra stopped watering and gazed through the big picture window in her living room to see Orion and the fairies.

"What are they doing? All I see is a big fire. I can't see any of them." Tallulah stood next to Esmra with her eyes squinted.

Esmra elbowed Tallulah for some added comedy to the moment. "Can you see them when you squint?" Tallulah grinned and rolled her eyes. Esmra left her picture window and went back to water her plants. "I am not sure. Fairies are strange and I don't ask a lot of questions. I am just glad they are here. Don't worry though, everything is fine."

Orion and the fairy nymphs were quiet as they sat outside around the fire. They had all taken a moment and lay quietly in the grass gazing up at the moon and the stars. Karma looked up as Esmra and Tallulah walked away from the window.

"I like those two. They seem to care about Meridian and Aiden. I like Aiden too. I hope he is the one for Meridian, and that our journey is the answer to all of this. With the keeper's blessing we can take the sword, I hope Meridian can break this curse and use the sword to take back Etheria. That realm has seen its better days." Karma said.

Orion smiled sharing Karma's gaze into the now vacant window, but his attention quickly turned toward the nymph of love. "So, Venus when are you going to talk to Meridian about helping her out with finding her twin soul?"

Venus snapped out of her stare. "Well, I was hoping to while we are on our journey, if she is open to it. And of course, Aiden. I can help them with my powers. What I am afraid of . . . is finding out that maybe Aiden isn't the one. What would that do to the two of them? Then where does that leave us? I am working on the perfect blend of magic and a spell for them. Esmra said she would help me when the time was right."

Venus reached inside the inner lining of her dress through her top and pulled out a small crystal ball. "Look, I don't get it out often, but it tells me things about the mortals if I need to ask questions."

Karma snapped, "You know the consequences of using that ball for seeing the future. Careful now." Karma warned Venus.

Venus gave out a sigh and became snippy. "See, Orion, what happens when you have siblings with more power? Karma here, she can dish out the Karma to anyone if the Universe sees fit to do it." Venus rolled her eyes.

Karma said to Orion. "Orion, it is against our laws to look into the future. Especially a mortal's future. It is forbidden."

Echo jumped to her feet with a grin to boot. "But now, if it is for the better, we can use it to lead us in the right direction." Echo walked over to Karma and tapped her knee into the back of her arm. "Lighten up. I mean we hold the fate of humankind in our hands."

The fairies came to their feet and went into the house where Esmra and Tallulah were in their own rooms to finish up their packing, leaving the television on. The fairies gathered around to watch the disturbing scenes.

Karma pointed to the television. "Orion, look here. This news channel is reporting that there has been an epidemic surfacing in strange stillborn deaths. It started out with just a few, that really is nothing to worry for. But now the death tolls are rising. The mortals cannot reason out what is the cause. It happens sporadically, not in any geographical location to what appears to be healthy mothers and babies."

Lotus took Orion by the hand. "It is happening. Now that the souls that pass on are not entering to the hall of souls, it grows short of supply. We are running out of time."

Esmra heard the fairies chattering from the other room. She came in wearing her old, black pajama bottoms and a Salem T-shirt, holding a bag full of her favorite oils. There she stood staring at the television, frozen as she listened to a report on the news about the stillborn infants.

"It is happening already." Esmra said.

Tallulah carried her packed bag and set it down by the front door. "Wow, you were right Esmra. What Selena told everyone is coming true. If it is making news, then it must be catching attention."

Aiden and Meridian were happily jogging down the stairs laughing while Aiden was sharing one of his funny stories about when he and Chris went on a fishing trip together. They paid no mind to Esmra and Tallulah who were still engrossed in the television. The love birds went into the kitchen and were rummaging around for snacks and something to drink. Meridian was first to bounce into the room.

"So, what are we going to eat for supper tonight?" Esmra and Tallulah did not acknowledge Meridian. Soon Aiden followed carrying a drink with a smiling mouth full of food. He bent his knee and gave a playful nudge to the back of Meridian's knee.

Aiden stopped smiling and looked over Meridian's head to see what distracted her. With a big gulp of a swallow, he freed his mouth up to ask questions. "What is happening? Stillborn deaths? Isn't this what you mentioned Tallulah? Chris and I were watching the news, similar stuff we saw."

Esmra broke her stare and without a word she returned to her room to finish packing. Within a few moments she returned with her bags in tow and set them next to Tallulah's suitcase. "Yes, this is what Selena mentioned would happen. The hall of souls is thinning." She took Meridian by the hand and led her to the kitchen where she made a pot of tea for everyone to drink.

Esmra stood over Meridian pouring the steaming water into her teacup. Esmra admired how relaxed the couple appeared, Meridian and Aiden were staring at one another smiling, despite the surrounding drama. She gave a soft smile and continued to pour water in teacups.

"I have not thought too much about dinner." Esmra watched Meridian drop a dollop of honey in her tea. "I think everyone can fend for themselves here tonight, we are leaving first thing in the morning, to go back to Tallulah's."

Meridian added another spoonful of honey. "Gee Meridian, would you like tea to go with your honey?" Aiden laughed as Meridian rolled her eyes and plopped the honey into her tea with a splash.

The guides remained in the house to watch over the group and Relic paid close attention to the playful exchanges taking place between Meridian and Aiden as he became fidgety. "Geez, really? Who does he think he is anyway? Setting aside the point that Aiden might be the one, what does she see in him anyway? I mean isn't the blonde-haired and blue-eyed thing a tad overrated? What about tall, dark, and handsome?"

Pramlee and Ridge rolled their eyes in sync. Orion and Talon chuckled to themselves. It was Lotus who jumped in with an ironic snarky remark.

"So, Relic, I thought you had other interests? Or is it, that you have to have all the attention?" Lotus said as she played with her long blonde hair.

Relic's face blushed accompanied by a twitchy smile. "Um, well come on. I mean check me out. Who could resist?"

Pramlee rolled her eyes again with a sigh. "Oh, I am so sick of hearing your peacock talk. Bad enough Kieren was acting nutty over it. What about Kieren? Has anyone seen or heard from Kieren since he stomped off? I actually miss having him. I miss my brother, too. I can't imagine the state he is in back in Etheria. I wish things could go back to normal. I might even tolerate Relic's ridiculous commentary." Pramlee pushed out her bottom lip and blew air up to move the lock of blue hair that covered her right eye.

Relic looked around and stopped at Ridge. "Have you seen Kieren? Do you think we should go try to find him? Maybe he went back to Aiden's grandparents' place to hide in the barn with Brennan who is suffering post-traumatic stress disorder from his visit with Warrick and Lahash in the dark realm."

Ridge said, "We will be back in the area soon enough. When everyone arrives safely back at Tallulah's, a couple of us can break away and find out about Brennan and Kieren."

Chapter 19

Chris left town, headed back to school after a disappointing spring break. Driving back Aiden's truck alone was not the way he planned to end his trip. He pulled over at the same gas station he and Aiden stopped at for fuel and road snacks.

Chris grabbed a drink from the same aisle where Aiden had stood, frozen at the time as Talon drew in closer to his only son. Chris stopped looking at the row of dated snacks and stared at the spot where Aiden stood not too long ago. After a few moments he approached the cashier to pay when his phone rang. He quickly threw his items on the counter to pay so he could dig in his jean pocket for his phone. Eager, Chris caught the call by the second ring.

"Aiden! Man, so good to hear from you!" Chris finished paying for his snacks and rushed out the door so he could listen to every detail.

Aiden broke away from Meridian for just a spell while she helped Esmra and Tallulah clean up from a quick bite to eat for the evening. He stood outside in the cool spring breeze where the air brushed Aiden's locks that had grown longer since Christmas. His locks, darkened from the winter, appeared nearly brown in the dark. He wore an old Metallica

T-shirt from the concert he attended with Chris he so fondly reminisced to his grandpa about. As Chris talked on the other end of the phone, Aiden pulled the bottom half of the T-shirt away from his body and stared at it with a smirk.

"Oh, man, yes, well as you must believe, a lot has happened for sure around here. I found Meridian and she was with Raina. Remember the crazy witch? Yeah so . . . she has had Meridian under some spell and apparently some anxiety medication. She has kept Meridian under her control. Now apparently, we have to take a trip out of town to retrieve a sword. That is why I can't come back yet." Aiden walked the perimeter of Esmra's yard, staring at the full moon.

"What? A sword? What are you talking about? A sword for what?" Chris nearly dropped the phone from between his ear and shoulder while he drove and tried to open his drink.

"Look, there is a lot that you don't know about. Raina is a nut and that is just the half of it. I should share the rest of the story in person. I am not sure how you would take knowing about Meridian and who she is. The reality of the way of things. I learned so much about our existence in such a short time and it is so unreal." Aiden smiled as he ran his free hand through his hair. He stopped momentarily and glanced at the second floor of the house when he saw a light come on in one of the bedrooms. Meridian walked past the window.

"Aiden, are you there? Look, what you are saying makes little sense. Are you drunk or what? What is going on with Meridian?" Chris said.

Aiden stopped staring up at the window. "Yeah man, sorry. Look Meridian isn't a normal girl but I do not want you to worry. When I get back I have so much more to tell you. I found out about my father. It is so surreal." Aiden walked back up to the house. "So be safe on your way back to school. I am headed out of here back to Tallulah's, but I won't be going back home. I and not quite sure how to explain everything to the grandparents. Which by the way, what did you tell them?"

"Well, I am a terrible liar, but I pulled it off, I think. I told them you had to go help a friend from school and that you would catch a ride back to school with the friend. I didn't make up names. Your grandmother didn't seem to believe me." Chis explained.

"Ah well, I will handle it. Talk later, thanks for everything." Aiden hung up the phone and he was just about to make a dash up the stairs, but Esmra stood in front of him with a smile.

"Aiden, come here, young man. I would like to visit with you." Aiden moved out of her way and followed her to the kitchen and sat in the same seat where he had his dinner.

The table was all wiped clean and the plates had been washed. "So, Aiden, how are you?"

"Well, I think I am okay. Should I not be?" Aiden answered with a soft smile and a hint of innocence in his eyes.

"You have kind eyes and beautiful blue eyes. I can see why Meridian is so taken with you. You have come to learn many things in such a short time. You made this trip all the way here with Tallulah because you are in love with Meridian?" Esmra set out a glass and poured water for Aiden.

Aiden picked up the glass and grinned as he brought the glass to his lips. "What no tea for me?"

Esmra paused with a smile. "Ahh now, I didn't take you for the tea type."

Aiden set the glass back down on the table. "Did Meridian tell you that?"

Esmra laughed and sat down at the table with a small box. "No, I just know things." She opened up the wooden box with a pentagram engraved on the cover. Inside it was lined much like Raina's box, red velvet fabric that held crystal quartz. It wasn't large, however perfectly symmetrical, in the shape of a pyramid.

Aiden stared at the crystal inside the box. "So, what are we doing?"

"Aiden, now that you know who your father is, you are learning more about Meridian and who she is. Have you thought much about the curse she carries and what this means?" Esmra pulled the crystal out and held it in her hand.

"Yes, well sort of. I know what could happen to any guy Meridian is with if it isn't true love. Tallulah explained it. I have told Meridian that I won't leave or give up on her that easily. I feel a connection with her." Aiden stared at the crystal that Esmra held.

"Aiden, how would you take it if you were to find out you may not be Meridian's twin soul? How would you react if you found out you both are not meant to be? There may be another person that is to help set her free may be someone else? Would you be able to walk away and let Meridian live out her destiny?"

Aiden let out a big breath and his eyes widened. He stretched his long legs out under the table and let his arms relax at his sides. "Well, that is a fair question and a hard one at that. But if I am not the one for Meridian, and I have to let her go because it is not meant to be, and letting her go would allow her happiness, and her survival. As hard as it may be, yes. I would let her go. It would kill me, but I would do it. I have lost her before and let her go. I think I could do it again." Aiden stood up from the table and crossed his arms as he paced.

Esmra remained seated and placed the crystal on the table and she turned around in her chair to face Aiden. "Son, I tell you that I see it in your eyes, way you look at her. Anyone can see that you love her. You have to love her not to run off after the wild things you witnessed . . . things you have learned."

Aiden sat back down and assumed his position of his elbows resting on his knees. He clasped his hands together and created a cradle for his chin. His large, blue eyes peered up at Esmra and he said, "Well, I can't ruin it again. After I witnessed the events at Tallulah's when Raina put a spell on everyone . . . I'll admit, that was scary. It spooked me. I didn't talk to Meridian for a bit, and she thought I was running off. Raina lied telling her I was seeing Amy again. I left Meridian in doubt. Her self-doubt is the main reason she has so many struggles. I don't want to add to anymore of her doubting herself. I think she is wonderful. I can't turn my back on her now, no matter who is meant to be with her."

Esmra said, "Well, you made this talk easier than I thought it would be. You are a wonderful young man Aiden." Esmra took Aiden by the hand and said, "I hope you are the one for Meridian. It would be heartbreaking to her if it is not you. But I know you will do right by her, no matter what. You are ready. Follow me." Esmra let Aiden outside past where he stood when he spoke to Chris on the phone.

Fairy Nymphs & the Demon Court

Outside, the fairy nymphs were waiting on Aiden. Karma and Venus were the first ones to greet Esmra. "So, he is ready? This is it?"

Esmra nodded and Aiden sat down on the ground in the plush grass in the large garden full of lavender and ivy. Small solar lanterns lit the garden area and the pathway. Aiden was not sure what was going on but he continued to walk while he smiled nervously. "So, what are we doing?"

Esmra kneeled down next to Aiden and said "Aiden, you cannot see them, but you are in the company of fairy nymphs. These fairies rule love and lust, and their elements. One fairy, Karma, rules what her name implies. Karma delivers what the Universe deems fit for a being is. Karma and Venus are here to assist you and Meridian in lifting the veil of your destinies. Now they cannot answer if you and Meridian are meant to be. That is not for them to share, it is for you and Meridian to discover."

Down the dimly lit pathway Meridian walked into the garden and Aiden turned his head away from Esmra and stared at her. She was wearing a pair of sea green cotton shorts and one of his white T-shirts, that was too big for her. Meridian had pulled her black hair back away from her face in a loose ponytail. Only wisps of her hair dangled around her delicate face. She carried a relaxed appearance as she walked, accompanied by a hint of a smile as she locked eyes with Aiden. Her feet were bare, with bright red nail polish decorating her long and slender toes. Her ankle was adorned with a bracelet with small chimes that jingled with every step through the grass.

As Meridian finally made it to the garden, Aiden snapped out of his trance and jumped to his feet. Taking Meridian by the hand, he helped her sit down next to him. Meridian leaned toward Aiden and rested her head on his shoulder as he put his arm around her.

Esmra took a seat next to the couple, just beside the small fire in the circular fireplace that sat in the middle of the garden. "Now Aiden, you cannot see Karma and Venus, the fairy nymphs. I know that you cannot hear them either. Meridian and I can hear and see them so we will help you along." Esmra nodded to Venus.

Venus sat across from the mortals on the other side of the fire. Her face glowed from the dancing flames of the fire. Venus appeared like Selena with her black hair and fair skin, but her hair was long and wavy. Her wings were light blue, but muted and the moonlight brightened them when she turned around to see Meridian with her turquoise, cat-like eyes.

"Meridian, I have shared this information with Esmra so I will once more with you. Karma and I cannot see who your true twin soul is and even if we could we would not share with you this information. It would be against our laws and a disrespect to Earth and our Universe. Before I explain what we will do, do you have any questions for me?"

Meridian lifted her head from Aiden's shoulder and played with the plush green grass she sat on. "Well, yes. So, if fairy nymphs rule lust, how can you can help us in this situation?"

Venus chuckled. "Yes, we rule lust. My element is air, I rule love as well. Echo rules Earth, Lotus rules Water, Siren rules fire and Karma rules karma through the Universe. Now each one of us can assist with different things depending on our element. With mine being air, it is natural for me to assist in matters of communication and feelings. I am here to help in the regard to love. Karma is here to help remove the veil, so the Universe can speak to you in ways you will understand. Are you ready?"

Meridian nodded and Venus opened her book of shadows and then pulled out her crystal, shaped in a sphere. When she removed the sphere from her pouch and held it in her hand, to Aiden who could not see her only took sight of the ball itself, and it appeared to float in the air. His eyes widened as he pulled his head back in disbelief of what his eyes told him.

Esmra patted his leg and said, "It is ok, Aiden. It is Venus, she holds the crystal. Do not be afraid."

Karma moved closer to Venus and the pair closed their eyes. Karma took both of her hands and placed them under Venus's hands that still held the crystal. With whispers, they began a fairy chant. Their lips moved in perfect sync with one another. As they chanted in a whisper, the crystal ball glowed bright white.

> *"Universe who sees all, bring us a vision this night,*
> *allow the chosen to see her twin soul when the time is right."*

The crystal ball ascended upward away from Venus over the fire. With Meridian holding both of Aiden's hands, Venus stood behind Aiden and Karma stood behind Meridian. The ball changed colors of the rainbow swiftly and it hovered over Aiden and Meridian.

After the crystal finished moving, the color changed, turning black. The fairy nymphs tilted their heads back and from each nymph came a charge of electric light from their bodies. Each nymph propelled her own ray of light into the crystal ball.

Once the pair of lights met the crystal ball, immense winds picked up and blew their hair back. The tree branches in the garden sway back and forth and petals from the garden flowers knocked loose from their stems and flew bountiful through the high winds.

The black crystal ball lit up and inside, an electrical dance played out. From the ball a bright white light shot up and surrounded them.

For Meridian, the scenery took a change. She could no longer see where she was at and found herself to be standing in darkness, without a soul in sight. "What is happening?"

Esmra said, "It is okay, Meridian! You are still with us; the nymphs are showing you the way! Stay calm."

Meridian studied her surroundings that gave way from darkness to visions starting with the hospital where she saw Aiden, as an infant for the first time. She watched herself, as her mother, Arianna motioned for her to follow her and Caius into the portal from the hospital back to Etheria. As soon as they entered the portal, the scene changed again. Next, Meridian found herself in the fairy realm with Kieren where they shared their first kiss and the scene continue to unfold when Relic jumped in and tore Kieren away from her.

In a snap, the scene was gone, Meridian now walked alongside Relic in the club where she, Relic, and Caius met Talon for the first time. Relic laughed and played around with Meridian when she questioned about the mysterious ghost that flew over their heads as they marched through the club.

She heard the sounds of the techno music playing as though she was there.

With another split, Meridian saw herself as a young guide, childlike where she played with her parents, Arianna and Caius. They walked to Etheria's palace where the gatherings took place for new guides that came to be in Etheria.

Meridian turned her head and she was taken from that memory, further back to the time of her creation and spirit guide birth. She stared at a large, perfectly sized crystal quartz. Inside the quartz was Meridian as a newborn. Meridian looked away from the quartz that held her infant self and saw past the night sky, into space where a bright star burned, shooting out immense heat and light from both sides. She blinked and the memories stopped, and she stood within the hall of souls, surrounded by the keepers.

Meridian squinted at the brightness they exuded, turning her face away from them.

"Meridian, dear child, we have been waiting for you. The time has come for you to awaken, open yourself to what you do not know. See what you cannot see, hear what you cannot hear. Do you know what I speak of?" the Angel asked.

Meridian shook her head in disbelief and said, "No, I don't understand. Where am I?"

"You are home, child, where all human souls come to rest and then begin new once more. Here we are the keepers, the watchers over human souls."

Meridian turned her confused face to the angels. Her eyes barely broke away and scanned the large doors that adorned the walls of where she stood. "I don't understand, you create souls?"

The Angel spoke, "We do not create souls, dear Meridian. We are the keepers. Souls are created by a higher energy, from within another plane in the cosmos. The souls we watch over are the ones who have transcended throughout each human life, ready for the next life as a newborn child. When a spirit guide's time has drawn to a close, we take the soul in. Guides live thousands of years, but you do not live forever."

Meridian asked the Angel with disbelief but curiosity. "Is it my time? Have I passed?"

The angel came closer to Meridian and reached his hand out to rest it upon her head. "I am Gabriel. No, it is not your time to pass. It is your time to heal. Do you understand what you must do?"

"No, I am sorry. Please. Help me. I feel . . ." Meridian was cut short.

"You are lost and seek to find your way once more. Who do you believe will help you find your way?" the angel said.

Another vision appeared where she watched the scene play out when she went to the dark realm with the other guides and Talon. The moment it was time to answer the dark one's riddle played in slow motion.

The Angel asked once more, "Who do you believe will help you find your way? What was it that darkened your journey to the dark realm? Who is it that holds you back from answering your own question about your dark curse? Who do you believe will help you find your way home once again?"

The scene stopped at the moment of truth, when Meridian stood in the dark realm as the guides were desperate to answer the dark one's riddle. Meridian stood still with the Angels as she stared at the frozen scene, where it was she that needed to answer the riddle. She blinked her sad eyes and with it came a single tear that streamed down her face.

"All this time, the entire time. I think I understand now. I know who it is." Meridian said. The scene from the dark realm vanished, where only she and the Angels stood. "The person is me. It is me. It has always been me."

The Angel moved closer to Meridian and his ominous voice became louder with intensity. "What is it you need to see but cannot see. What is it you need to hear, but do not hear, dear Meridian?"

Meridian's solitary tear became a river as the tears saturated her pale skin. Her cheeks flushed red, her body shook while she cried. She drew a deep breath and closed her eyes and said, "Faith."

When Meridian opened her eyes, she no longer stood before the Angels. They were gone, without so much as a whisper. There at a distance stood a figure of a man. His appearance waved like water when he moved toward Meridian and as the figure emerged more clearly to her, the figure stopped and stood still.

His hands dangled at his sides, he was tall and dressed in all black. Meridian struggled to connect who the being was that stood in place of the Angels.

Another string of visions played out in front of her. In her mind's eye she recounted her dream she had while she lay asleep at Tallulah's. The bright light shone, burning her eyes. A voice from within the bright light spoke to her and said, "I am always here and I carry you in my heart. I sleep with the Angels and I am never too far from you.

Still crying, in an instant she knew who the figure was, the man that stood before her. She ran with tears pouring from her eyes, arms wide open as she let out a childlike laugh. "Father! Father!"

There he stood, tall and humble. Caius was ready to embrace his only daughter. Meridian collided into her father with force as she threw herself onto him. With a deep embrace, she held onto him, burying her face into his shoulder.

Meanwhile, Aiden stood still within the protection of the bright light with his own visions from the time he was a child until the present time with Meridian. He was reliving his own memory the day at the old oak tree where he stood and believed it was his mother contacting him after her passing.

To onlookers, both Meridian and Aiden were in a deep meditative state. Their eyes closed while they held one another's hands. The fairy nymphs still in a posture of propelling their power into the crystal, the winds howled, and the trees sang with high notes of wisps and swift beats as their branches brushed together. It pulled away the petals from Esmra's rose bush from where they decorated a corner of the garden, into the magical fairy winds that Karma and Venus created.

Aiden's next vision was once again the procession of events in his reoccurring dream that did not bring to any answers on who the strange woman was that lay quietly in her hospital bed. Aiden's eyes tightly squinted while they remained closed and his jaw locked shut while his cheeks fluttered with the tiny motions of his jaw biting with frustration. His grip on Meridian held stronger.

Once more the events in Aiden's dream played out; he awoke from a sleep from the couch in the waiting room, journeyed down the hall of a busy hospital and approached the room again, pushing the door open. As he struggled to see who was in the bed, he collapsed to the floor. The five apparitions that continued to glow stood at his feet while the three orbs floated above the stranger in the bed. The stranger that only for a moment gave a hint to her identity with her blonde hair that hung over the bedside railing.

Aiden rolled over onto his back while on the floor and one of the five apparitions again pointed to the stranger in the bed and said, "Would you die for her?"

Aiden strained to lift his head from the floor, with only the sounds of his own breathing and heartbeat racing through his mind. The harder he struggled to raise his body upward, the tighter the invisible hold gripped him. The doctors and the nurses continued their hurried pace around the bed, while the two individuals who stood at the end of the bed stood frozen and still.

Aiden fought to get free, he gritted his teeth and arched his back fighting the force that held him to the floor. He screamed as loud as he could, but no one noticed him, only the five glowing apparitions that stood quietly at his feet.

He continued to fight to move any part of his body he could to free himself.

The fairy nymphs still at Meridian and Aiden's side sang in operatic high-pitched voices in a language that no being or human would understand. As their pitches grew in harmony of one another, the nymphs' voices were in perfect sync. With every elevated pitch, with every syllable that left their delicate lips their wings slowly extended from their resting positions. The magical rays that connected to the crystal pulsed slowly and increased in sync with the octave of their song.

As the pulses of magical light increased, their wings fully extended and fluttered back and forth in sync with their beautiful song and rays of light beaming from their bodies.

Aiden still standing quietly but stiff in his trance, engrossed in his vision of an endless dream, slowly was released from the invisible death grip that held him on the floor. Just as he realized that he was no more in a grip, he raised slowly and placed both hands in the floor to push himself up and get to the strange woman in the bed. As he jumped to his feet, his eyes shot over to the bed where his view of the woman remained obstructed, however another being appeared to Aiden.

On the other side of the bed stood what appeared to be a ghost with blonde hair but her face remained a mystery, giving a watery appearance, remaining a blur to Aiden. No matter how he struggled the face this ghost, she eluded him.

Aiden continued to try to make out the mystery ghost as he took one step forward toward the bedside. In a blink of an eye, he was no longer standing in the hospital, but at the oak tree, down the long dirt drive, just yards from his home. The special place where his first blind encounter with Meridian took place. In his mind's eye he watched himself go through the motions the day he first sensed Meridian.

Aiden stopped in his tracks, while Meridian who remained an enigma to him, placed her hand on his chest and stood before him. Suddenly something disturbed the glorious moment he experienced again in exchange for the sinister delights of the dark realm.

Aiden looked up to the once blue and quiet sky now stolen from his dream, for the dark clouds swiftly blanketing the once sunny sky. Winds hurled, bringing what appeared to be tornadic waves of gale force winds, hurling dead birds through the air. Once again, a ghost with blonde hair made her appearance, frantically flying over his head, giving a warning.

She pointed to the empty space in front of him. Aiden dropped his head to see the space, and there stood Meridian with her hand on his chest, like the time before. She stood dressed in the same black outfit the night they met at

Stephanie's bar. Her raven hair dangling around her shoulders moving in slow motion, even with the winds of terror, she appeared nearly immune from the wind. A tendril of hair swept over her green eyes and her beaming smile took over her face.

Aiden brought his hand to her face as she softly smiled and stared into his eyes. Leaning in, he closed his eyes and his lips met hers. At the moment he pressed his lips against her lips, he hesitated. His jaw tightened and his lips tightened. He pulled his head away and opened his eyes and there in front of him stood someone else. Someone that turned a dream into a nightmare. There the witch herself stood smiling.

Aiden shouted and fell to the ground with shock. "Raina! What? How? What are you doing here?"

Raina threw her head back and her evil laugh echoed throughout his mind and grew louder the more he shouted. "Stop! What are you doing?" Aiden said as he jumped to his feet and moved away from the dark witch.

Raina abruptly stopped laughing and brought her chin down. She tightened up her lips with a smile only showing a hint of her black teeth. She locked her eyes on Aiden who now had moved several feet away from the witch near the old oak tree.

"I would come back for Meridian. I will never let you have her. She is mine. Pyro has blessed me with power and soon Ipos and I will join and take over Earth." Raina laughed again. "No one can stop me. We will rid this planet of all spirit guides and mankind will be ours!"

Suddenly Aiden awoke from his meditative state. The fairies' light had disconnected from the crystal and the howling winds subsided. Meridian opened her eyes.

Meridian turned around and Karma stood behind her. Karma asked, "What did you see?"

Meridian paused and swiftly nodded back and forth. "I was in the hall of souls! I saw my father! It was surreal. It was amazing!" Meridian's voice, full of zeal and the elusive light and free demeanor returned for just a spell. "I saw Kieren, I remember him now. We shared a kiss and of course Relic! Relic I remember! He came in and tore Kieren away from me. I was with Relic in a techno club, I saw Talon for the first time. The ghost! The ghost, the one who was flying over my head when Relic and I were following my father through the club. My father! My father! I remember. It was him. He has been the one talking in my dreams. He tells me to remember! I can remember!" Meridian said as she cried with joy. She ran over to Esmra and hugged her.

"Esmra, I can remember my parents! I saw my mother! I saw my mother." Meridian paused and tore her hug away from Esmra and noticed Aiden who was saddened by his experience.

"Aiden, I am sorry." Meridian walked over to Aiden and hugged him.

"It's all right." Aiden stared at the ground hiding his eyes and still tried to keep a smile.

Meridian pulled away from Aiden for a better look at his eyes. "Aiden, what is it? What did you see?"

Aiden turned away and took a few steps away from Meridian. "It was nothing really. A replay of the reoccurring dream I told you about. I was finally able to see past the stopping point from the last time I had the dream. I think that the woman lying in the bed. I think it is my mother. The apparitions there, they asked me again if I would die for her." Aiden drew a ragged breath and looked up toward Meridian. "I don't understand if whatever it was, we did was supposed to help us see things more clearly, why I am more confused?"

Esmra motioned for Aiden and Meridian to accompany her back into the house where they sat once more at her large, round kitchen table. The fairy nymphs were silent as they followed along. The spirit guides joined the group, and Talon could not stay away.

Esmra pulled the chairs out for the two love birds and with a silent demand, she nodded for them to both have a seat. "Aiden, the fairy nymphs are powerful creatures. They can do wonderful or equally horrible things to beings . . . if they choose. They cannot foretell the future, but they can make the way for a human to have a better understanding. Now what is this about your mother?"

Aiden shook his head and said, "I am not sure. I keep seeing myself in the hospital where I was born and my mother passed away. I get into the room and I cannot ever see who it is exactly lying in that bed. All I know is that it is a woman with blonde hair like my mother. This time, once I could get on my feet, I can see a blonde-headed woman standing in the room next to the bed, but she is blurry. I can't see her face. The next part, I don't like at all." Aiden held her hand. "I find myself back at home, by the oak tree where I sensed a presence, one I thought was my mother months back. I look up and there is a blonde-headed ghost pointing at something, then I see Meridian. I lean in for a kiss and it is really Raina!"

Esmra's eyes widened and her mouth dropped open. "Raina!? Oh dear. What happens next?"

Aiden continued, "Well, she says Meridian is hers and she claims she has the power of Pyro and she will summon Ipos and they will take over humankind. I don't understand."

The guides stirred and Talon growled with anger as he paced the kitchen.

"Meridian, so your memories are returning?" Pramlee smiled.

"Yes, I remember Kieren and that we were falling for one another. I remember Relic, he is my best friend." Meridian smiled but her eyes appeared shameful when she spoke of Kieren.

"Aiden must have gifts. He is seeing the future it seems," Pramlee said.

Relic interrupted, "Maybe he was in the hospital, he is seeing the past. It makes sense. There must have been ghosts surrounding his mother when Aiden was born. He is seeing himself at the oak tree when Meridian approached him. He is seeing the past." Relic stopped and looked at Meridian while she was struggling to recount the memory that Relic described.

Meridian shook her head and said, "No, why don't I remember that moment? Why would Aiden see Raina in his dream?"

Esmra seemed confused with what she heard. "Meridian, maybe Aiden is seeing the past and the future?"

"Maybe, but what does his mother have to do with it?" Meridian said.

"I don't know, that may not be his mother. That could be anyone, but I am more concerned about Raina. One thing for sure is that part of Aiden's vision makes sense. Raina will be back for more. As for your visions, there was a success in opening things for you, Meridian. What else happened?"

"Well, I don't know if it was real or not, but I spoke to an Angel. He asked questions about me and my first trip to the dark realm. Who will guide me home was the question."

Aiden watched Meridian as her face brightened up as she spoke. He asked, "So what is it?"

Meridian smiled but remained conservative in her answer, "Well, it is me, it has always been me. I have gotten myself in a lot of situations because I lack faith in myself. Faith to do things right. After finding out about this curse it became worse and more elusive, to somehow find the one I guess."

Esmra interrupted the reminiscing. "Well, look here, we have a big trip ahead of us. We can talk more later. You two need some sleep, we leave bright and early in the morning."

Chapter 20

Not far away from Esmra's back at Nevoc, Raina was back at her establishment as though she never left Earth. The building remained shut down, as her long standing obsession took over. She sat in her office, reviewing her business records as though nothing out of the ordinary had taken place.

Someone interrupted Raina's concentration from footsteps coming down the hallway. The wooden floors creaked with every step. She stopped working to walk to the door and quickly open it to find an old friend.

Raina huffed, rolled her eyes and left her unwelcome guest standing without an invitation to come in. "What do you want Amelia? How did you get in?"

Amelia let herself in and lay her purse on the couch. "I told you that messing with elixir would not serve you well. Your one and only employee let me in." Amelia sat down on the couch and crossed her legs maintaining her stare on Raina.

"What are you talking about? It has served me well. Pyro has blessed me with power and it will serve me well." Raina sat down pretending to go back to work on her business books.

Amelia smiled and bounced her leg up and down. "Raina, you have been gone for weeks. The bar is shut down, you have lost more income. Where were you?"

Raina put her pen down. "I went on a trip and that is all I will say about that."

"Raina, I wouldn't continue in this way. I am here trying to help you," Amelia said.

Raina rolled her eyes once more. "Whatever, why would you even want to help me? They kicked you out of the coven for the same reason I was. Now you live a different life. You don't even practice magic anymore. You think because you left this life and married your billionaire husband that you can smugly lecture me. Spare me. I need nothing from you."

Amelia rose from the couch, put her purse strap over her shoulder and pushed her long, slick hair back over her shoulder and walked toward Raina's desk.

"Look, I realize that you are angry about being kicked out. We both made mistakes. I did things that nearly cost me everything. I left this life because for whatever reason, I struggle to stay closed to the dark forces. Once you invite that in, you will never escape it. You need to trust what I am telling you. I didn't walk away because I do not believe in using magic. I left because I do not believe in using black magic. I ruined it for myself. I took it to a bad place and once that happens, you can never go back. There is still hope for you." Amelia walked toward the door to leave.

"I hope it isn't too late for you, Raina." Amelia shut the door and left Nevoc.

The dark realm was at an unusual unrest. Seated at the large rock table, those of the demon court awaited the dark one's wrath. Pyro, was not acting as his usual self as remained quiet, staring at the high flame in the center of the table. The orange-flamed flicker burned still only casting a light shadow on the slate grey stone table. Pyro seemed even smaller than his normal stature as he slumped over in his chair only cutting his eyes upward to glance at the precession of demons taking their seats.

Ipos strolled in with a quick pace, his footsteps heavy and swift. He jerked the chair of choice backward in a rushed manner where he quickly sat down and clasped his large hands together as he rested his elbows on the arms of the chair. As he tipped his head back to stare upward at the crimson atmosphere, he let out a groan that Lahash could not ignore as he entered.

"Ipos, such a heavy feeling from you. Certainly not your usual demeanor. I can't possibly imagine what ails you. What's the matter? Your legion of downtrodden not doing your reign any justice?" Lahash said with a smile as he nodded at Warrick who casually strolled in with a tight grin.

Ipos pulled his chin back and looked directly at Lahash who casually took his seat and then straightened his jacket. "Lahash, don't play your ridiculous games with me. You know damn well what the issue is. I don't have time for your childish banter."

Lahash pulled his head back and lost his grin for a moment. He brushed his hands across the stone table, exposing his white, French cuffed shirt underneath his jacket. His gold buttons on his sleeve scratched the table as he brushed his hand slowly back and forth. "Ipos, whatever do you mean? Oh yes, the silly little mark. Well, what can be done? The guides answered the dark one's riddle and fairly, Luna was released along with the one individual who was the center of the riddle, now didn't they?"

Ipos stood up from his chair and leaned over the table pointing his finger at Lahash and said, "You are up to something! You want that witch to summon me. You want my legion! Don't you have enough of the scum bags you draw your energy forces from?" Ipos walked around the table toward the side where Lahash was seated.

Lahash stared up at the angry demon in amusement. "What? You have the powers of seeing the future, surely if you are this upset, it means that you shall perish, no? Maybe your powers of seeing the future elude you. After all, I don't know how your powers or senses have served you well, with your fashion choices, anyway. Surely you realize, your attire is dated."

Pyro remained silent as he stared at the quarreling demons. Warrick stood next to his chair overlooking the quarrel, but his eyes were distracted with the entrance of more demons.

Ipos clenched his large fists and hovered his large body over Lahash. His long razor-like nails pierced his palms as he clenched his fists. The veins across his hands emerged fueled by silent anger. Before he could come with a rebuttal, the additional demons' amusement interrupted him with the scene.

"Ipos, this is new, we never have the privilege of seeing you in such rare form." The amused demon stood next to Warrick with his hands placed upon his hips. He was tall, towering over even the large Ipos, with a large neck and head. His skin was a dark red and his eyes were yellow.

Ipos unlocked his eyes from Lahash with disdain and said to the demon, "Moloch, this doesn't concern you. Stay out of it!"

Moloch threw his head back with a guttural laugh as his body shook with every thrust erupting from deep within his large body. "Doesn't concern me? Oh, I am sorry to disappoint you, but all of this concerns me!"

As the remaining three demons scurried in, the vivid exchange was further interrupted when the dark one spoke. His voice low, and thinly veiled what was raging beneath his cryptic tone.

"That will be quite enough. Be seated." The quarreling demons quickly dissipated and took their respective seats. The room went quiet with only the light wisps from the flame that now flickered with every syllable from the dark one's message.

Moloch did not waver as he sat erect, smugly scanning the table. Warrick and Lahash had a similar demeanor, however, they were avoiding eye contact with one another.

"Lahash, you have some explaining to do. Choose your words wisely."

Lahash repositioned himself in his chair and removed his hand from the table and nervously folded his hands in his lap. He pulled his small chin into his chest.

"Master, with the visit from the guides and Talon, we were at a great disadvantage with their aid from the witch. She could decode your riddle and with that, they won Luna back and released Raina."

"I do not need a recount of the events in my dark realm! Why is it that the witch could work with the guides?

The spirit guides were not meant to make it back here with the answer! With Luna back, Selena's power will grow!" The dark one's voice escalated. "Your nymphs managed to escape with the key to the hall of souls, Warrick! You both have created much destruction of my plans in your wake and this will not go without punishment! You both are losing favor in my court, and you know what this means for you if you do. I need not show you the future that will certainly be a different view for the both of you."

Lahash was frozen and his usual upturn of his thin lips disappeared. Warrick stared at Lahash waiting for the cutting comebacks that were nothing short of a demonic art form. The silence crowded the room and the demons shuddered from the dark one's anger. Warrick ironically stood up from his chair to speak.

"Oh, Lord, please allow me to speak for Lahash and I both."

Lahash's head jolted up in shock, his mouth partially open and his face devoid of the usual self-righteousness.

"Warrick, this is unusual for you to speak for Lahash. I'll allow it, but only for morbid curiosity."

Warrick let out a sigh of relief, his shoulders were no longer around his ears, he paced and his arms moved up and down brushing his long grey beard as he spoke.

"Lord, Lahash has been quite instrumental in the delay of many events and an intake of needed information. He spoke with Talon to find out why he supports the guides. Lahash showed up and removed the witch from further damage that she would have done if she had summoned Ipos. He was able to slow down Pyro as he possessed the witch. Raina may be loose on Earth to do as she pleases now, however we cannot rightfully keep a mortal whose soul is still attached to the body. Raina would have to be dead in order for us to take her soul. I realize that Lahash's obsession with Echo has you concerned, and rightfully so, however Fairies operate under no laws except their own, and this information and obsession could be further instrumental in our plan."

Warrick moved around the table while the demons' eyes locked on Etheria's traitor as he paced.

"Lord, Lahash could use the nymphs. He could urge Echo to kill Raina before she summons Ipos. It would preserve Ipos, Raina's soul would be trapped in the dark realm. If we can manage this, we can take out the rest of the fairies and we can stop the guides from ever making it to the quartz sword."

The room was still, even the candle flickering had diminished to a still flame. The demons' eyes were shifty and uncertain, but their bodies remained frozen. Moloch as confident as he was even stood still in the face of the anticipated response to Warrick.

The dark one's voice was slow and he said, "Warrick, what an intriguing synopsis. I would agree with most of what you say, however I struggle with your plans. I have always said we are to be wary of fairies. However, if Lahash can use his connections, that very well may play in our favor. I want to push forward. Get this done before they reach the quartz sword."

The room fell momentarily silent. The flickering of the fire that once burned brightly in the center of the table had vanished. The room was dark with only hints of the crimson atmosphere. Moloch stood up from his chair.

"Warrick! Look what you have gotten us into! This is your problem and now with your selfish and idiotic ways, you have sucked us all into this! My only job is soul collector. Now you have managed to complicate matters further for all of us now."

Ipos left his seat in relief and quietly walked out of the room when Lahash stopped him.

"Oh, Ipos! Aren't you feeling better now? Warrick has possibly bought you some time. Isn't this wonderful? I can still pursue the nymph, Warrick gets his way, things are going well." Lahash was smug as he spoke to Ipos.

The scraping of Ipos's feet across the rock floor halted, however, he kept his back turned and raised his head.

"Neither one of you fools can see the things I can see. I may have more time but do not be so foolish to believe we are unstoppable." Ipos turned around and his deliberate dark grey eyes stared down Lahash.

"Even the dark one knows of things to come. Being his favorite today does not equal being his favorite tomorrow, if there is one." Ipos turned and disappeared.

Chapter 21

Esmra's house was dark and everyone had turned in for the night for some much-needed rest before they hit the road back to Tallulah's house. The fierce group of the unseen quietly waited for dawn while they kept one another company outside, in Esmra's garden.

Up the old wooden stairs and down the dark hall to the last door on the left, Meridian and Aiden lay awake holding one another in a quiet embrace. Outside the moon illuminated Meridian's face when her head slowly moved up and down with the rhythm of Aiden's breathing as she lay on his chest. He carefully cradled her in one arm and rested the other behind his head as he stared at the ceiling drunk with euphoria holding the one he had longed for.

Meridian's wide eyes were planted on the moon barely blinking. Her profile barely exposed, Aiden glanced downward at her and waited for the slightest flutter of her long lashes for a hint if she were lost in slumber or awake. He did not have to stare much longer when Meridian shifted out of her lunar trance with a soft sigh that accompanied her break in thought.

"Are you awake?" she said.

Aiden smiled. "What do you think?"

Meridian let out a giggle as she snuggled into Aiden trying to get closer to him. "I can't sleep. I keep thinking about what happened in the garden. Seeing Angels. It was surreal, nothing like I would have imagined . . . I guess."

Aiden gave Meridian and a tight hug. "Tell me about the Angels."

"Well, I can't really see them, they are bright, glowing energies. They have a human silhouette and they float or they are suspended in the air, but not high up. They are large and nearly impossible to look at, they are so bright."

Aiden listened to Meridian talk of her experience in the hall of souls. His eyes were soft and relaxed as he continued to stare at the ceiling, listening to the soft sound of her voice. Esmra's sheer white curtains were partially pulled open, giving a lunar glow to his face and white shirt.

After several moments of silence after her explanation, sat up on one elbow while she rested her hands on his stomach. She ran her hands up and down his chest and stomach.

Aiden brought his arm away from holding his head, to caress Meridian's thick tresses that hung over her shoulders. As her curls wrapped around his fingers, he studied her hair and he stroked her locks with his thumb. Meridian put her hand over his hand that held a strand of her hair.

"You sure seem; Well, relaxed, I guess. You are quiet. What's up with you?" Meridian nuzzled into Aiden's neck.

"Oh, I don't know. It's nice. This is nice. Just laying here with you. I never thought I would get to do that again. I lost a lot of sleep after you left. Many nights I lay awake and thought about you." Aiden said.

Meridian pulled away from Aiden's neck slowly and kept her head down. Her face had lost its smile while she kneaded the sheets with her fingers. Aiden sat up next to Meridian and kissed her forehead.

"Meridian, it's okay, I am not upset with you. I never was, actually. I didn't understand what was happening. I have not ever felt this strongly for a girl before." Aiden lay back down next to Meridian.

Meridian broke her eyes away from the sheets she fumbled with and looked at Aiden intensely. "Really, what about Amy? I thought at one point you two were serious."

Aiden took a deep breath. "Well, I guess then that was serious as I knew it. I don't think I knew what love truly was back then. In my mind, I guess I thought I knew. After meeting you, I realized I didn't. This is different for me. Something deep within me tells me that this is meant to be. Esmra asked me what I would do if, we find out different. I told her that I would be by your side until that time comes, if it does at all." Aiden rolled over onto his side propping his head up on his hand. He took his free hand and rested it on Meridian's hip.

"Aiden, I am sorry for what happened before. A lot of my behavior made little sense to you. I was doing what I did to protect you. There are so many things about being a human I still do not understand. Maybe I never will. I have had so many insecurities as a spirit and as a human. I believe that what I learned in my vision is that I have to have faith in myself. Stop fighting my own feelings out of fear. I want you to be it so badly and it would kill me if I find out it is someone else that is my twin soul." Meridian lay her head back down resting it on her arm as she looked up at Aiden.

"I know all this is scary for you. It has been unreal for me to learn all these things. To learn who my father is. To know now, that he is near. I want so badly to know him and I want so badly to know what happened to my mother after she passed. No one has ever mentioned her from the afterlife . . . like if she became a guide. I wouldn't think she went to the dark realm. I don't think she was a bad person by the way my grandparents talk of her. She was sensitive, quiet and unassuming. They said she was otherworldly and spiritual, a little psychic. I think I inherited that from her. I sense things that don't always make sense at the time. I would like to think I was like her," Aiden said.

Meridian sat up and crossed her legs while playing with his hand that remained propped on her hip. "Maybe your mom was a ghost? I remember that the day you were born. There was a ghost going in and out of all the maternity rooms. She was crying so maybe that was her?"

Aiden sat up on the bed to face Meridian. "Maybe that is who I am seeing in the dream I keep having. It has to be her. Maybe she is trying to help me. I don't understand why the glowing apparitions ask me if I would die for her. Maybe it's the guilt I carry in my subconscious coming out. I have always felt bad. Like I killed her." Aiden looked down at his hands with shame.

"Aiden, stop it! You did not kill your mother! Now that is just crazy talk and you know it. Women pass giving birth, these things happen, it wasn't anything you did." Meridian ran her hands through Aiden's hair.

"Well, if it is her in the dream, it is nice that at least in my dreams I can see her. It is a way to know her, I guess. I would do it," Aiden mumbled.

"Do what, Aiden?"

"I would do it." Aiden looked up at Meridian. "I would die for her."

Meridian leaned in for a kiss as she put both hands on Aiden's face, holding his head still. She whispered in his ear, "I know you would."

Aiden met Meridian's lips with a soft embrace. Their lips pressed to one another's slowly and held frozen for several moments. As their kiss intensified their arms held each other close as they remained locked in a kiss.

Aiden ran his hands up and down Meridian's back and he lifted her shirt up over her head. For a second, the pair unlocked their lips and arms to catch their breath and so Aiden could remove the shirt she borrowed from him.

They were once again locked in an intense kiss. Aiden caressed Meridian's back with soft strokes up and down, kissing her neck softly and slowly. Meridian held on to Aiden's neck with her fingers clasped together.

As Aiden brought his hands up to the middle of her back, his hands stopped moving for a moment and they locked eyes as he removed Meridian's bra, and then they fell back into the bed as Aiden lay on top of her, kissing her neck and shoulders.

As Aiden became lost in the moment, Meridian's heightened pleasure faded as her mind drifted. She pulled Aiden up and away so she could see into his eyes.

"Aiden, the curse." Meridian whispered.

Aiden dropped his head breaking eye contact with her. "I know, I know." Aiden flopped back onto his seat rubbing his mouth with his hand staring at the wall.

Meridian leaned forward. "I want to be with you. I really do. I am afraid. What if . . ." Aiden put his index finger over her mouth.

"I know, Meridian. Look, I understand. At the same time, I know how I feel about you. Just as the angel said to you, it is you that is the one that can save you having faith in yourself. I would never pressure you for anything. When and if the time comes that you feel it is right. I will always be here," Aiden said as he leaned forward and kissed Meridian and held her tightly.

Meanwhile outside in the garden, Talon walked around the perimeter of Esmra's grand garden. As he strolled, he stopped every few steps to look at the flowers and herbs that adorned every corner. Esmra's garden took up her entire back yard with an old, dated, privacy fence to boot. Along the fence line were grand exhibits of roses, lilies, and the divine aroma of lavender and rosemary.

The fence like the walkway was heavily decorated with old, antique-style, solar lanterns, some tarnished from the years of hanging on the fence. Talon continued his stroll taking in the scents of the garden that brought a long overdue smile to his face. Under his feet with every other stride, stepping stones told their story of all the witches in the coven. Each witch that had come and gone through the house had decorated and left their own stepping stone.

The stones seemed never ending around the garden. Talon raised his eyes as he studied the stones that lay ahead of his steps. He arrived at one that caught his attention with the beautiful artwork. Hues of blue, sea green, and a sandy color representing the ocean. As he kneeled down further to take a better look, he saw the name 'Amelia' painted into the stone with delicate stokes of aquamarine blue. Something interrupted his quiet moment when out of nowhere Relic and Pramlee stood over Talon.

Pramlee leaned over and tapped Talon on the shoulder. "Hey, what are you up too? We were over by the fire talking with the fairy nymphs. We wanted to check on how you were doing. A lot going on."

Talon stood up from his kneeled position and turned toward Pramlee and said, "Oh I am okay. I was taking in this grandeur. Esmra may not have a house to match, but her garden is spectacular to say the least. I can see why she spends so much time out here."

The soft wind brushed the several windchimes strategically hung on her trees. They stood looking toward the chimes. Relic glanced over his shoulder at the fairy nymphs whispering and giggling amongst one another with Ridge.

"What do you make of that? I never took Ridge to be a fan of, well anything, but fairies? They seem to like him too," Relic smarted off as he laughed.

Pramlee shrugged her shoulders nonchalantly, picked at her fingernails and said, "Well, I would think anyone could like Ridge. He is a little more logical than some." Pramlee dropped her hands down by her sides and gave Relic a pop with her hip.

Talon took an opportunity to dig a little at Relic and said, "What's the matter, Relic, worried about a little competition?"

"Please, I got this. They all want me. I have a thing for Lotus." Relic nodded to Lotus who was laughing and smiling while she stared at Relic.

"Hmm. I see that. Looks like she likes you too," Talon joked.

"Well, she should, I mean look at me, I have a lot to offer," Relic boasted with his chest puffed out.

Pramlee carefully studied Relic's face with disgust. "You know, you are very disappointing. What about Luna?"

"What about Luna? I did my part, I married her and Selena let us out of our vows. No big deal." Relic shrugged his shoulders and put his palms up with a crooked smile.

Pramlee let out a loud huff, shook her head and stomped off. She continued stomping until she made it back to the fire where everyone else was seated. Talon pulled his head back and raised an eyebrow.

Talon said, "What gives? What is up with her?"

Relic swiftly shook his head, "Ah nothing. Don't worry about it."

The pair walked together to join the others for the night. "We have quite the group, an ifrit, a fallen, dazzling fairy nymphs, sprit guides and …"

A hypnotic voice spoke, interrupting Relic's cocky banter that no one enjoyed. It halted all eye rolls. A mysterious being stood behind Relic, in front of what was left of the rosebush from the fairy ritual earlier.

Talon turned around and jabbed Relic as he faced the addition to their group and said with a whisper, "Lahash."

Chapter 22

The fairy realm was unusually quiet. The fairy nymphs no longer remained ornaments of the fairy realm in Selena's court while out dazzling Earth. Selena sat alone at her large, round, gold table adorned with beautiful floral arrangements.

Selena studied the fairy book so dear to her. The book was a leather-bound collection of spells, magic and writings of the fair folk that dated back a millennium. A lock held it together and Selena kept the key in her possession for as long as she had been the queen.

Slowly turning the tattered pages of her grand fairy book, her mind drifted back to the day she tricked Caius and Meridian to take the journey to the dark realm to steal back her coveted fairy book stolen by a demon and one she had not spoken of to anyone, not even Orion.

She continued to turn pages of endless scripture of spells and ritual work that the fair folk most often used. As the pages opened up, a soft, glowing light emerged and the words were set in motion around the illustrations that told a story. On one particular page, Selena stopped.

From the pages, a plethora of stars emerged and ascended in front of Selena's eyes, swirling around in a circle slowly creating a galaxy like pinwheel. In the center of the forming pinwheel was a blue star, perfectly circular and still with only its mesmerizing swirls of gas that made up its own atmosphere.

As the pinwheel formed, the blue star shot a burst of iridescent aqua light into the air and atop, a projection of baby Luna wrapped in a cradle of stars. There Luna lay still and quiet with rosy cheeks. She opened her large eyes and the memory seemed to look back at Selena as though it was happening again.

Selena stared at the memory of Luna's creation, a solitary tear emerged, glistening on her high and pronounced cheekbone. As the tear rolled down Selena's face, it quickened, falling through the air before the tear ended its short journey, dampening the tattered page. In moments, the memory faded and the projection collapsed, making the sounds of subtle ocean waves. The glorious pinwheel of stars propelled forward swiftly, the stars merged together creating one unified prismatic glow, brightening Selena's deep amber eyes. In a blink of her eyes, the beautiful vision disappeared.

Selena continued to turn many pages of her book turning through many fairy years of memories, births and magic. As she arrived halfway through the book, she stopped and the words rose up into the air and levitated as she brushed her finger over each sentence while she read. With each word she read out loud, the story lifted from the pages into the empty space above the book and played out in front of Selena's eyes. The quickness of her index finger tickling the words, picked up the pace of the world building. In moments, there were streams, mountains and flowers in the empty space above the book. Hundreds of lights took flight with the flutter of furious fairy wings peeking out from the glow. The smell of moss flourished through the air and a running steam, audible, filled her ears as she reflected on the creation of her realm.

The page turning progressed. Selena arrived close to the end of the book where spells were written and where her fairy quartz lived, hiding and waiting within the pages.

The crystal awakened, rising from within the pages, floating in front of Selena's illuminated face. She smiled as she reached out to hold the quartz in her hand. Not ready to give it back to the book for safekeeping, she turned the next page decorated with illustrations of the fairy nymphs. All the nymphs were in flight holding one another's hands with Karma hovering in the middle of the circle they created. Selena's thoughts drifted back to the night of the ritual when Warrick was exposed.

As long as I have existed and knew that there would come a time that Etheria would see its own end. An ending that would bring a chance at rebirth. In all my years, I suppose I never really knew what it would mean when the day would come. The secrets and the coverups, evil that reigns there has begun a journey to the surface and the fairies will be called upon. It is our choice to help or to stay neutral. With all the animosity that existed between us and the guides I never thought that I would make the choice to help the spirit guides and so here it is.

Before Selena could turn another page, her thoughts were interrupted by her large doors opening. Luna walked in, light in her step with a calm demeanor about her. She pranced over to the corner of the room and poured herself a cup of fairy potion. As she brought the small cup to her pink lips, her eyes smiled as she peered over the cup at Selena. Luna removed the cup from her lips, swallowed a large gulp and wiped the corner of her delicate mouth with her index finger.

"I can see why Relic was so fond of this drink. It was nearly impossible to keep any around. He was always into it." Luna said as she skipped over to Selena and gave her a kiss on the forehead. She bounced over to the other side of the table and quickly took a seat, propping her feet up on the table with a smirk.

Selena squinted her eyes at Luna as she closed the fairy book and said, "What's with you, child? I do not hardly ever see you this sprite. What have you been up to?"

Luna cut her eyes down toward the floor covered in garden art work adorned by moss, ivy and stones. She quietly drummed her fingers on the table as a sideways smirk emerged. "Well, Mother, I am really happy to be back is all.

I missed home, the fairies and I missed you." I smirk left her face.

"Wonderful. I am happy to hear that, I was worried how you would feel about everything. We have not had much time to talk about what took place in the dark realm. I would like to hear more about what it was like for you there."

Luna's face changed once more as she dropped her feet from the table and sat straight up. She spun the cup around with both her hands.

"Mother, I don't want to talk about it. I am not ready. No one hurt me or anything like that. My experience of being trapped there seems like a dream or a vision of sorts. I remember being held in a dark room much of the time and I could hear whispering coming from the outside. I heard screams from time to time. I wondered if it were Charity, Chance or the other guides Cora and Janus. I can't tell or remember. I believe that they kept me within iron to keep me weak. I couldn't use my glamour or magic to escape. I don't want to talk anymore about it. Can you just be satisfied with knowing how happy I am to be home?" Luna said walking over to Selena offering a loving embrace.

Selena was smitten with Luna and as they embraced, Selena patted Luna's hand. "Yes child, I am satisfied. I am happy."

Luna turned to leave and Selena watched her with contentment. When Luna arrived at the door she turned and said, "Is that the book?"

"Yes, it is. Sometime soon, I think it would be time for you to connect to the book. I want to share the many mysteries of our existence and power. I want you to know who you are." Selena said as she rose from her seat and walked toward Luna.

Luna shrugged her shoulders with a smile and said, "Sure, that sounds great. Time with you." Luna skipped out and went down the long hall and exited into the large garden.

***

The sun was rising and brightening Esmra's kitchen through the window over the sink. There Esmra stood holding her coffee cup in her hand, staring out the window. Her light grey eyes glistened in the sunlight despite the tiredness that swarmed her face. The house was quiet with only the chattering of the news channel from the living area.

Esmra broke her stare for a refill of coffee before walking into the living room to watch the news. She was dressed in her comfortable travel attire that consisted of a pair of sandals, lightweight cotton pants and a loose fit button-up shirt that had seen better days. The buttons were heavy, barely hanging on by the cheap strings that once held them snug. She carefully sat down in her comfortable recliner and brushed her long grey hair back over her shoulder as she situated herself.

Her mild adjustments were stopped when the chattering of the news caught her attention. A news anchor stood outside of a local hospital relaying the disturbing news of the mystery around the growing number of stillborn births. Esmra froze at the end of her seat and quickly grabbed the remote to turn up the volume. She leaned in hanging on every word when the news said:

"Stillborn births are on the rise at this local hospital in Springfield Missouri. We are on the scene here as locals share their growing concerns for untimely deaths of infants. As you can see here, the influx of mothers lining up at the hospital to make their complaints. All while expectant mothers are running away from what they perceive as a death sentence for their unborn. Is there some plague here? Have the doctors and nurses been negligent? We are on this story and others of the same nature. See it first with Springfield's best newscast. We will be right back."

Esmra slid back in her chair while she covered her mouth and stared down at her lap. The sounds of shuffling house shoes across her mildly gritty and dirty wood floor interrupted her shock.

"I heard enough as I was walking down the hall. I guess things are getting bad and it is real," Tallulah said while yawning and wiping the sleep from her eyes.

Esmra's face was blank, "I think we better get a move on and get out of here. We need to get going on this trip."

The pair shuffled upstairs and woke Aiden and Meridian to get them around and loaded in Tallulah's car. Within the hour, they dashed out the front door.

Relic was hand in hand with Lotus and seemed oblivious to the disturbing news. Pramlee was still mildly agitated with the peacock and took a shot at him. "Relic would you two please stop all this touchy-feely business, really, you heard the news. Things are bad and getting worse. You need to focus on what we need to be doing and that is making sure that Meridian and Aiden are protected, and we make it to get the quartz sword. How can you act this way at a time like this?"

Relic paused and his famous smile left his face as he drew a breath to put Pramlee in her place, but Ridge interrupted the brewing spat.

"Look you two, we have a lot going on here and we need not be at odds with one another. Relic, she has a small point. You are being a little too free here. Pramlee you are unusually cranky. I can't say what the right reference would be here."

The rest of the fairy nymphs stood close with Orion trying to hide their amusement with the situation as they covered their mouths; but their chuckles and devious eyes were a giveaway. Relic cut his eyes down at Lotus with a tight grin. Just as quick as he flashed his grin, Pramlee slugged him as she passed by making no apologies for her attitude.

Ridge turned his face away from all, not giving away his own amusement. He faced Tallulah's car while the humans piled in for their journey.

"Well, they are all leaving, so let's take off ourselves. I think a change in the scenery would do us some good." Ridge said right before they disappeared in transit to Tallulah's.

***

Everyone loaded up in Tallulah's brown Buick. Aiden was giddy thinking about a long trip back home. His smile beamed and his eyes were bright as he watched Meridian get into the back seat and scoot over enough for him to get in.

Aiden jumped in and put his arm around Meridian, who had slumped a bit to fit perfectly under his arm. Meridian immediately found her comfort zone with Aiden, leaning her head against his chest. She ran her hand up and down his chest, playing with the soft T-shirt he wore.

Esmra was in and ready to roll, dressed in comfort, carrying a large purse with a new book on herbal gardening. Meridian noticed Esmra's purse and she grinned.

"Esmra, is it customary for all witches to have a large purse?" Meridian giggled.

Esmra held up her purse to examine it turning it to each side. "What do you mean, this is a normal bag?"

Meridian continued to chuckle and said, "Tallulah's bag is a little bigger than your bag. That is a big bag! I could fit a small child in that thing! How do you find anything?"

Esmra chuckled back and put the bag down in the floor board next to her feet.

"Well, at least I have what I need. I carry my oils and supplements in there. I have to admit since I don't go out of town often, I feel a little challenged in packing."

Tallulah shut the trunk of the car and dug for her keys in her purse. She paused outside her door while her arm disappeared inside her bag. Esmra opened her book up and read as if she took no notice to what Tallulah was doing. Esmra beat Meridian to the punch line coming.

"Yes, I see her digging and no you don't need to comment."

Aiden and Meridian laughed at Esmra while Tallulah finally found her keys and plopped into the car and started the ignition.

"What is everyone laughing about?" Tallulah asked.

"Nothing, it is nothing," Esmra said as she casually turned the page in her book she read.

They hit the road and the drive was an easy six hours south to Tallulah's. The trip was mostly uneventful and they only pulled over twice for restroom breaks and fuel. With an hour left, they drew closer to the point in the trip where Aiden and Chris drove to go back to school.

Aiden leaned forward in his seat to see the scenery. "See, here . . ." Aiden pointed. "That is the road I turn off at to go to school."

Tallulah came to a stop sign and turned heading down the two-lane road with a handful of places to stop for fuel and even fewer places to grab a snack.

"Tallulah, there is a filling station that Chris and I always stop at, it is sort of a tradition. If anyone needs anything, the food selection is bare, but . . ." Aiden drifted off.

Tallulah glanced up in her rearview mirror and Aiden could only see her smiling eyes looking back at him.

"All right then, that sounds like a plan. My bladder could use a break." Tallulah said.

As they continued to drive down the road, Meridian had questions brewing. For the most part of the trip they talked about lighter subject matter to give their minds a rest from the challenges they were dealing with.

"Aiden, so what did you tell Chris? Your grandparents?" Meridian turned to face Aiden.

"Well, a white lie to my grandparents to keep them from going into shock. Chris told them I was helping a friend. Which I am. For Chris, he knows some of what is going on, but I told him I would share the rest in person. I mean, all this going on is pretty grand and a lot for anyone to take in."

Meridian did not seem satisfied with the answer. She let out a sigh.

"What's wrong?" Aiden asked Meridian.

"Well, why you would want to lie to your grandparents. I would think it would please them you have located your father. Couldn't you tell them that much?"

Aiden's face dropped. "Meridian, I can't lay on them I found my father and he happens to be a fallen, a form of a demon. If I told them that, they would ask what drugs I was on, probably wouldn't believe me and possibly take me to have my head examined."

"I want to meet them. Will you introduce me?" Meridian insisted.

Aiden sat staring at Meridian, his mind ran away.

I had not thought about grandparents meeting Meridian . . . I don't want to say the wrong thing. If I take her to meet them, then that will open up a can of worms. She can't understand that this is just not the time.

"Meridian, I don't think now is the best time for you to meet them. Why don't we take care of this trip, let me get back to school and things settle down." Aiden said in a low voice while he fidgeted his hands.

Meridian sat back in her seat and folded her arms while she stared out the window. The car had made it to the place Aiden mentioned, so Tallulah stopped so everyone could use the restroom and stretch their legs.

Everyone except Meridian filed out of the car. Out in the parking lot, the dear followers were there, watching, protecting the precious cargo. Aiden was behind Esmra and Tallulah by several feet waiting for Meridian to catch up. He looked over his shoulder and realized she was not there and stopped.

"Meridian?" Aiden said. "Aren't you coming?"

Meridian stared out the opposite window, facing the road. She acted as though she didn't hear him. Her mind went down a road of negativity.

Why wouldn't Aiden want me to meet his grandparents? If I am so important, how it will make a difference when I meet them. Maybe he is doubting he and I are really meant for one another. Maybe he is protecting himself from me. Was all the talk last night just a farce? I guess I should go in.

Meridian opened the car door and she placed one foot out of the car door and paused once more when she saw the spirit guides.

"Oh, hey, I was wondering when we would bump into one another again." Meridian left the car and slammed the door shut. She dropped her head low and her signature arm crossing remained. With her hair pulled back in a messy bun, her profile was easy to read.

Aiden took steps toward her and as they met in the gravel parking lot of the old convenience store, he put his arm around her, just for it to be pushed away. Meridian left Aiden behind, marching into the store, straight away to the restrooms passing Esmra and Tallulah who were looking at the selection of drinks.

Aiden walked through the doors toward the restroom, Tallulah stopped him.

"Aiden, what is wrong? What is going on with you and Meridian?"

Aiden shrugged his shoulders. "Well, I told her about waiting to meet my grandparents. I don't know why this would make her upset. I thought it would be best to take care of this trip we have to go on. It will be a lot for me to try to explain things to my grandparents. I didn't want to add to anything was all. Now she is upset with me."

Tallulah reached into the cooler and took out a water and handed it to Aiden and motioned for him to follow her to the coffee area of the store.

"I need this. I have been so exhausted with everything. No decaf. For me, no way. I will take totally leaded. If they had an espresso, I would drink a gallon at this point," Tallulah remarked as she shook her sugar packets into the coffee cup and stirred. "Now, Aiden . . . about Meridian. She is very different and she struggles with so much because of her circumstances. She has changed a little since I saw her last. She is a little more aware of the ways of the world here, but she still struggles with her esteem. At first, she came to me and was so childlike, acting too free with herself. After she realized what her curse meant, there was a time she wouldn't even look for you. She was afraid she would somehow cause you pain, death or problems. Then you two meet, she perks up and seemed so happy until Raina interfered. You know the rest."

As they were still conversing, Meridian had stomped out of the bathrooms back out to the car where she stood outside, conversing with the fairies and the spirit guides watching over them.

"Aiden, you are doing the best you can, and it is a damn miracle that someone like you would go through what you do. Men don't always know the right things to say, so allow me. Meridian doesn't trust herself much but she is getting better. She needs to hear and feel that everything between you and her means something to you," Tallulah said.

They left the store and the breeze picked up and blew Aiden's long strands in front of his face. He did his signature toss to move his hair out of his way. Tallulah smiled and moved a single strand away from his eyes.

"Aiden, I am sure you have said all the right things, she needs reassurance. I don't see why you couldn't take Meridian to meet your grandparents. No one says you have to mention your father. We are not planning on leaving right away. I need a break from traveling and I need to tend to some things at my shop. I have been gone and I am sure there are things that need to be taken care of. So why don't you both, go visit your grandparents. Tell them what you need too." Tallulah winked at Aiden and got into the car.

With everyone in the car, they resumed the trip. Aiden reached over to Meridian's hand that rested on her lap.

She looked out of the window, avoiding any eye contact with anyone. As Aiden reached over and held her hand, she didn't move it away from him and she didn't move it at all. They stayed this way until the moment Tallulah pulled back into her driveway.

"So good to be at home. Esmra, you know where your room is, so make yourself at home. I am going to put some tea on. Why don't you kids get squared away upstairs, we should have supper going pretty soon. I may need you both to run up to Stover's market," Tallulah said as she smiled and nodded at Aiden.

Aiden jogged swiftly up the stairs right behind Meridian who quickly stomped up the stairs. As she made it up the stairs, she quickly moved to her room and threw her purse and her bag on the bed. Aiden moments later trailed in behind her and closed the door.

"Meridian, what is wrong? Why are you so upset with me?" Aiden followed Meridian into the bathroom connected to her room. Meridian went through her cabinets, examining the contents she left behind when she took off to Salem. She paused from the shuffling through her drawers to see Aiden's sad eyes looking back at her through the mirror.

Meridian slowly turned around, bracing herself against the sink with both hands. "Aiden, I do not understand why you wouldn't want me to meet your grandparents. Am I not good enough? Are you worried about this curse? What it means?"

Aiden leaned his right shoulder up against the doorway. The doorway held his tilting head while a lock of his blond hair covered a portion of his eye. He lifted his head away from the doorway, crossed his arms with an escalated voice, "Why would you think? I am here, aren't I? I came all the way to Salem to find you. I have been in agony over you for months while you were away. Why is it we have more pressing matters to handle now, and you come up with these ridiculous situations as your reasons to be upset? I can't believe the crap that just came out of your mouth!"

Aiden stepped back out of the doorway, turned his back away from Meridian and sat down, slumped over on the bed. Meridian was frozen and stood still in the bathroom.

Aiden let out a sigh and moved toward the edge of the bed. "Meridian, I am not worried about that stupid curse! I meant what I said before we left. Why don't you believe me?"

Meridian took her time. "It is not just the curse that bothers me. It's everything. When I go to sleep and have my dreams, I feel at home even though I don't understand what is happening. All this talk of finding the answer to the curse. What if it breaks? What if I disappear? I go back? I don't want to be away from you. When I am with you, I feel it's right, when I sleep in my dream it feels right too. I feel so caught in the middle of everything. I want to be with you and to be together in every way. But then, all the uncertainty clouds me, no matter what I do someone may get hurt. I can't make a decision to save my soul, let alone the world or a world I barely remember." Meridian paced the room.

She put her hands on her hips and stared at her feet as they took each step. She nervously took her hair out of the bun. Her long, wavy hair hung all to one side over her shoulder. She brushed it back and her hair fell down her back when she stopped at the end of her bed. She watched Aiden stare at his feet. His elbows rested on his knees with his lips hidden by his clasped hands.

Meridian let out a sigh and put her hand on her forehead. "Aiden, how do I know you won't spook again? We are supposed to make this trip to get this quartz sword. What if you realize how insane all this is and you go away, like you did before? I know it was only a couple of days but it felt like forever to me." she sat down next to Aiden.

Aiden unclasped his hands and tilted his head toward Meridian with a stern look in his eyes, his lips pursed together, and his jaw was clenched shut. He let out a quick and sharp sigh through his flaring nostrils.

"What is it with you? Why don't you believe me? Believe how I feel for you? You made me leave the bar at

Stephanie's, I respected your feelings and told you I would still be there for you. I rescued you from Raina that night at that questionable establishment referred to as a bar, I took you to Tallulah and Esmra so they could explain everything to you. I let you run me off at your house, I show up at the bus station and you walked away from me. I begged you to stay to let me help you. After all that, I drive to Salem with Tallulah to find you and now, you are still acting as though I would do something to cause you harm!" Aiden got off the bed and ran his hands through his hair as he walked over to the window. He tilted his head back as if to stare at the ceiling, but his eyes cut down toward the left where Meridian was seated. "What do I have to do? I told you I am here for you, that curse does not scare me because of what I feel in my heart." Aiden lifted his head and turned to face Meridian.

Meridian left the bed and joined Aiden. Her eyes on the floor, she leaned up against the wall next to her window. Aiden took one look at her staring at the floor, his frustrations were at their peak.

"Nothing, huh? You have nothing to say? Fine, I have tried every way I know to show you how I feel for you. I understand how I made you feel and I would spend a lifetime making it up to you, but you won't let me." Aiden stared at Meridian.

Meridian said, "Is this about sex?"

Aiden's frustration on the rise once more. He threw his hands up. "No! This has nothing to do with that! See, you aren't even listening! I would be with you for as long as it took, until the last second if there was no other choice I had to leave you . . . If I am not the one. I would be here for you knowing it is possible I am not the one. I would do all of that, just to have one moment with you! But you won't listen, you push me away more." Aiden was on his way out of Meridian's room to leave.

"Where are you going?" Meridian's voice was shaky.

"I am going back to school. I told you I would be here for you, no matter what it cost. But I can't do it like this, if you won't allow it." Aiden turned his back to leave.

Meridian began to cry, her face flushed. She could no longer hold in what she felt. She hollered, "No, Aiden, please don't leave. Don't leave. Please." Meridian ran toward Aiden, then abruptly stopped in her tracks as her eyes fell on his one hand gripping the doorknob.

"I understand, I push you away. You may not really understand, but for me, in this life everyone always leaves, or they don't come back." Meridian lowered her voice, she stood standing with her arms crossed holding herself, her eyes stared down toward Aiden's feet. "I lost my father, whom I barely remember, my mother. They were taken from me. The men. I know you don't want to hear about that," Meridian mumbled.

Aiden turned around and put his hand on his hips. "You are right, I really don't want to hear about that."

Meridian uncrossed her arms, dropping them at her sides, defeated in where she was going. "Look, I don't want to bring it up either, but understand, back then, I didn't understand before why those guys never came back. Now I understand, I understand that I hurt others. I am afraid. I don't want to hurt you, for something to happen to you. I do not want to lose you either. In such a short time of being here, I feel like I have lost my life, my family and my friends. All I have now is you, Tallulah and Esmra . . . of course Stephanie too. You are all I know right now and I am so afraid." Meridian broke down sobbing into her hands. She quickly turned around from Aiden, trying to hide her emotions that were pouring out uncontrollably. Aiden reached out to turn her around to hold her, when she put her hand up while turning away further to hide her face. "No, please, I don't want you to see me this way," Meridian bellowed.

Aiden did not speak but walked around to face her. He cautiously pulled her hands away from her face and whispered to her, "I understand, Meridian. I understand." He wrapped his arms around her and pulled her in to him, he stroked her hair and kissed her on the forehead. "It will be okay, I promise."

Meridian slowed her crying and wrapped her arms around him, pressing her cheek to his chest. "You are right, you don't deserve this. I am just a fool."

Aiden said, "Please, don't push me away anymore. I can take anything for you or from you, but I can't take you pushing me away."

Meridian looked up into Aiden's eyes and she whispered, "I am so sorry." Her tears streamed down her face. "Please, forgive me, I don't know what is wrong with me. I am trying to fight so many things I do not understand. You have been so patient with me. I don't deserve you." Meridian buried her face into Aiden's chest again. "I don't want to lose you."

Aiden pulled Meridian's chin up so he could look into her eyes and he said, "Then don't."

"I am sorry. You are here, and I believe what you say. I thought things were starting to happen again, like they did right after Raina showed up the first time and that issue with Josh happened. I guess I am afraid you may take off again for a few days. Or this curse becomes my worst fear." Meridian stared at her hands, fidgeting with her bracelet.

Aiden turned to Meridian. "Look at me." Meridian did not stop examining her hands. He pulled her chin to his face once more. "I am not leaving you. The only way I am leaving is if I have to, if I am not the one. I won't let you leave me, not like that. I won't allow those things to happen again. I have never witnessed anything like that in my life, I was afraid of what I witnessed. I realize how my absence made you feel. Please, let all that go and have faith in me."

Meridian's eyes perked up and her mind raced at the memory of her time in the hall of souls with the angels. The word faith had so much more meaning to her than ever after her visit with Gabriel. Her eyes filled and with an overload of tears, one broke away from her eye and rolled down her face, brushing Aiden's hand that still held her chin.

He leaned in and pressed his lips to hers. Continuing to hold their lips together for several moments, no other sound in the room audible, but their racing breaths. Aiden's hands released her face, and he swiftly embraced her with both arms. She squinted trying to hold in the tears, but she lost that fight as they gushed against her skin.

Aiden released his embrace so he could wipe the tears from Meridian's cheek. He raked his thumb under her eye to catch the last few tears. After a moment he leaned back in, with a passionate kiss, telling her without words he meant what he had said.

Their kissing fueled with passion, driven by the repression of the curse and the fury to set her free, Aiden removed Meridian's shirt. He pulled her shirt off in one swoop, fluffing her wavy black hair into her face. With a quick nod of her head she swiftly moved hair from her eyes.

Aiden grabbed Meridian's face and with his body, he pushed her toward the bed, falling on top of her, kissing her frantically as though this would be the last time they shared a kiss. Their kissing grew with heat and intensity, where Aiden only broke away for a moment as he tore off his shirt and lay back down on Meridian.

There they lay, partially dressed with locked lips cemented together, barely giving either room to take in air. Aiden continued to kiss her, moving his lips down her neck to her shoulder where he pulled her bra strap down, exposing one of her breasts where he continued to intensely kiss her. He paused and looked up to Meridian who smiled and played with his long hair.

Once more he paused, wrapped his hands behind her back to unlock the clasp of her bra. With one hand, Meridian offered assistant and removed it herself. With swift hands, he unbuttoned her jeans and the sound of the zipper followed swiftly and Meridian arched her back to pull her jeans off her curvy hips, collapsing back down onto the bed.

Aiden sat back and stared at Meridian, taking her in. He kissed her stomach and caressed her body when the intensity lessened. He was softer and sweeter. He moved his mouth to hers where the kissing slowed along with their breathing. He held the kiss for what seemed an eternity before he pulled away from Meridian and stared deep into her eyes and said, "Are you all right?" Meridian nodded. She brought her eyes upward to meet his gaze once more.

"I am always okay when I am with you," Meridian whispered. "You give me hope and a reason to believe that no matter what, I will be okay." She brushed her hand down the side of Aiden's cheek. "If you believe in me, I can too. I do and I believe in you."

Aiden's lips softly rested together and his chest fluttered with every beat of his heart. Meridian smiled and pulled his face in closer. "I love you."

Without further words, the fear subsided, it had set her face void of fear, punch drunk with love free to go home. Only no home she had ever known. A long sigh left her lips and she closed her eyes. Her arms falling to her sides, she lay still and calm with a sense of peace.

Aiden removed his jeans then removed the rest of Meridian's clothes where they remained together naked, holding one another as they continued to kiss.

Aiden lifted his head away from Meridian and smiled. She brushed her hands through his hair and kissed his forehead. Aiden whispered to her, "Are you ready?"

Without words, she answered him with her smile, her eyes deliberate as she studied Aiden's face and brushed her hand across his cheek once more, like the day she left for Salem. The hurt in his eyes surfaced bringing back the memory that haunted her for so long.

She nodded and they spent the rest of the late afternoon in bed wrapped up with one another as they ventured into the unknown hoping they would find it meant they were meant for one another as twin souls that found one another through time and destiny.

Hours passed, and Meridian and Aiden lay in the bed quiet and still not making a peep. Meridian was turned on her left side facing the window while Aiden lay on his stomach. With dusk, the room was dim with only the light from her bathroom peeping through the crack between the door and the frame, leaving a thin strip of light running down silhouettes of the furniture decorated the dim room. Meridian slowly stirred, rubbing her eyes and rolling over onto her back taking a deep breath inhaling Aiden's lingering scent of cologne. The orange sky with wisps of blue streaking away from the half-moon exposed a few stars, and the birds quieted with the night sweeping in.

Meridian's eyes widened and she sharply turned her head toward him, looking for any sign he was all right. Frozen with fear she gasped and her mind took over.

Aiden lay with his head facing away toward the door, not having moved, he was flat on his stomach buried under the fluffy down comforter. Like a statue it was unclear if he were alive. Meridian slowly moved herself upward to lean on the headboard of the bed while she continued to look for any sign that Aiden was okay. Her mind took off on a ride, riddled with fraught with fear compelled her into questioning herself once more.

"Oh, no . . . oh no . . . it happened again. What do I do, it can't be. Oh, it can't be please! He is gone! I can't touch him! Do I reach out and shake Aiden? What if . . . What if . . . no . . . no... be positive. Be positive. After all we have been through, he has to be the one. Oh please. Okay, Meridian you need to calm down. Take a deep breath, wait I did that . . . I need to continue to breathe. Okay . . . I can do that. I can reach out and touch him, or do I shake him awake?"

Meridian stopped the mental tug of war, and after internally arguing with herself she unlocked her arm she held tightly against herself with fear. She let out her breath and slowly took in another. She reached her arm out to Aiden, with a trembling hand. Suddenly, a loud noise from downstairs startled her and she sharply pulled her arm back into herself and gasped for air.

Downstairs, Tallulah and Esmra were cooking up dinner, or trying. Tallulah took inventory of what she would need for the next few days for everyone to eat. There she stood in her pantry on her toes searching for spaghetti noodles when she pulled down a small box of what she thought were noodles and a stack of pots and pans came down onto her head and all over the floor of the pantry.

"Well, good night. I can't do anything right today. I feel so out of sorts," Tallulah said as she stopped hunting for noodles to clean up the mess of pots and pans.

Esmra was at the stove, cooking her meatballs and examined store-bought jar of sauce that Tallulah managed to round up. "Are you, all right? Do you need my help?"

"No, but I think I can manage this," Tallulah said flustered.

The kitchen smelled of an Italian restaurant and the ambience of the kitchen would satisfy any food lover with the lit candle in the center of the table. The garlic toast in the oven nearly finished, Esmra paused from her meatballs to open the old fridge and brought out a fresh herbal garden salad she made earlier.

"I hope they like my salad. I took the recipe from my new book."

Tallulah came marching out of her pantry flustered and she threw her grocery list on the countertop next to her antique sink.

"I thought I had spaghetti noodles. Oh, well, I said we would send the love birds to the market. Salad? Oh of course." Tallulah dropped her hand into the salad bowl, refusing to stop for a fork or a bowl of her own. She pulled out a black olive and quickly placed it in her mouth.

"I am starved! This will be a great meal. We need to send Aiden and Meridian to the store for dessert. I want us to have a nice meal and a break from worry. Wine, yes I think wine." Tallulah smiled before she stole another olive from the salad bowl.

She continued to bounce through the kitchen and the clicking of her flip flops picked up as went around nibbling at all the food. "By the way, they have been upstairs a while. I hope that whatever was the trouble on the way home hasn't escalated." Tallulah threw her plaid kitchen towel over her shoulder and rinsed her hands off in the sink. As she was drying her hands she went upstairs. "I'll be right back, I am going to check on them."

Esmra continued cooking her meat balls, stirring in the store-bought sauce into the sizzling pan with a smile.

Tallulah knocked on the door and after several moments she said, "Hello? Meridian? Aiden? I need you two to go to the store." Tallulah knocked once more. "Meridian?" Tallulah slowly turned the knob and cracked the door open. Tallulah's large brown eyes squinted while she tried to catch a peek at what was going on in the quiet room.

After not making out exactly what she saw, she turned on the light. There sat Meridian, still frozen and unable to move from fear and her green eyes glistened as fear filled her eyes.

Tallulah pushed the door completely open and with a gasp at the sight she covered her mouth. She didn't make a peep, instead she turned around and she ran downstairs.

"Esmra, oh no, the kids! The curse! Oh my. Come on! Those damn meatballs can wait!" Tallulah threw her hands up in the air and went back up the stairs. Esmra tuned the burner down on the stove and calmly began her way upstairs and found Tallulah standing in the doorway.

"Tallulah, what is it?"

"What are you talking about?" Tallulah whispered. "Look! What if the curse, they did it, they did it. Aiden is dead. Oh my god! No!" Tallulah's voice raised as her eyes scanned the floor, seeing their clothes strewn.

Esmra leaned up against the doorway with amusement watching her friend in an uproar and Meridian frozen with fear, now made worse with Tallulah's uncontrollable outburst. "Tallulah, calm down."

Tallulah in her frenzy didn't quite hear what Esmra said.

"Tallulah? What in the world? This is awkward. You aren't helping. I haven't, I haven't . . . we fell asleep after, you see. I don't know . . ." Meridian pulled the sheets up over herself, watching Tallulah pace the floor.

"You did it. He's gone! You did the . . . you know, the, the . . ." Tallulah was cut off.

"The nasty!?" Meridian shouted with a furrow and irritation in her voice.

Tallulah stopped and laughed at herself. "Look at me, I am acting like some parent."

Esmra snickered. "Well, you kinda are."

Aiden is . . ." Meridian stopped to look at Aiden who had not moved since the two women barged in his room.

Meridian put her hand over her mouth and gasped, her eyes watered. Tallulah froze as if she had seen a ghost and Esmra, the calm one of the group, casually strolled over to Aiden's side of the bed, sat next to him and pulled the covers back.

There he lay on his stomach with his head hanging off the side of the bed. His arms spread eagle and his legs spread out the width of the bed, still. Esmra put her index finger up to her lip and turned her head to Tallulah.

Carefully Esmra lowered her index finger away from her lip, dropping her hand slightly just over his back. She whispered, "Look." Pointing to his back that slowly moved up and down. Esmra leaned over to examine his face that rest quietly. Aiden let out a soft sigh, parting his lips slightly.

Meridian and Tallulah let out a collective sigh of relief and their shoulders made it back down to where they normally should sit.

A moment passed and Aiden groaned and lifted his head. His eyes squinted and once focused; he saw Esmra. Incoherent, his face still incarcerated with drunk love, he drew in a deep breath and rolled over on his back. He lay still for just a moment, with a smile and his eyes partially closed once more.

Then suddenly the drunken look disappeared, his smile vanished, and his eyes no longer squinted, rather they popped open wide as plates right along with his mouth. He flew straight up, and he realized he was laying there in bed with Meridian, though naked with an audience.

"Uh, oh... what? Oh man, was my butt hanging out? I thought I felt a small draft for a second there. I mean, I can explain. Tallulah you aren't going to hurt me, are you? I had a great time!" Aiden's nerves unraveled. "Uh, did you have a good time?" Meridian pulled the sheet over her face trying to hide her amusement and stop the laughter and the tears of joy from her eyes.

Meridian and Esmra looked at one another and then turned to look at Tallulah who stared at Aiden with a shocked look accompanied with an ironic smile. Aiden scanned the room and shrugged his shoulders. He glanced at Meridian. "What was I that bad?"

The three women in the room bursted into laughter at Aiden. Meridian leaned over and picked up a pillow and swatted Aiden right in the face and said, "Bad? Have you not noticed anything? You are alive! The curse! You also could sleep with a train coming through, apparently."

Aiden's puzzled look left his face, he stared at Meridian with his mouth open, then quickly darting his head around to Esmra, who quietly sat smiling at him.

"Yeah! Yeah! Oh yeah! You had faith in yourself. I always had faith in you!" Aiden's voice was escalating with vigor.

Meridian pulled the sheet down, with her eyes over her hands which helped cover her upper lips, still trying to hide her amusement.

"We made it! Right? I don't know what to say here. I knew everything would be all right." Aiden, out of breath with excitement, panted with every syllable that left his lips. His hands trembled, but he also laughed through his nerves.

With all his excitement, he forgot his wasn't wearing pants and jumped out of the bed, ran over to Tallulah and gave her a very awkward hug. "Oh Tallulah, it is finally over." Aiden stopped talking and moved away from the embrace with Tallulah who awkwardly patted his back and stared at Esmra with discomfort. "I am still naked. I am hugging you. This is awkward. Oh my, I am still naked. Oh man . . ." Aiden while he still hugged Tallulah, turned his head toward Esmra, "Can I have my pants?"

Chapter 23

Lahash and Warrick continued their stroll to the grand room and upon entering, it was dark without the many torches lit up that were used during gathering times.

The hall echoed their footsteps as they strolled over the grey marble floor with flecks of gold. Gold sparkled from the few rays of light that shown through the large windows. Lahash studied the iridescence from the floor while he casually walked alongside Warrick.

The unlikely pair arrived at the footsteps that led to the large double doors.

"Lahash, why do you study the floor?"

Lahash cut his eyes toward Warrick with curiosity. "The resemblance of the architecture reminds me of some places I have been on Earth, many years ago. It reminds me of Italy. I love Italy. The food, the drink. The life."

Warrick's face was full of surprise and amusement and he said, "I never took you for the type of demon who cared about those things."

Lahash, offended at Warrick's dismissive attitude, walked up the steps. "I wouldn't expect you to understand many things about me. No one does. That is why I am a loner, I prefer it that way. Always have, always will. Do not forget that I do what I do for myself. If someone benefits, so be it."

Warrick's watchful eyes full of discontent and disgust snarled at Lahash.

"Lahash, do not think I enjoy all this. I can't wait for the day we can go back to the way things were," Warrick muttered.

The pair stopped when they made it to the top of the stairs. Lahash relaxed his clasped hands he held loosely behind his back. He rubbed the door and studied the engravings. "Wonderful, so this is it. On the other side, the angels reside, watching over the innocent souls that transcended, ready to continue the circle of life and be assigned to a newborn." Lahash paused, dropped his hand from the door and studied Warrick's face. Crossing his arms, he said, "Warrick, do you know stillborn deaths are on the rise? Apparently, there is a shortage inside. With your ban, the guides do not serve their purpose, leaving humans without someone to watch over them. The demons within Ipos's and Moloch's legions are quite busy, wouldn't you say?"

Warrick's face furrowed, his lips tightened. "What is it you are getting at?"

Lahash shook his head, "Nothing really. It is the rogue demons that have started. However, Astaroth, she has been busy working on Aiden. He fights it though. Even in his sleep."

"What are you getting at, Lahash?" Warrick asked again.

"Nothing . . . nothing. You hope to remain here in Etheria and continue your rule. I wanted to know if you considered other outcomes . . . ones that do not land in your favor?" Lahash coolly said.

"What do you mean?" Warrick moved closer to Lahash.

"Not a thing, Warrick, not a thing." Lahash moved to quickly change the subject. "Now why have your brought me here? You and I cannot enter, we are not pure."

"Why do you say that? The fairy entered after she stole the key. The key I still have not recovered."

"The fairies can go either way, you know this." Lahash grinned.

Warrick's eyebrow raised. "Yes, you would know. I brought you here to show you exactly where the lock sits here in the door."

Both the grand doors were engraved with infinity symbols that were sizable enough they covered nearly half of the door. As Warrick's hand brushed over the infinity symbol he stopped when he reached the center of the symbol. It contained a small entrance, just big enough for an index finger to fit into.

Warrick motioned to Lahash, "See here, look, inside. Deep within the circular cutout, this is where the key goes in. When we got to the nymphs and we retrieve the key, this is where it will go."

Lahash and the undercover demon returned to the dark realm greeted by another demon of the high court and Astaroth. There he sat, casually in the meeting room of the high court.

Lahash, the first to enter the room, squinted his eyes. "Valefor? Why are you here? Has the dark one called for a meeting?"

There stood Valefor, his eyes, large and black, stared at Warrick with disdain before quickly jerking his head and eyes on Lahash. "Lahash, no, not a meeting. I want to discuss matters." He nodded to Astaroth.

Lahash with a guarded endorsement said, "Fine. What is it?" Lahash was slow to sit in his usual chair.

"Well, Astaroth has brought to my attention that she and Moloch had quite the exchange. I suppose that Astaroth and he will always be at odds. The craving for power in court may have hindered what we should be attending to," Valefor said, standing from his chair to walk to the grand fireplace in the stone wall.

"What is it you need? What is this about?" Lahash's curiosity appeared.

Valefor moved through the meeting room with a light and regal gait. His long blonde hair reached the end of his waistcoat brushing it as he walked. "We all have our own powers, things we use to accomplish tasks for the dark one, for ourselves." Valefor continued his speech while he stared at the roaring fire. "You with your sophisticated methods . . . I suppose. Astaroth with her ability to infiltrate dreams, Ipos holds much power over his legions by keeping humankind down. Moloch, his taking of souls. I need not bring up Pyro. He is too much of a wildcard, and likely to do anything. For myself, when the hall of souls is to be invaded, they will call for my powers for stealing upon. It is I that will take the Universe's power."

Valefor turned to study the reactions of his audience. "How is it I can trust what the dark one has employed you to do? You are to stop Echo and Karma from taking the quartz sword. You have taken up with Warrick, who everyone hates.

Has Warrick figured out what will come of him? Or does he still believe that he will remain in Etheria?"

Lahash smiled and maintained his dismissive demeanor toward the powerful demon. "Ah, yes, I know that you are the dark one's favorite at the moment. You will be the one to absorb the Universe's power from the angels. You can't trust me, I am for myself. We all want the same thing. That you can trust. We all want Warrick out of here and back in Etheria and as of late, no, Warrick hasn't figured things out, yet. We want the power of the Angels for our own. And we all want . . ."

Valefor's eyes sharpened. "Lahash? What is it?"

Lahash gave a quick head shake. "Nothing, I lost my train of thought. I must go now, I have other duties to attend to." Lahash quickly left the room without another word.

Astaroth left and chased down Lahash. "Lahash, wait!" She continued until she appeared right beside Lahash who had turned to enter his own quarters.

Lahash turned around with dismiss. "What is it?"

"Lahash, that isn't like you. You never lose your train of thought. The other demons grow wary of you. You are under the spell of a nymph, but the dark one seems to believe that you aren't and that you can take out the nymphs. I know you Lahash. You are in lust for Echo, she has you under her spell. Valefor is the one who will steal the power, however he will be vulnerable when he does. He trusts no one, especially you," Astaroth said.

Lahash crossed his arms and leaned up against the rock wall with a cool grin. "Astaroth, you and I had good times, why don't we again?" Lahash nodded back toward his chambers.

"Stop it, Lahash, that was a long time ago. The others do not trust you. They worry with the dark one putting you in much charge you will fail us. Ipos sees the future, yet he refuses to share it with any of us. He knows something and this has the rest of the court worried." Astaroth paced back and forth in front of the swaggering demon.

"I will retire for a bit, as always you are welcome to join me, how I do miss our demonic escapades." Lahash reached his arm out to Astaroth, who jerked away from his reach.

"Stop, Lahash, I will eat you for supper. No more. This is serious," Astaroth protested.

"Oh yes, I do hope you are hungry. Although, I do not take rejections nearly as hard as Moloch. Do you still tease him as well?" Lahash turned to open his door with a flick of his wrist. He put one foot into his chamber and turned facing Astaroth. "Last chance?"

Astaroth glared at the deviate demon and turned in concern and disgust as she quickly strode away back to the meeting room.

Chapter 24

After the awkward hug between Aiden and Tallulah, he retrieved his pants. Esmra and Tallulah jogged downstairs back into the kitchen. Their smiles were grand, and eyes full of joy and the relief that things were finally moving forward.

Tallulah put her hand on over her heart. "Oh, Esmra, everything is going to be okay. Aiden is still with us. He isn't gone. I don't think anything will happen. Right? I do not even know how much time passes before a guy . . . you know."

Esmra, happy but reserved went back to the stove carefully stirring the meatballs. She turned and saw Tallulah bouncing around the kitchen, sampling more dinner treats as she hummed.

"Tallulah, I don't want to burst anyone's bubble here, because you know how badly I would like to see things continue for the betterment of everyone. If it is broken, then why does Meridian remain the same?" Esmra stopped when she sensed the invisible friends and her eyes landed upon the fairy nymphs.

Siren strolled through the kitchen and stood next to Esmra. Tallulah put her hands up and waved. "I know, I know it's the fairies. They are here? What about the rest, I sensed something usher through. You can fill me in later. I will give the list to Meridian so they can get the rest of our food for dinner.

"Esmra, I am sorry for us to drop in on you like this. We haven't been far off, but we felt the sensation. The twin soul. Meridian has found him so our magic helped. It is Aiden," Siren said.

Echo rushed to Esmra's side all grins. "Oh, this is wonderful, I am so happy!" Echo jumped up and down, while Lotus and Siren stood with quiet smiles remaining reserved. A few moments later, Karma appeared.

"Esmra, we are happy that this curse has broken but does that mean Meridian goes home? As long as Aiden survives the night the curse is broken, but with Meridian still here as a human. What does this mean? We cannot fathom why she remains."

Esmra turned off the burner and sat down at the table. "Well, me either, I guess young love and ignorance is bliss," Esmra said rubbing her forehead.

Growing crowded, guides appeared and some didn't look very happy. Kieren and Relic, though happy at what they knew, also felt a loss finally having come to the realization that Meridian may be destined to be with another.

As always, Pramlee could be counted on to be giggling and bubbly at the progress in their dilemma.

Outside, Talon stood in Tallulah's yard staring up at Meridian's bedroom window. He could see Aiden. His laughter was audible all the way down into the front yard. Talon's worried eyes softened and his face showed a smile of relief. He hung his head down for a moment and he chuckled and mumbled to himself.

"Oh son. I always knew you were special. You are so much like your mother in so many ways. I wish she could see you. I wish I could find her to tell her that everything that took place between us was not all in vain. I can't wait for the day I can tell you . . ."

"You will. You will soon." Orion broke away from the serious conversation inside the house.

"Orion! I can't believe that I didn't notice you. Yes, I hope that I can tell him soon."

Orion stood beside the fallen. "I am glad that Meridian is finding faith in herself. I hope she can maintain it. The rest are inside discussing the why's behind the reason Meridian remains here on Earth. I overheard Pramlee say she would go up in the room and test out if there has been any change in Meridian at all."

Moments later the rest of the guides and the nymphs joined Talon and Orion in the front yard. Pramlee lost the pep in her step. Her face was sad.

"What is it?" Talon said.

"Well, I went into Meridian's room. She and Aiden were getting dressed and she was in the bathroom combing her hair. I don't understand it. She can't hear me anymore!" Pramlee exclaimed.

Relic defeated said, "Is this it? Meridian's destiny is to remain a human? I don't understand. Why does this curse continue to plague us?"

"Gee, I guess news travels fast." Relic put his hands in his pockets, shook his head and strolled off down the sidewalk toward the newcomers, Selena and Luna.

Selena stopped and watched Luna and Relic walk off together. "I saw this in the book."

Ridge, who just strolled out of the house, said, "What book?"

"My book, the fairy book. It not only holds spells and magic. It literally tells stories of the past, the present and the future."

Kieren drew a quick breath. "What! You knew this would happen? Why do you keep playing games!"

Selena's sharp eyes turned dark green as they blazed into Kieren with rage. "Fool! Do not question me! My book cannot foretell all futures, there are too many possibilities! I found out myself, the moment it broke. I saw it play out in the book."

"Selena, does your book show anything else?" Ridge asked.

"No, it usually only shows a fairy's future, if any. There is no formula or scientific reason. The book has a mind of its own," Selena said.

"Does it talk too?" Kieren smarted off.

"Not in so many ways but yes. When a fairy reads from the book, the words can take shape, or illustrations can form. It isn't verbal," Selena said. "The demons are on their way to stop the retrieval of the quartz sword and take back the key to the hall of souls. Unfortunately, I know nothing more and I can no longer see anything else where she is concerned." Selena dropped her head and walked away to stand with the nymphs.

Pramlee zoomed alongside Karma, who was telling Esmra the things she knew. The stairs squeaked from footsteps walking down the stairs and accompanied by the sounds of two happy love birds. As quick as they bounced in with zeal, their expressions turned grim when they noticed Esmra's face.

Meridian stopped and crossed her arms. "What is it, Esmra?"

"Did you notice any of the spirit guides around you before you came down?" Esmra asked.

Meridian shrugged her shoulders. "No, I haven't seen them since I came back. Why?"

Esmra took Meridian by the arm and pulled her to sit down. "Meridian, it is strange, since it appears your curse is broken, you can't see or hear the guides anymore. I am puzzled that if it is broken, why didn't you change? Go home, back to Etheria? Why do you remain a human?"

Aiden interrupted, "I guess we got so caught up in what we were doing and that I am okay, that we didn't stop to think about where she would go or what would happen to her. This whole time, everyone has been worrying what would happen to me. What if it isn't really broken? Meridian, how long did it take for any of the guys to pass that you know of?"

"Well, that John guy from Salem. I can't say what happened to him. Not any of the guides or Talon said anything. I can ask, but the boy from the school who was hit by a car the morning I left for my flight to Salem, it was within a day. The next morning." Meridian said.

Aiden and Meridian locked eyes and both of their faces turned white. Tallulah made it back into the kitchen. "I heard the last part. I don't think we need to worry about that now."

Everyone stared at her. She shrugged her shoulders and said "What? Why should we worry about things we have no control over? Meridian, why don't you and Aiden take yourselves down to the market and get back here so we can dig into this meal? I will remain positive here, I will worry when there is something to worry about!" Tallulah said with a smile and a bit of an attitude.

She handed Meridian the grocery list. Meridian stood with her arms crossed and she relaxed her right arm so she could take the list from Tallulah with a smirk, while biting her lip.

"Tallulah, are you all right?" Meridian asked.

"Yes, I am fine. I am just so fed up with all the gloom around, I want to have a few moments with my favorite people enjoying what I do best, besides palm read. Eat! Now I get hangry, so hurry!" Tallulah exclaimed with her smile still present on her face.

Stover's market was within walking distance from Tallulah's house. Aiden and Meridian grabbed light jackets and strolled past the unseen supporters standing in the yard.

Hand in hand the pair seemed happy despite the unsettling comments from Esmra. Aiden pulled Meridian's hand to his mouth and gave it a kiss.

"All that talk in there, are you scared?" Meridian asked.

Aiden drew in a long breath and raised his eyebrows, watching his feet as he walked. He shook his head and said, "No, not really. You may not understand, but I agree with Tallulah. We need to think positive. Thinking otherwise brings self-fulling prophecies. I have faith and trust in myself that I know how I feel. It is just something that is not easily articulated. This is right, you and I." Aiden watched her face.

"Yeah, I guess you are right. I have spent what time I can recall either acting like a fool or not believing in myself that I could overcome things. I wanted to tell you I am sorry for how I reacted over your grandparents. You are right. We have a lot going on right now." Meridian said.

Aiden stopped walking and pulled Meridian back. "No, I was wrong. I understand that I made you feel the way I did. We will meet them, if we have time. Gosh, I have a lot I need to take care of." Aiden pulled his cell phone out of his pocket. "My grams called several times. I am sure she is worried."

"Okay, but I too wonder why I am still here. If it comes to pass that everything is gone, I can live normally here or back in Etheria with my old life? Being able to recall my father and see him, I was able to remember things from a life ago. I am torn. I want to be with you. What about me being 'chosen' or the one who is to take care of everything? It is overwhelming. I don't want this to end." Meridian's voice trailed off.

"Look, I know I may be some stupid guy who just likes to fish and listen to rock music, trying to figure out what I am going to major in so I can graduate. I don't know about a lot, but we are not promised tomorrow no matter what life we live or where we live it. We can only do what we can do. No one knows where the wind will take them. As such is life. I do not want to think about a time you are not in my life. I want to continue to believe what is meant to be will be and you and I will come out of whatever this is together. I will hang on until the bitter end."

Aiden leaned in for a kiss, putting his arms around Meridian, holding her close. She brought her arms up around his neck and met his lips with hers. After a brief kiss, their embrace relaxed and they looked into each other's eyes.

Meridian held both of Aiden's hands. "Are all guys like this? Okay dumb question, I know that not all of them are. Are guys this young like this?"

Aiden shrugged his shoulders. "I can't speak for a lot of guys. I would say probably not. I was raised a little different is all. I never understood a lot of the games guys play with women anyway. A guy should always let a woman know where he stands no matter what. So many of them play games or want to test the woman because they are too chicken to be a man, say how he feels and let her decide. Just chickens. Or they have ill intentions." Aiden chuckled.

They resumed walking and Meridian leaned into Aiden as he put his arm around her as they continued to talk. "I try to be up front with anyone. I don't have time for games anyway and I am not a fan of wasted time."

Meridian glanced up at Aiden as he held her. "Well, I feel safe with you . . . something I haven't felt in a while. Of course, I feel safe with Tallulah and Esmra. You know what I mean."

"What about the time you spent the Raina?" Aiden asked.

"Well, that is what I mean. I can barely remember anything from the couple of months I was with her. It is like a blur. She kept me drugged up on pills and I guess some spell. What worries me more is what she is capable of and her silence is a little scary to me."

The store was in sight and nearing the hour to close. Only a few patrons' cars were parked in the front and the neon light open sign turned off by the owner.

Meridian nodded toward the store and said, "We better hurry. I saw Holly, the owner hit the switch turning off the open sign."

Aiden opened the door for Meridian. They laughed with one another, recounting the awkward moment when Aiden jumped out of her bed and ran to Tallulah. Meridian's laugh echoed through the store as they entered through the front door.

"I know! You should have seen yourself!" Meridian wiped tears of joy from her face. While she attempted to collect herself, she glanced at the list Tallulah gave her when out of the corner of her eye she glimpsed someone. After a double take, it didn't appear to be anyone.

Aiden continued to laugh, but his laughter died out when he noticed Meridian's demeanor changed. "What is it, Meridian?"

"Uh, oh, nothing, I thought I saw something is all." Unsure, Meridian continued to read through the list.

A whisper within Meridian's ears said her name. "Meridian, Meridian, oh Meridian." Meridian stopped in her tracks and looked around to find where the voice came from. Once again, the voice started, deliberate and high pitched, "Meridian, you will come back to me."

Meridian dropped the can of icing she had in her hand and Aiden, who had been shopping for the complementary baking items, jumped and turned around. "What's wrong?"

Meridian's body shook, "I keep hearing my name from this voice, I thought I was hearing things."

Aiden quickly leaned over and grabbed the icing and tossed it in the basket and took the list from Meridian's hand. "Let me handle this, we only have a few things left."

Aiden quickly pushed the cart and kept a careful eye on Meridian as he marched through the store. Aiden quickly shuffled the items on the counter. His face flustered as he hurried.

Meridian stared out of the glass door to the market. With the dark outside, she could see her own reflection staring back at her, long, flowing, and black hair. She was wearing a pair of black ripped jeans. Her look was topped off with Aiden's T-shirt. Her eyes shifted back to Aiden, who paid for the groceries.

Suddenly, she heard the voice again sharply entering her mind, "Meridian!" In the reflection she saw Raina standing behind her looking over her shoulder staring back at her. Raina dressed in all black, a long satin cape with a hood colored red on the inside. Her teeth shone brightly in the reflection when she said Meridian's name again. Raina put her arm around Meridian across her neck and leaned in as if to kiss her. "Meridian," she whispered.

Meridian jumped and dropped her purse on the floor. Aiden paid the bill and he turned around and grabbed Meridian.

"What is wrong!?" Aiden said hastily.

Meridian froze and she could not speak. Aiden grabbed Meridian under his arm and pushed the cart out while he held her close. After a brisk walk home, the couple moved quickly into the house.

The guides, Talon, and the fairies quietly waited for their return. Aiden and Meridian marched past them swiftly.

Relic and Luna returned to the group, where Relic stood and tapped his foot on the ground. "Raina. She is near. Here we go again."

Talon who had already left the house and paced the perimeter where Orion and the nymphs quickly joined. Kieren who had been subdued with sadness at his lost love finally had words to share. "I can feel it too."

Ridge's face puzzled and he stared at Kieren waiting for further comment, "What has come of Raina? If Pyro possessed her and with a trip to the dark realm, what would that bring of a mortal who returned?"

Before anyone could answer, fussing from the kitchen was audible.

Tallulah was hysterical. "I knew it! I knew that crazy bitch would return!"

Esmra continued putting plates out while Aiden and Meridian watched Tallulah during her hysterics. "Tallulah, calm down! Listen we will eat and we will do a spell of protection. The guides are near it will be okay, please," Esmra said.

Tallulah stopped her scuffle and came out from the pantry, "Okay, yes. I am sorry. I hope he makes it through the night. I don't want her back here causing more trouble." Tallulah plopped herself down in her chair.

"Ms. T, I am okay. Have faith." Aiden put his hand on her shoulder breaking her stare from the flower-decorated plates on the table. She reached across her chest and patted Aiden's hand.

Tallulah smiled at Aiden, "You are right. Faith. I am still trying to figure out it starts with having it in myself as well as others."

"Tallulah, for the first time I feel like things are going to be okay for me. I don't know how, I can't say when, but it will all be okay." Meridian wrapped her arms around him and rested her face on his back. With a tight squeeze, she closed her eyes, smiled and took a deep breath while she took in his scent that gave her a sense of home.

Chapter 25

Moloch was up in arms as he squared off with the dark one in the usual meeting room. "Master, my existence is to see that the souls of those humans of ill will are collected. It is what I feed from. This is my time! I can fulfill my destiny as your servant stealing souls. No more waiting around on Warrick to cast away spirits. Useless!"

"Moloch! Calm yourself. You have had plenty of souls to steal. I realize you would enjoy such a feast to come sooner than later. You should have realized that this would come, this is the beginning. Soon you will not worry about these things. The power from the Universe will be ours, we will take the power from the Angels and rule. The dark realm is full of all the dark souls we could ask for. It is time for a change. Be patient," the dark one said.

Moloch continued to pace, "Lord, Warrick believes he is returning to Etheria as things were. He does not understand what will transpire. What will come of Warrick? Will he remain with us when we destroy Etheria?"

"No, he will not. He is nothing more than a tool for us to use. When the time comes when we invade, you will be needed, you will take his soul and destroy him. That will be the last soul you will ever need to take," the dark one said as he laughed.

***

Tallulah's brown Buick, though a little dated, it was enough for the humble palm reader. Esmra, seated in the front passenger seat, stared out her window. It was quiet with only the sound of the car moving along down the road, and sometimes, a few beats of wind with the spring storm that brewed ahead.

Esmra glanced up in her rearview mirror to examine not just the condition of her tired eyes, but to take a moment to take a peek at the love birds in the back seat. Aiden seated right behind Tallulah, had his arm around Meridian while his head leaned on the headrest. Like Esmra, he was also staring out his window in silence.

"Well, do you think you all could make it a little easier on your driver?" Tallulah said.

Esmra snapped her eyes away from the mirror and looked at Tallulah. Her blank face brightened, her eyes smiled, and she said, "Well, Tallulah, why don't you tell us how you really feel?"

"Well, do you know how hard it is to drive without music or any talking? I could go to sleep with the road humming."

Aiden leaned forward and positioned his body behind the center console with a smirk. "Okay, Tallulah, what would you like to talk about? Is seems you have something to say, right?

Aiden pulled his phone from his pocket and searched the internet for news on stillborn births. His face furrowed in deep concentration as he clicked and read articles. He scratched his head and said, "Look here." Aiden handed the phone to Esmra.

Esmra read and after a few moments she said, "My little news station isn't the only one. It doesn't appear by what I see here that it is being observed as some kind of epidemic. Minimal souls are transcending through lives and completing the journey back to the hall of souls. This is sad." she handed Aiden his phone back.

Tallulah picked up her speed a bit as she pressed on the gas pedal giving the engine a bump. Esmra fidgeted with her purse strap while she stared at Tallulah.

"Esmra, settle down, I am not speeding too far over, but I don't want to waste time. It is a drive." Tallulah patted Esmra's fidgeting hand.

The trip continued along smoothly aside from a few large drops of rain that hit the windshield sporadically. Aiden cracked his window open slightly, giving the much-needed sound to break the monotonous humming from the road.

The air was thick and smelled of rain to accompany the darkened sky. The rain drops came in droves with howling winds rocking the car. Soon enough golf ball-sized hail followed crashing into the car. Tallulah slowed down looking for an underpass or any shelter.

Esmra looked out her window which faced west and said, "Hey, good news, it is clearing off over there."

They continued to drive. The two-lane road had a long stretch of curves and no-passing zones with ditches filled with heavy streams of water backlogged into the road.

Tallulah took her eyes off the road to pick up her coffee and take a sip when she hit a large bump. Coffee went everywhere. While she and Esmra were dodging hot coffee not paying attention, Aiden sat up from his seat and shouted, "Look out!"

In the middle of the road perfectly positioned on a sharp curve, lay a large tree, lightning had struck that blocked the side of the road they were on. A woman with black hair who did not appear to be bothered by the storm or a car about to run her over, stood in front of the tree.

A smile crept over her pale face and there was no movement in response to the out-of-control car. Tallulah slammed her brakes taking them into a spin from the wet roads. Barely missing the obstruction in the road, they were barreling down the other lane. The woman watched the car in delight not making a move to save herself or even for concern for the car.

The sharp curve blinded a single car headed in the opposing lane without a second to prepare for Tallulah's car coming head on. Tallulah gained control for a moment, and there again, the mysterious woman somehow was now right in front of the car once more. This time, her face was clear, Raina stood in an instant startling Tallulah, she hit her brakes once more, this time hitting the oncoming car.

The Buick rolled off the paved road down a ravine sending the car into several flips. As the car took several rolls, Meridian was slung top to bottom like a rag doll. The glass from the broken windows showered the inside of the car, hitting everyone. A tree abruptly stopped the car from rolling further down.

Raina walked toward the other car to assess the driver. She was pleased to see that something knocked out the woman driving the car. Raina reached her hand and placed it on the woman's neck as she lay with her head back on the headrest with blood running down from a large gash in her head.

She casually strolled to the edge of the road and looked down into the ravine. Inside the car the bodies were still and unconscious. The driver's side window had been completely broken. Tallulah's face was full of scratches and her blood ran down from her forehead. Esmra's mouth hung open as her blood poured from her mouth.

In the back seat, Aiden's face was marked with cuts from the shards of glass, that now rested in his lap. His head pressed up to the window, his hair soaked in blood and the palms of his hands sliced with long cuts accompanied by seatbelt burns across his neck.

At Aiden's feet lay Meridian with her face smashed into the floor board, her arm mangled and dislocated from the jolt of the car rolling from not wearing her seatbelt. A river of red coated her raven hair and pale skin on her cheek.

The sirens sounded in the distance. People were getting out of their cars, crowding around the scene. Quickly, Raina left the scene of the accident past the car that collided with Tallulah around the corner. She jumped in a black car with dark-tinted windows and took off driving away.

Chapter 26

Back in the dark realm, the demons faced a conundrum of feeling empowered with the dark one's plan while harboring unrest. Moloch, normally the cool headed but proud demon, sat in his large, dark slate grey, stone chair. His large red face rested in his thick hands adorned with long black finger nails.

A knock at his door disturbed his quiet thinking. Breaking his stare, he slowly turned his head toward the door, "What is it?"

A light but stinging voice muttered from the other side. "Moloch, may I come in? It is Astaroth."

Moloch didn't move quickly to answer the uninvited guest. He leaned forward while he studied the floor by the door where Astaroth awaited an invitation. Moloch rose from his chair; his long black cape brushed the stone floor as he strode unhurried to his unwelcomed visitor. Moloch tucked his chin to his chest, his large eyes darted while he listened in front of the door. There was no movement, not a sound.

Moloch backed away from his stance and brought his arms upward as he quickly turned away with a quick pace back to his chair. Astaroth's hesitation went unanswered as she took her first step into Moloch's chambers. Her gait was soft but swift as she walked dragging her huge demon wings across the floor.

"Moloch, I understand this is not happiness to see me here, but I felt that we should visit more since the dark one has set out new plans for the demon court. Why do you avoid encounters with me so often?"

He appeared mildly interested in what Astaroth had to say, as he looked the other way. "I do not understand why you ask such ridiculous questions. I do not confer with any of you, because I do not have to. What do you want?"

"Moloch, with our master's new plan, I am uncertain where I would fit into this work. It may be best I sit this one out. What you think?"

Moloch snapped his head around in surprise with venom in his voice. "What of this? Are you playing some ridiculous game?"

Astaroth continued, "Not at all. My work has been quite successful in these passing months for the humans. My powers over dreams have so far succeeded with the boy. His gifts are awakening although, making it more and more difficult to wear him down. His skills in anticipation of the future hinder my work. I have struggled with this aspect in his dreams. However, with Meridian, I have not been the needed success, even with her previous influence with Raina.

Meridian confounds me, and this is not something I could overcome. Her dreams and visions are protected by the Angels and now with the help of the fairy nymphs, I cannot continue any psychological inferences upon her."

Moloch continued to stare at his unwelcomed guest. Words seemed to have escaped him.

"Moloch, the boy. I understand we will need to get to work on him. If I am still needed at the court, then I offer my assistance. I can continue to penetrate his dreams and weaken his state to take either opportunity of possession or death. How would you prefer?" Astaroth asked.

Moloch remained suspicious, and with reservation, his deep voice further darkened with a slow recount of times past.

"I have not forgotten your ways. You will stop at nothing to gain favor in court. There have been many demons come and gone from court because of your ways. How you have escaped the dark one's wrath is beyond my comprehension. Do not give consideration that my tolerance for your assistance means a careful watch of you will be no more. I will be watching." Moloch stood up from his chair and moved deeper into his chambers.

****

Warrick having been left by Lahash for the demon meeting, remained in Etheria, where he and his son crossed paths.

"Slaten, son. How are you?" Warrick smiled and reached his hand to Slaten.

Slaten's face was full of disgust and his voice loathsome and telling. "I am not your son."

Warrick put his hand back to his side, refusing to acknowledge the statement.

Slaten crossed his arms, he spread his feet past the width of his shoulders and his was face devoid of movement.

Slaten's face wrinkled. "I will never join you to betray our kind. If we cannot get Meridian home, who is our chosen one, my sister and I will do whatever we have to and protect the Etherians from this gross and unjust deceit that has no doubt gone on for too long. Remember that, Warrick. I will see to it your day will come."

Slaten stomped off in a few steps and then disappeared from sight leaving Warrick with his illusion the dark protected his place in the realm one, having no idea what was in store for him.

Chapter 27

Arriving quickly at the scene of the accident where the humans were loaded up in the ambulance, the guides swarmed. The drivers of both ambulances quickly sped off with their sirens on leaving behind the tow truck, the fire department and police on the scene.

"I told you," Kieren said as they all arrived.

Pramlee put her hands over her mouth while Ridge embraced her. Relic stood next to Kieren in shock at the wreckage that was once Tallulah's car. Orion moved quickly down into the crash site with the nymphs.

"This is a work of the dark one," Orion said.

"How do you know that?" Relic shouted from the road.

Orion and the nymphs moved back where everyone else stood watching. "Talon, do you want to help me out here?"

"Orion is right." Talon said as he pointed to a mark in the pavement.

Siren kneeled down and ran her hands across the pavement and then stood back up nodding. "He is right. You all can't see it, but Orion and the Fairies can."

Siren reached into a small pocket on her dress and pulled out a velvet bag. It was green and tiny. She opened the pouch and tilted it ever so gently, giving it a shake, pouring its contents into her other hand. As she shook, a lavender-colored, powdery substance poured out. After she put the pouch away, Siren rubbed both hands together, sifting the powder from her hands. In the space between her hands and the road an image formed while the fairy dust created a silhouette. A sigil formed as though it was suspended in mid-air.

"Spirit guides or humans cannot see this, but with the help of the powder, what is elusive comes to light," Orion said pointing at the hovering sigil.

The purple iridescence of the powder glistened despite the lingering overcast from the storm. They all shuffled together closely examining the mark. Relic's eyebrow raised, and he stepped back from the crowd.

"Okay, Okay, here we go again. So, which one is this?" Relic gave a slight tap on Pramlee's shoulder.

Pramlee had been bent at the waist studying the mark.

"Will you quit! I didn't know about the last one was on Meridian, it was Ridge who figured that out. Which by the way, how is it you knew what it was?"

Ridge stood a few steps away and his hand rubbed his chin while he studied the mark.

"That isn't the concern for now. However, I know the mark. It is a demon of the high court, or one. This isn't one I have seen in a long time."

Kieren pushed Relic's shoulder and nodded to Orion who paced around the area where the vision of Raina emerged right before Tallulah's car took a nosedive down the ravine.

"What is it, Orion?" Relic's sarcastic look left his face.

Orion shook his head and walked around the area examining the skid marks left behind from the car.

Echo tapped her foot at Ridge with her arms crossed and stern face to boot. "Well?"

Ridge stopped rubbing his chin and cut his eyes toward the impatient fairy. "It is Pyro. The same demon that possessed Raina before, that night at Tallulah's. Now that Raina is free from the dark realm, there is no telling where she would be or what she would do. I would have to say Raina seems to be involved if this is the work of Pyro."

Relic rolled his eyes and said, "So demons control the weather and other drivers?" Relic pointed at the sky and in the distance the storm moved swiftly to the next town.

"We do not know if weather caused this or not. It could have been anything. Right now, I don't care what caused it, we need to go to the hospital to see how they are all doing," Pramlee said.

The entire group disappeared and arrived at the small local hospital. The guides, Talon, Orion and the fairies floated down the busy halls and found where each human was located.

Their rooms were close in proximity with two in intensive care. Pramlee ran into the room where Meridian stayed, to be hit with shock seeing Meridian hooked up to so many machines.

"What is this, what is wrong with her?"

Ridge made his way to her bedside and studied the beeping monitors.

"This isn't good. She is on a life-support machine." Ridge rubbed the back of his neck barely looking at Relic and Kieren, standing side by side with their mouths hanging open.

Ridge and Pramlee quickly moved to the other rooms. Tallulah seemed to improve, with a broken arm and some stitches in her deep cuts, awake and coherent, asking if everyone was okay.

Next door, Aiden lay still unconscious but came around with oxygen. He lay on the gurney with his head moving back and forth rapidly in a panic. The nurses kept him strapped down to the bed., "Meridian! Where is Meridian?"

A doctor on duty came into the room and checked Aiden over, shining a light in his eyes.

"Aiden, you all took quite the spill. You should consider yourself lucky. You have a cracked rib and some scratches. You do not show signs of a concussion. How are you feeling?"

Aiden stopped struggling and looked at the doctor.

"Will you take these straps off of me, please? I am fine, really. I am sore and my head is killing me."

The doctor put his clipboard down and positioned himself closer to Aiden.

"That is normal. We can get you something for that. I need you to sit back and relax. We need to keep you overnight and make sure everything with you remains stable. If everything checks out and we do not need to do a scan to check your head, you should be okay to leave in the morning."

The doctor started his exit from the room while the nurses continued to check Aiden's vital signs.

"What about Meridian, where is she? Is she okay?"

The doctor stopped and turned around to face Aiden. "Meridian was not near as lucky as you were. I am sorry, but she is on life support. She has suffered blunt force trauma and internal bleeding. We are going to have to move her to another hospital that will be better equipped to handle this situation. She will be airlifted. I am sorry."

The doctor swiftly left to find Tallulah in her room. "Hello, I am Dr. Smith, I am the attending physician here on call this evening. You took quite a tumble. I need to ask you some questions about Meridian. She does not seem to have a blood type. We drew blood from her during the initial intake. Do you know anything about this?"

Tallulah froze. "No, not really. Why? Is everything okay?"

"I am afraid not. Are you responsible for her?"

Tallulah nodded and the doctor moved closer to Tallulah's bed. "Well, unfortunately not at this time. She took quite a blow and she has gone into a coma, we have her on life support. X-rays reveal she has some broken bones, but that is the least of it. Her kidney is severely torn and there is a lot of internal bleeding, she also appears to have swelling of the brain. The report shows she was not wearing her seatbelt. We will have to airlift her to another hospital, one that has the facilities to handle something of this magnitude."

Tallulah cried uncontrollably, her body stiffened and she bent over as if to hold herself while she sobbed. The tears came in waves saturating her face. The doctor put his hand on her shoulder.

"We will do all we can for her. I assure you once she arrives at the other hospital, they will do everything they can to help her. Is there anyone I can call for you? Family? Friends?"

Tallulah shook her head, "Yes, Stephanie. My friend at home. Please call her. And what about Esmra and Aiden?"

Dr. Smith motioned for the nurses to come back into the room. "I am going to let the nurses fill you in, I have to get to surgery, but I will return to check in on you."

Chapter 28

Tallulah and Esmra were signing their discharge paperwork when Aiden showed up.

"Hey," he said staring down at his wrapped hands.

Tallulah signed her form and collected what little things she had to leave with. "How are you? You have some cuts."

"Yeah, looks worse than it is, I am just very sore with a cracked rib . . . I will survive."

They continued to talk as they found Esmra who had sat in the waiting room with Stephanie. "Stephanie!" Tallulah briskly walked over to Stephanie giving her a hug while the tears streamed down her face.

Stephanie tightly embraced Tallulah. "Esmra told me everything. Are you okay?" They broke their embrace to leave the hospital while they continued the conversation about the wreck.

"So where are we anyway exactly?" Aiden asked.

Stephanie started the car, "Well, this little town called, Belington. Small little town not too far from the house actually. So where was Meridian airlifted too?"

Tallulah said, "Well, back at home, at our hospital."

Aiden perked up and leaned forward from the back seat and said, "What? Our hospital, C. Heyworth Medical Center? Meaning our town?"

Esmra looked over to Aiden. "Why? Is there something wrong?"

Aiden sat back in his seat and stared out the window. "No."

They made it back to Tallulah's house and hobbled in slowly. Aiden went upstairs and called Chris.

"Hey man . . . yeah. I know. You heard. Do my grandparents know?" Aiden paused listening to Chris talk. "Okay, I am going to see them, I am sure they are still worried even if you told them I was okay. Can you leave school and come back?" There was a long pause while Aiden listened to Chris. "It would mean a lot. I need my truck anyway, just get here as fast as you can and pick me up so I can visit with my grandparents." Aiden hung up the phone and got back downstairs.

"Hey, so when are we planning to go up to the hospital and see Meridian?" Aiden was hasty.

"Well, we will leave here, Stephanie is finishing up a few things at her place and she is driving us over. Everything all right?" Tallulah asked Aiden who stood at the foot of the stairs.

"Yes, I am all right. Chris is coming and bringing my truck. I will need to go see my grandparents and let them know I am all right." Aiden struggled to scratch his head with the blood-soaked bandages on his hands.

"Well, while you wait, if you need anything . . ." Tallulah patted him on the back and walked back toward the kitchen.

Chris made it back in a short amount of time and the best friends left and directly went to Aiden's grandparents' house. Aiden sped down the long dirt drive and they jumped out and made it into the house where they were met by his grandmother.

"Young man, I am going to kick your butt! Now, Chris filled us in about you being in some kind of car accident. Why didn't you call us?" Aiden and Chris continued to walk by as she asked her question.

Strolling into the kitchen they sat right down at the table and Aiden huffed. "I know, I know. I should have. But I am okay, really. But Meridian, she is not doing okay."

Aiden's grandpa came in from working on the farm and threw his ball cap at Aiden. "Son, you sure are having a week, aren't you? Are you all right?"

Aiden nodded and looked down at his hands. His grandpa walked over to the sink to wash his hands and smiled. "Well, good then. As long as you are okay." He grabbed a towel off Grandmother's shoulder to dry his hands and quickly took a seat in at the table to eat lunch.

Aiden's grandmother, agitated, grabbed the same towel he used to wipe his hands and slapped him with it. "Is that all you are going to say?"

Aiden's grandpa opened his mouth for a bite of green beans. "What? He is fine, isn't he? He is alive, a few cuts . . . he is all right the best I can tell. So, what do you want me to do? He is a young man now. You want me to ground him?" Aiden's grandpa winked at Aiden and took the bite of green beans that still remained on the fork in his hand.

Aiden's grandmother huffed and went to the fridge where she got both Chris and Aiden something to drink. "Well, I think that he could have called is all. I have been worried." She slammed their drinks down on the table and both Aiden and Chris slightly hunkered down and snorted with smiles when the glasses hit the table.

Aiden's grandpa continued to eat as though nothing else was happening out of the ordinary. "So, when are you headed out to see Meridian? Your new friend, right?"

He peeked over his shoulder to be sure that his grandmother finished her rounds. He glanced back at his grandfather and said, "Well, here in a bit. We are going to go over."

Aiden's grandmother walked over to the table. "Well, then maybe you should go upstairs and try to rest. You look like hell. I will make up some snacks for you boys to take while you are up there. You will need your rest, Aiden."

Aiden took his grandmother's advice and both he and Chris went upstairs. Aiden lay on his bed with the television turned down and Chris took his spot above him on the bunk bed.

"I could use some rest too. I stayed up late studying for the math test. I am beat. I can give you my notes." There was no answer from Aiden. Chris leaned over and dropped his head down. There lay Aiden passed smooth out from exhaustion. Chris sat back up and then lay down for a nap himself.

An hour passed and Aiden had not moved. Not uncommon for the deep sleeper he was, his eyes rolled back and forth swiftly fluttering his lids. Once again, the reoccurring dream of being at the hospital started.

There he lay on the couch where he picked himself up in the waiting room. He walked down the hall where all the nurses and doctors bustled about. He placed his hand on the door and pushed it open.

No longer watching himself, but seeing through his own eyes, he fell to the floor in the hospital room and could not move. Three glowing orbs appeared in the corner across from the bed as he lay on the floor, held down unable to move.

Aiden continued to struggle against the tight locked grip that imprisoned him. Out of breath, weakness set in as he fought to get up from the floor.

A voice from one of the apparitions spoke to him as he struggled to move. "Would you die for her?"

Aiden stopped struggling, and the force that held him down was no longer there. His body free, he quickly rolled over to push himself upward, and the two people that stood at the foot of the bed looking at the mystery blonde were there once more.

As soon as he made it to his feet, and no matter how loud he shouted, no one appeared to hear him, let alone notice him. The three orbs floated over the bed and hovered for a few moments.

Aiden attempted to move his feet forward to get a better look at the woman in the bed, when the same ghost from before in this dream appeared. This time, the portion of the reoccurring dream stopped, and he found himself in a dark room alone. No one was near him. Suddenly standing in front of him was the ghost and he could see her face as plain as day.

She had long blonde hair. She smiled and took Aiden by the hand. Aiden stared at her face and his memory of the day he and Chris were in his room discussing his mother surfaced.

He immediately recognized his mother. His eyes puddled as the tears glistened in his blue eyes.

"Aiden, you are not alone, I have always been at your side. I have searched for you for so long and I have finally found you. I can only talk to you in your dreams, though not always easy," she said.

"What? I am confused. Was that you at the tree? Was that you? Are you trying to tell me something?" Aiden, frantic in his words, pushed his syllables out as if they were his last.

The ghost did not reply, she only dropped her head down and let go of his hand and cried and sobbed.

"Mother? Are you mad at me? Did I cause your death? Is there something you need to tell me? I am sorry. I am so sorry," Aiden said.

The ghost continued to sob, "You can save me. If you can show me the way home."

Aiden pulled his head back in confusion. "I don't understand."

The ghost stopped crying and her hands dropped away from her face. She quickly snapped her head up and hissed. Her face changed right in front of Aiden's eyes, no longer the beautiful young blonde woman that looked like the pictures of his mother. Now what stood in front of him was a demon hissing. "You killed your mother! You should die! What kind of child kills his own mother!"

Aiden shot straight up out of his sleep hollering, startling Chris who nearly fell out of his bed. "Aiden!" Chris jumped down out of his bed. "Aiden! What is it?"

Aiden was out of breath and didn't seem to pay any attention to Chris while he put on his shoes. "C'mon, man let's go. Let's get back, I need to see Meridian."

Aiden stumbled from his bed, leaping forward to grab his jacket that covered the width of the chair. Sweat running down his face, his skin flushed red, hurried in his pace and speech alike. Leaving Chris behind a few steps, Aiden hustled downstairs. The sweat from his brow dripped with every bounce off the steps. Finally hitting the first floor he rounded to the left and straight out the front door. The screen door slammed behind him just about the time his truck door opened.

Chris shuffled behind finally making it down the stairs but not quick enough to move past Aiden's grandmother. She grabbed Chris's shirt. "Now slow down! What is the hurry?"

Chris stopped barely making eye contact with Aiden's grandmother. He kept his chest pointing toward the door. "Grams, I don't know. I think he must have had a bad dream or something. He has been acting strange. He wants to see Meridian." Chris stared out past the front door. Aiden's truck fired up.

"Well, here," Aiden's grandmother said. "I made you all some snacks. Take 'em."

He gave her a quick peck on the cheek. "See you in a while."

Chris bolted out of the front door as though something were chasing him instead of leaving him behind. Aiden rolled down his window and hung his head out staring at Chris without even so much as a word. Just a long stare.

Chris jumped in and before he could shut his door, Aiden already backed out. Once he put his truck in drive, he peeled out gravel taking off. Chris stared at Aiden with nervous curiosity. "Look, I know things are bad, but I don't want to end up in the hospital with Meridian either." Chris slunk down in his seat and fumbled through the sack of food he took from Aiden's grandmother.

Aiden had not said a word, no response to Chris's nervousness, instead he stared at the road. His face was tense and he appeared in a state that few were accustomed to seeing from Aiden. Anger. Anger that Aiden had now allowed himself to ever feel, anger toward himself.

The ride was quiet and a knife could cut through the tension that came from Aiden. Chris opened the sack and pulled out some cookies and began to snack on them when his phone vibrated. He fished his phone out of his pocket.

"Hey, Tallulah messaged. They are going over to the hospital now. I can tell them we will just meet them over there. Okay?" Chris sat staring at Aiden.

The truck engine roared with Aiden's heavy foot driven by a heavy heart. He nodded to Chris and continued his silence all the way to the hospital. Aiden pulled in and jumped out of his truck taking long strides leaving Chris trailing a few steps behind.

As they entered the hospital, Aiden slowed down as he noticed the couch in the waiting room. He stopped and his eyes flinched at what he saw. The couch was sitting on the opposite side of the waiting room and it was a different color than what he could recall in his dream. The couch in his dream was dark red and plain with wooden framing. This couch that sat before him was a light blue with metal framing. Aiden stopped and scratched his head as he stared.

Chris caught up to Aiden. "What's wrong?"

Aiden let out a sigh and smiled, breaking his eyes away from the couch. "Nothing." He snorted. "It's okay. I will explain. Let's get to Meridian."

They both quickly approached the information desk where they were given directions on where Meridian was. Aiden swallowed hard and took a quick breath as he waited to find out which floor and room Meridian was on.

After the elevator ride, Aiden stopped and looked to his left and then to his right before he took the turn to the right. Chris was watching and finally could not wait another minute.

"Aiden, what is the matter with you?" Chris demanded.

"Okay, I keep having a reoccurring dream I am in this hospital, I am asleep on the couch in the waiting room. Then suddenly, I am walking into a room from a hallway in the hospital. When I get in, I can't see the person in the bed, only long blonde hair and it appears to be a woman. I have no idea what floor. There is a ghost with blonde hair standing next to the bed. Plus, glowing apparitions asking me if I would die for her. Then finally my dream moves on, and it is my mother and she is speaking to me. Then a demon appears accusing me of killing my mother. I was relieved to see that the couch is different and I turn a different direction," Aiden said.

They continued their walk down the hall. "Why would all that bother you? It is a dream and hardly true. It is your mind playing tricks on you is all. This has nothing to do with Meridian. Besides, if she is as special as you say, I hardly believe that what injuries she will have will last long. Think about it. She really isn't even a human!"

Aiden stopped and stared at Chris. "You know, you are right. I will bet she is going to be okay. She was a spirit before. Special gifts, right? Man, this whole time I have been so worried that it would be the worst. I worry about my mother and I guess finally knowing who my father is even though I can't see him, well it's my mind playing tricks on me." Aiden relaxed and they made it to Meridian's room where all the unseen could be counted on to be close.

The guides watched Aiden walk into the room where Meridian lay asleep, hooked up to monitors. Tallulah, Esmra and Stephanie were by her side. "Well, it isn't intensive care. Right?" Aiden asked.

Everyone turned to look at Aiden and Tallulah rose from her chair and walked over to Aiden and gave him a hug. "Well, it isn't as bad as they thought. They are keeping her in an induced coma so that the swelling can go down. It knocked her out for a while, but the coma was more for safety reasons. The doctor has looked her over, she had internal injuries they are monitoring, but we are uncertain."

Aiden kept his sad eyes on Meridian while he listened to Esmra explain. He softly broke away from Tallulah's embrace and walked over to Meridian. There she lay quiet. Her face streaked with the long scratches from the car tumble, her hands bruised and her left eye black with subtle hints of purple from the swelling.

Aiden pulled a chair close to her bed and he placed his hand on her hand, clenching it as if it was the last time he would hold it. His body hunched over the bedside and he settled his chin on the side of her bed. He stared at her hand as he continued brushing his thumb over the back of her bruised hand.

Chapter 29

The doctor entered the room with all eyes on him. He placed his clipboard down at his side as his eyes carefully scanned the room. "I am sorry, the injuries are worse than we expected. With her other confounding results with the blood work, there is nothing more we can do. Without a will or something from Meridian signed in terms of life support, I need someone responsible for her to make a decision."

All eyes now shifted to Tallulah who now sobbed into her hands. Esmra reached out to her to comfort, however Tallulah put her arm out and nodded her head. With a deep breath, she wiped her eyes dry. Her nodding increased with speed as she said, "Okay, okay. I know what I have to do. Okay." Her voice was shaky while she held in emotion. Tallulah cleared her throat. "Give me the forms."

The doctor slowly lifted his hand with the clipboard. Tallulah reached for a pen in her purse not realizing the doctor had a pen for her to use. Tallulah continued to dig further into the depth of her large bag and she broke down in tears. "If Meridian could talk, she would tell me I need to get a smaller purse." Tallulah stopped digging in her bag and broke down with convulsing sobs that continued uncontrollably.

Esmra and Aiden rushed to her side, Aiden's eyes were swimming in tears he could no longer hold in as he broke down with Tallulah. He wrapped his long arms around Tallulah. "It's okay, Tallulah." Aiden wiped his eyes and looked back at Meridian and he broke down again.

The guides were restless while they stood at the end of Meridian's bed. Relic couldn't handle it. He turned his back and placed his fingers in the corners of his eyes as he tightened them shut. He dropped his head back and stared at the ceiling and hollered out, "Why!? Why!? We came all this way, and now we lose the best of us. Now what do we do without her? How will we save our home?"

Relic floated through the wall and left with Kieren behind him while he also fought back his tears. Pramlee on the other hand could not leave her best friend. She sat on Meridian's bed and held her hand. "I love you, Meridian."

Ridge stood at Meridian's head and stared at her face. "If she passes, will she come home? Has anyone thought of that? What if she passes . . . maybe she can come home?"

Pramlee's sad face left and her eyes brightened through the glistening of the tears. "If she passes away, anything could happen. She goes to Etheria, or she may end up lost, or to live another life. So many possibilities."

Before they could continue their conversation, the room went black and shadowy figures emerged from the walls making eerie noises. Ridge jumped to Pramlee's side. It startled Tallulah, Esmra and Aiden and they shuffled to get to the light switch, and no matter how many times they switched it, the light would not turn on. Aiden peered outside the room to find that it affected no other lights in the hospital.

Then suddenly, there stood Raina at the end of the bed. Aiden went to knock her down, but he was thrown back into the wall. Esmra and Tallulah grabbed one another and screamed. The nurses and the doctors tried to walk through the doorway, but could not enter, there was an invisible barrier keeping anyone from coming into the room.

Tallulah broke away from Esmra and tried to tackle Raina, but she too was hurled back into the wall by an invisible force. Raina did not break her eyes away from Meridian. She opened her jacket and pulled out the same bottle of elixir she had used on Meridian in the past. This time she need not say any spells to make the elixir take its form. Raina opened the bottle and she threw it up in the air and it froze still hovering over Meridian's bed. The contents of the bottle ascended into the air, floating while spreading out. As the liquid remained suspended in the air, it took the shape of what appeared to be a person.

Raina smiled and spoke to the emerging image. "Oh, Pyro join me, summon Ipos and set the demons free. No more will any being hinder, we will take over and all will fear me as it should be."

Slowly, Pyro emerged from the liquid, that now turned blood red. He stared at Meridian and waved his arms and the hospital room walls broke away and disappeared, replaced by a crimson atmosphere. The surroundings of the hospital were gone, leaving them all with the appearance of being in the dark realm.

Meridian, still unconscious, rose from the bed, her body lifeless and from underneath her gown, the tattoo of the sigil that represented Ipos burned and lit up with a red glow. With only the heart monitor attached to Meridian, it beeped wildly.

Pramlee shouted out, "She is still in there! Meridian is still okay! Look!" The room swirled with heated wind, whipping Meridian's hair back away from her face. Pramlee tried to rush to Meridian's side, but Pyro threw out a ball of fire and hit her in the chest knocking her out. Pyro returned his focus onto Meridian and he spoke in Latin.

Relic and Kieren came through and were in shock at they witnessed the scene. Relic yelled over the howling winds. "What is happening?"

"It's Pyro, he is summoning Ipos through the sigil on Meridian! We think Meridian is still alive! Look at the heart monitor! She won't be for long if Ipos comes through!

We have to stop this before it is too late!" Ridge pointed the heart monitor.

Meridian's eyes opened as wide as plates in terror of what was happening. As Pyro continued to summon Ipos, the sigil burned hot into Meridian's skin. She opened her eyes and screamed in immense pain unable to break free.

Aiden and Chris got as close as they could to Meridian. Aiden yelled, "Meridian! I am here!"

Meridian couldn't move, the winds grew stronger, and the heat was unbearable. Slowly the sigil disappeared as the area that surrounded the sigil burned away with the flames coming out of Meridian. She writhed in pain, screaming as her body slowly burned. Aiden and Chris took off with force toward Raina and tackled her down to the floor.

Pyro hurled Chris and Aiden away from Raina, then she rose to her feet and stood at the foot of the bed. With the jolt, it knocked Chris into the far wall where he lay unconscious next to the long red couch with a wooden frame.

Aiden fell over and he lay on the floor unable to move. Suddenly, out of nowhere, an unlikely and ironic twist of fate occurred. Lahash showed up.

Invisible, the nymphs lurked, watching the scene unfold. Siren stood in front of the group. "We must allow Pyro to summon Ipos out. It is then we can destroy all of them. When he goes to summon, it will weaken him, he cannot protect Raina, we strike then."

The nymphs nodded and continued to watch. Echo's face showed concern as she watched Meridian suffer in pain. "How long can Meridian hold on? With her injuries and this, we may lose her."

Karma stared at Meridian, "It will be okay, she is stronger than you realize. She can pull through this. Just stop Pyro at the right time." Karma grinned at Echo. "How did you convince Lahash?"

Echo smiled, "Well, as they all say, fairy glamour."

"Stop this, Pyro! You will destroy Meridian and Ipos! There is nothing good that will come for either of us! Even if you summon Ipos and destroy him along with Meridian . . . it will not result in the ending you want! If she goes, the fairies will still pursue their agenda! There is still a chance for demons to succeed in all this without sacrificing our own! We need Ipos!" Lahash screamed.

"Stay out of this, Lahash! You know not what you speak of. I do not care, I want Ipos gone, I want my legion!" Pyro screamed out.

Lahash threw his arms out and hurled an invisible ball of energy to Pyro, knocking him down. Meridian followed and fell down when Pyro was incapacitated. She collapsed back into her hospital bed while the two demons continued to battle it out.

"Lahash, stop! You are under nymph spells!" Pyro screamed as they swirled in the air over Meridian's bed.

Relic and the rest of the guides remained in shock from the words they heard coming from Lahash. "What? I suppose that Lahash is under the nymph's spell?" Relic shouted.

Ridge was incredulous as he stayed next to Pramlee who remained unconscious. He watched helplessly as the battle continued between the demons.

Aiden looked up and over from where he lay on the floor and he saw two people who stared at Meridian. No longer did Raina stand there, but it was Tallulah and Esmra crying. Aiden saw Chris who still lay unconscious, and his eyes moved a little over to the right, where he saw the red couch. The same red couch he saw in his reoccurring dream. Suddenly everything for Aiden slowed down as if his dream were playing out once more.

He continued to struggle to get up, no one in the room noticed him anymore or heard him. He remembered what the five apparitions said to him in the dream. "Would you die for her?"

He stopped struggling and he peacefully lay his head back onto the floor. The moments of his reoccurring dream played out in his mind one by one. He realized that he lay in the hospital's floor just as he did in his dream, the same place where he struggled to be released from an invisible grasp. He closed his eyes and everything in this moment made sense. He knew what he had to do and after he drew in a large breath, he yelled out "Yes! Yes, I would die for her!"

Suddenly he no longer remained held to the floor with an invisible force, and his body was free. Just like before in his dream, he jumped to his feet to see who lay in the hospital bed. Esmra and Tallulah who had stood at the foot of the bed, moved away and looked at Aiden.

"What are you talking about, Aiden?" Esmra asked.

There next to the bed, stood the ghost and everyone could see her. She was beautiful, with long flowing blonde hair and translucent skin. Her hand was placed on the forehead of the woman in the bed. Aiden stared with his mouth open as he laid his eyes on the mystery woman whose real identity eluded him for so long.

Tallulah and Esmra stopped staring at Aiden to find out what created such a shock in his face. There she lay as plain as day, and like moments suspended in time, Aiden felt free, his life purpose presented itself and had been through his dream. Lahash stopped fighting Pyro and let him go with a nod from Karma.

Pyro rushed back to resume his summoning. Meridian's heated skin burned once more and it pulsated and burned as Ipos came through the sigil.

Karma looked to the nymphs and hollered, "Now!"

Everyone in the room stopped moving frozen in time except the demons and fairies. The nymphs moved around Meridian's bed and sang in high-pitched, operatic voices, their wings spread out. Their power burst, connecting their bodies and Karma ascended to hover over Meridian and Pyro. With one shot, a loud clap rang out.

Karma's sliver eyes glowed as she opened her arms and extended her wings. A monstrous ray of light full of the power of the Universe emerged from her body and shot straight into Meridian. Pyro was thrown, jolting him back hitting the wall and disappearing.

Karma turned her body and propelled the Universe's karma into Raina. With a burst into flames, Raina burned alive. Her blood curdling screams pierced everyone's ears as she burned and screamed for her life.

Raina continued to scream from within the flames inadvertently calling the dark realm's soul collector, Moloch.

There in an instant he appeared, ready to take Raina's soul to the dark realm.

As her body died, a black ball of smoke emerged and Moloch made his advance toward the darkened soul. The smoky, darkened remains of her soul dissipated and entered his body through his opened mouth and eyes. In moments, the ball disappeared. Without a word, he vanished with Raina's soul.

Meridian now free from Pyro, her sigil vanished from her body as if it were never there before. The hurling winds stopped, and the walls of the hospital room brought back as though the scene of the dark realm never was.

A bright iridescent light beamed from this woman who lay still with her eyes closed, hair nearly white as snow, with her arms at her side, with one of her wrists turned up. The once black tattoo of the infinity sign now glowed like a hologram on the inside of her wrist.

Esmra and Tallulah gasped at the sight they took in. The glowing mystery woman opened her deep, mesmerizing, green eyes to stare right at Aiden. He moved closer to Meridian and said, "Meridian. It is you, it has always been you. You were in my dream."

Time stood still, Aiden thought about the conversation that he had with his grandmother when she told him she knew he would do great things in his life. That he was special. A solitary tear left his eye as he took her hand. He looked up to the ghost who was his mother. "Mom, it was you. It was always you looking out for me and Meridian. I understand now. You couldn't leave, you had unfinished business." Aiden smiled through his tears.

He looked around the room where now the guides and his father he never knew stood and witnessed Aiden come to his profound understanding of who he was. He remembered the dream of the three orbs floated above her. He smiled and said, "I would die for you." He leaned over and kissed her on the cheek.

Meridian embraced Aiden, and tears rolled down her face. Aiden whispered, "I told you, I would be here until the bitter end. The irony." Aiden smirked. "As such is life. I was the one who had to love you and set you free." His eyes fell to look at her hand he still held. He raked his thumb across the back of her hand and with a whisper he said, "I can let you go now."

Meridian's anxiety surfaced, "What are you talking about? It's over. I am myself once more."

Aiden scanned the room, seeing Chris pick himself up from the floor and hesitated for a moment. Esmra and Tallulah looked to Aiden for more of an explanation, but Aiden's surreal understanding only left him with his last cryptic words. "It isn't the bitter end. This is a bittersweet beginning. I will see you again. I promise."

Right in front of everyone's eyes Aiden collapsed and fell down on the floor. Everyone rushed to his side, sending the room into a hysteria. Chris hollered out for help. The invisible barrier had diminished with Pyro's exile from Earth, the doctors and nurses broke through and scurried to Aiden who lay on the floor, his eyes barely open.

As everyone ushered to Aiden's side, Meridian floated up from the bed and a bright spinning orb surrounded her. Aiden lay on the floor, his life leaving his body. He smiled and was in peace, to see Meridian set free. The light engulfed her body, spinning rapidly, she disappeared into the light. In a blink of an eye, the orb shrunk down to a tiny sphere, and drifted down into Aiden's open hand that lay at his side. He looked at his hand and smiled and in that instant the orb vanished and Aiden's life left his body.

The sounds of cries drifted into the hall of the hospital where staff and patients alike swarmed the room where the ultimate battle for one's soul transpired.

Selena emerged, her cold demeanor no longer present. It saddened her eyes. "True love to break the curse, but an act of true love to send her home."

Selena said, "Meridian is going home, to restore Etheria, however the real work has just begun. Now we must do all we can to help Meridian destroy Warrick."

Talon, tearful and in agony, said, "If my son gave his life, where is he now? Why didn't we see something? There was nothing, we did not see his soul leaving. Is he lost?"

Ridge looked around the room for any sign of anything from Aiden. There he lay, and the doctors had given up. The doctor shook his head to Tallulah leaving her and Esmra in the irony that just played out before their eyes.

Kneeling at Aiden's side, Esmra brushed her hand over Aiden's forehead. She smiled and said, "All this time, we were looking for something that remained right in front of our eyes, you never wavered. You were so strong in the face of things that one person could be expected to take on." Esmra looked at the space in the bed where Meridian once lay, then to the space that once stood Aiden's mother. "We spent so much time looking for the unseen answer, and it was you. You gave Meridian the strength and the hope to find her way home. You are the definition of true love in this world. You, Aiden. My hope is you find your way back to us and to Meridian once again." Esmra leaned over and kissed Aiden on the forehead. "We all love you, until then . . . goodbye Aiden."

Meridian Chronicles: Keeper & the Soul Key (#4)

The last installment to the series!

What happened to Aiden? Did Meridian go home?

Find out when it releases

Spring 2020

Stay tuned for a new series to come!

Dark & Twisted

Fall 2020

www.mdfryson.com

Goodreads

Bookbub

Twitter

Instagram

Meridian Chronicles

MD Fryson **363**

Fairy Nymphs & the Demon Court

MD Fryson 364

Meridian Chronicles

MD Fryson

Fairy Nymphs & the Demon Court

MD Fryson **366**

CPSIA information can be obtained
at www.ICGtesting.com
Printed in the USA
LVHW050823190819
628120LV00001B/6/P